UNAUTHORIZED

Compton had been found by the Suffolk County police on a bad stretch of road near Little Port. A limousine had turned the corner and run head-on into a truck hauling about a thousand gallons of spring water only fifty yards from where the body lay on a slope near some bushes. And if the rain and warm ocean breezes hadn't helped melt the snow, it might not have been found for another week. He'd already been dead for nearly a week.

◀ ▶

First Prize

First Prize

EDWARD CLINE

THE MYSTERIOUS PRESS

New York • London • Tokyo • Sweden

MYSTERIOUS PRESS EDITION

Copyright © 1988 by Edward Cline
All rights reserved.

Cover design by Jackie Merri Meyer
Cover illustration by Steve Macanga

Mysterious Press books are published in association with
Warner Books, Inc.
666 Fifth Avenue
New York, N.Y. 10103
A Warner Communications Company

Printed in the United States of America

Originally published in hardcover by The Mysterious Press.
First Mysterious Press Paperback Printing: April, 1989

10 9 8 7 6 5 4 3 2 1

Nothing is written

—*Lawrence of Arabia (1962)*
Screenplay by Robert Bolt

1

Manhattan lent itself to wandering, and I'd wander, just to be around people. I'd plunk down in a place like this to have the talk and clatter and movement of the living behind me as I sat and thought and watched the traffic lap through the city in diminishing waves beyond the plate glass.

The face reflected in the darkened glass was mine—taut but not edgy, bony but not desperate. The eyes were dark green, usually with curiosity, or surprise, or anger—rarely with envy. The hair was a thick, tightly curled blondish-red, and took care of itself as long as I kept it cut. It was the mouth that most people found more expressive and telling than they did the eyes; some found it charming, others a dead giveaway to what was really on my mind. I had no opinion of my face, other than that I liked it and that no one should have any reason to fear it.

Standing up I was a fraction of an inch over six feet, and trim enough to still be able to wear the same clothes I'd worn in college almost twenty years ago. I was fit enough that I could run down a mugger, but not enough to endure a marathon. Some women found me good company and loved to run their fingers through my hair; others didn't like my eyes or mouth and said as much without either of us having to utter a word. Which was just as well, since what I thought of myself was not based on a poll, my own or anybody else's. Whenever someone accosted me with "Chess Hanrahan, you're a smug so-and-so"—give or take a few epithets—I hadn't the slightest idea of what I was being accused of. In most instances I suspected that it was a graver offense than my imagined conceit.

I left a dollar bill under my saucer for the overworked waiter in the all-night diner on Ninth Avenue. All I'd had were a couple of coffees and a slice of walnut-mince pie. I was usually generous, but tonight I was feeling super-generous and not tired at all. It was just after midnight and I'd wrapped up a case that should have depressed me but didn't. Not even the front page of tomorrow's *Times* at my elbow could depress me. I'd bought it somewhere farther uptown just to do the crossword puzzle and had been surprised to see my case reported on the front page.

The story concerned the revelation by the police that the sensational kidnapping of a boy genius from the townhouse of his wealthy parents had been a hoax. The boy and another bright friend of his concocted a scheme to defraud his parents of a hundred thousand dollars. Once the ransom had been paid, and the money squirreled away until it was safe to spend, the boy genius would have been "released" and the "kidnappers" gone unapprehended. The pair had planned to speculate in commodities. They had a "system" but no cash.

But the kid who showed up at the prearranged drop point near Montauk out on the Island to pick up the suitcase of money led his tail—me—to an abandoned barn farther into the Island. As I picked my way through the weeds and got closer to the barn, I'd heard howls of laughter. I peeked in through some rotted slats and saw the two celebrating the event with uproarious toasts of beer. I retreated, called the police from a booth in the town down the road, and that was the end of that.

I was mentioned in the story, but not quoted. The genuis and his friend were awaiting arraignment for sentencing by a juvenile court. The parents were no jewels either. They'd hired me to find him and arrange the exchange with the least amount of fuss possible. I even suspected that they knew what the kid was up to, but they didn't bother to tell me. The boy genius, sixteen, had written about Einstein's theories at the age of eight and had won some kind of national science award at the age of twelve, but now he was going to join the company of other boys who at nineteen couldn't spell Manhattan. The parents were upset with me for having called the police. They paid my fee, but with extreme prejudice. You can buy the most unpleasant surprises.

On the other side of the page was another story on the latest fighting in Lebanon, followed by one about the billions wasted in farm subsidies. And on the bottom was an announcement of the winner of the Granville Prize, a literary award, which was a gold-plated inkpot and quill and a tax-free check for $25,000. I didn't read beyond the second paragraph. I'd read prizewinning novels before and if I were handing out an award it would be called the Big Yawn.

I'd started doing the crossword puzzle but couldn't finish it because a crowd of extra-loud goofs came in and the diner became too noisy. It looked as though they would be here until sun-up. They also looked as though they might have just come from a costume party, but we were closer to St. Patrick's Day than we were to Halloween.

I folded the paper and slid out of the booth. At the cash register I paid my check. As the waiter counted out my change, I glanced at the goofs and remarked, "Guess you get all kinds of oddballs in here Friday nights."

The waiter replied, with a rigidly impassive expression,

"Guess some customers are entitled to their opinions about other customers."

I frowned in surprise. Now, the oddballs I was referring to had their hair dyed on the wrong end of the spectrum and sculpted into shapes of permanent fright. The girls were heavily and ludicrously made-up and wore earrings of paper clips, nails, and razor blades. So did some of the carefully sallow boys. These people had an obvious identity problem. Ugliness was efficacious. The waiter, who was about my age, knew what I was talking about.

I couldn't believe him and couldn't let this pass. So I said, "What you're saying is that their right to be oddballs automatically exempts them from being judged, and that my mere 'opinion' about them precludes any validity or correctness simply because it's an 'opinion'?"

The waiter's eyes hardened. "If you want to put it in so many words—yeah." He slammed the cash register drawer shut, then walked away. In a reflection on the metal pie case, I saw him grin. And he saw my reflection of anger, and grinned even more.

I shrugged, went back to the booth, took the dollar bill from beneath the saucer, and left a dime instead. Let him be true to his nonideals. He could pretend the dime was a dollar.

Outside, a light snow was beginning to fall. I wrapped my coat more tightly around myself, shoved the paper into one of the pockets, put on my gloves, and headed back to Central Park South.

A little over a year ago I wouldn't have been able to say anything more to that waiter than maybe "jerk." A little over a year ago I was clutching what was good about me and hiding it from the world so it wouldn't get damaged. I was simply a chief of police of a New England university town that barely needed policing. I was disgusted with the world. I had been contemplating taking a sheriff's job in an even smaller town in Vermont.

But a murder had happened, and a few bodies and weeks

later I'd solved it. The first murder victim had been a philosophy professor, and his career and those of his colleagues at Sloane University fused a connection in my mind between what he taught and what he did—in fact, between what I'd been taught and what I was doing about it. The doors of some important mysteries of life cracked open then and I solved those, too. That case was the watershed of my life, which up to that point had been drying up.

As time went by I felt my back straighten and my confidence grow. I even became brave enough to move back to New York, where I'd once been a detective lieutenant of homicide with the police department. I'd quit the force because a district attorney had seemed more interested in blasting me than the killer I'd removed from the streets. But that district attorney could have been mayor now and I'd still have come back. I opened up a private investigation business, which was doing well. I was virtually immune to the city's tensions, its rudeness, its noise. When I wasn't on a case, I read. I'd been a reader anyway. Solitary men usually are. At the moment I was finishing up Aeschylus's *Oresteia* trilogy, which I grew curious about after reading a Rattigan play. I was reading philosophy, political science, poetry, even some novels. All that reading was telling me what was good about the world, what was bad, and why it could be better but wasn't.

I lived in a condominium on East Sixty-ninth Street with western and southern views. After I'd signed the agreement, moved my furniture in, and settled in, I applied for and got a private investigator's license. My momentum seemed to stop, though, when it came to signing the lease for my one-room office on Madison and Thirty-fourth. Did I mean it? Did I actually want this? I heard the sirens and racket outside the realtor's office window, and remembered that they helped to drive me away years ago. But they were only sounds. So I signed the lease. I'd put up with the city for as long as it would put up with the likes of me.

I didn't need to work. The portfolio of stocks my father, an investment banker, had left to me had increased in value, and since moving back I'd made a few shrewd substitutions, acquisitions, and sales that only increased my income. I wasn't quite a millionaire, but I wasn't poor, either.

Beneath the marquee of a hotel I stopped to light a cigarette, and stood awhile with the doorman watching the early March snow coat the limousines and street with a tenuous veil of white. Then I moved on.

I'd saved myself a life of misery and self-asphyxiation because I was still alive enough to be curious about the things that bothered me but which seemed to have no cause and no conclusion. Occasionally I looked back on myself as I was then and gasped at the distance I'd traveled. I liked the man I saw but liked myself even better. I was still the same man, but I'd crawled out of the armor of resignation. I went after the paradoxes and contradictions. I'd changed—no, grown—in a way that was frightening, but frightening only because of what I'd been ignorant of. I could have gone the rest of my life unchanged; loyal to something, yes, but would have grown senselessly insular and increasingly bitter.

Back in my apartment I slipped out of my wet clothes, put on a robe, and fixed some coffee laced with brandy. Walker, my big orange tabby with thoroughbred legs, woke up long enough to wonder what I was doing. I scratched his ears and he went back to sleep. I turned off the living room lights and stood at the window for a while to watch my city through the whirling snowfall, then sat down and finished Aeschylus under a reading lamp and learned how the gods brought reason to men's justice.

Naturally I was surprised when on the following Wednesday morning, a few minutes after I'd got to my one-desk office and was settled back in my swivel chair to admire the brass plaque I'd just picked up from an engraver's, Edgar O. Atherton, president of the Eunice Davies-Granville Foundation, called and asked to see me. Or rather his secretary did. I asked what was the purpose. She replied that Mr. Atherton would explain. I took down the address she gave me and made an appointment for an hour later.

I was too preoccupied with the plaque on my wall to speculate on why the Granville Foundation would want my services, outside of an idle mental remark that perhaps someone had filched their gold-plated inkpot and quill. I put my hammer, screwdriver, and box of nails back in the desk, then took out a rag and lightly rubbed the two lines of 12-point Scotch Roman that read: NOTHING THAT IS OBSERVABLE IN REALITY IS EXEMPT FROM RATIONAL SCRUTINY. That was now the motto of Hanrahan Investigations, courtesy of the philosophy professor whose murder I'd solved up in Massachusetts. I'd carried it around on a slip of paper in my wallet for a year before I decided that I'd earned the right to mount his test question and make it my answer to everything.

I checked my answering service for messages, made a note to reply to the two callers, sorted through some junk mail that had been dropped through the door slot, then slipped back into my coat and left.

The Foundation appeared to be the primary tenant of an old four-story brick building that was in the midst of a hive of office building construction on Madison Avenue. The building couldn't have had much of a turnover; the tenants were listed on a bronze plaque on the wall by the front door, and the Foundation topped the list.

Its executive offices were on the top floor and were so quiet that it was hard to believe that the building fronted a major traffic thoroughfare. The wall-to-wall carpeting was over an inch thick and the walls were done in cork. A woman of perhaps fifty sat behind a curved receptionist's desk. "I have an appointment with Mr. Atherton," I said to her. "My name's Hanrahan. Chess Hanrahan."

She checked her book, then said, "Won't you have a seat, Mr. Hanrahan? I'll let Mr. Atherton know you're here."

I obliged and had a seat. There were magazines on a glass coffee table and also a pile of long gray pamphlets. Under the silhouette of a unicorn were the words, in flowing script, *The Eunice Davies-Granville Memorial Foundation*. I picked one up and read it.

It was a history of the organization with a statement of its goals and a list of the past winners of the Prize and of its grant awardees for the previous year. Some of the Prize winners' names I recognized; most I didn't. And I'd never heard of any of the people who'd won the grants. Under each name was a description of the project the grantee had been given money to complete. The projects included such things as "A Study of the Culture, Language, and Customs of Southern California Surfers," "A Photo-History of Political Campaign Buttons in the United States," "The Evolution of Basque Cuisine," and "A Portrait of Agricultural Life in Pre-Colonial Tanzania."

I was still reading through the two hundred-odd names and projects when another older, well-mannered lady appeared and ushered me past some mahogany doors, through a library, and into the spacious office of Edgar O. Atherton.

He was in his early sixties, distinguished-looking, probably belonged to the Union League Club, and was nothing if not impeccable. He sat behind a desk so big I felt like shouting good morning to him across it. Except for the window overlooking Madison Avenue, the office was enclosed on three sides by shoulder high shelves of books. On one wall was a portrait of a nice-looking woman in her mid-twenties, posed in formal flapper-style dress and hat. Facing it on another wall was one that I imagined was of her parents. They didn't look too pleased with their daughter.

"Good morning, Mr. Hanrahan," said Atherton, rising. I

reached across the desk and shook hands with him. "Please have a seat."

I obliged again and folded my coat over my crossed legs.

"Cold out?" asked Atherton.

"What fell last night will be with us for a while," I replied. I nodded to the woman in the portrait. "Was that Eunice Granville?"

"Yes," said the president. "Died tragically young. Twenty-three, I believe. The Foundation was established in her memory by her parents, Oscar and Matilda."

"What did she die of?"

"Consumption."

"Oh," I said. She looked pretty healthy to me.

"Oscar Granville had metal mining interests in South America and in the Far East," volunteered Atherton. Then he put on a serious look. "Mr. Hanrahan, have you ever heard of the Granville Prize?"

"I noticed it in the Saturday paper."

"Well, Gregory Compton won this year's prize for fiction, or rather his book did, *Walk Around the Sun*. Wayne Dozier's *Coldcuts* won the drama Prize, Alice Verlander's *For a New Fiction*, the literary criticism Prize, and Virgil Bospath's *Everybody's Playing Violins*, the poetry." Atherton paused. "It's Mr. Compton I asked you here to talk to you about. Have you read any of Mr. Compton's works?"

"No."

"Well, perhaps you will some time. Our problem is that Mr. Compton has not claimed the prize. We have heard nothing from Mr. Compton since last week. Well, no, that's not quite true. We were never in direct communication with him. We notified him and his publisher by mail that he had won the prize and, if distance or other circumstances prevented him from appearing in person in our offices to claim it, we asked that he please contact us. We would then mail him the award, or give it in trust to his publisher or agent.

"It still sits in our vault, unclaimed, however. I have

made inquiries to his publisher, his agent, and his acquaintances, but nobody seems to know where he is. He has simply vanished, or chooses not to reply. I am certain that he knows he should contact us. The Granville announcement has been reported in all the national dailies and in most regional newspapers. There is simply no way he could not know."

"Maybe he's out of the country."

"Perhaps," said Atherton, who then shook his head. "Even if that were true, someone among his colleagues or friends would know where and how to contact him."

"Maybe he's gone to the country to work on his next book. Didn't take a radio with him and unplugged his phone. Writers do that, don't they?"

"Yes, I understand they do. But this is the twentieth century, Mr. Hanrahan. Given the extent of our communications establishment, there is hardly a square mile on this continent one can retreat to and not still be within broadcast distance of civilization."

Atherton was right. I asked, "Must he claim it in person?"

"No. But we do have a little ceremony for the awardees, attended by the press and notables. And we went ahead with it on Monday afternoon without him." Atherton looked sour. "It was quite a dismal affair. The press had a dozen questions for *him*, but he was not there to be asked them."

"Have you any ideas?"

"Have I, Mr. Hanrahan? Only one, which is that Mr. Compton is pulling some kind of stunt. What or why I cannot fathom."

I thought about that for a moment. "Maybe he doesn't want the Prize," I suggested.

Atherton looked as startled as a great horned owl. "*Doesn't* want the *Granville Prize??*" he said, glowering at me. "How absurd. Of course he wants it! He would be glad to have it. Anyone would. One may as well refuse the

Nobel." He looked away for a second, then shook his head and said, "But if that is the unlikely case, then we would like to *know*. The press has been pestering me and his colleagues for interviews with him. I have been telling it that he is momentarily unavailable for interviews. I cannot go on saying that. I don't care if he's retreated to Greenland or Buenos Aires, the Foundation would like to have an answer from him, some kind of response. This is unprecedented and hardly civil."

"How did you come to pick me, Mr. Atherton?"

"You were recommended to me, Mr. Hanrahan. And I seem to recall your name from the papers concerning some scandal at a university."

"Who recommended me?"

"I'm afraid I can't say."

"Must be someone I know."

"Perhaps. Though not likely."

"Let me ask you this: did Compton submit his book to the Foundation?"

"Goodness, no, Mr. Hanrahan. Authors may not submit their own work. No, his book was submitted by his publisher to our selection committee, per our rules, some eight months ago. That committee then eliminated all but ten works of fiction, which were in turn remanded to the decision of the jury. His book was one of those ten."

"How many titles did this selection committee eliminate?"

"Well over three hundred."

I let out a low whistle. "What were the criteria?"

Atherton's eyes became rings of surprise. I supposed he was shocked that I knew not only the word but its verb. "The criteria? Well, such things as timeliness of subject, depth of analysis, originality of style, soundness of structure, contribution to an overall insight into the nature of the human condition. Other categories. But I don't see why you concern yourself with those matters."

"I'm the reading public, Mr. Atherton," I said, smiling. "Of course I concern myself with those matters."

Atherton snorted. "I wasn't aware that the reading public had such sensibilities."

It was a backhanded compliment, but I let it pass. "Who published Compton's book?"

"Pericles Press." Atherton opened a folder in front of him. "His editor there is Mr. Earl Teague." He wrinkled his nose in dismay as he said the name.

I took out my pocket notebook and wrote the name down.

Atherton went on. "Mr. Teague postures as a very angry editor, Mr. Hanrahan. He claims not to have any knowledge of Mr. Compton's whereabouts. I doubt the authenticity of that posturing."

"Why?"

"Frankly, he does not sound like a very wholesome individual. I have only spoken with him over the phone, and am not inclined to meet him. You, however, might succeed in extracting some truth from him. I have tried to, and failed."

"Who's his agent?"

Atherton took a sheet of paper from the folder. "I had this prepared for you, Mr. Hanrahan," he said, leaning over to hand me the sheet. "It contains all the information we have on Mr. Compton—his address, his agent, age, past writing credits, and so on. You may also take this." He slid a glossy photograph across the desk. "We asked his editor for a picture we could use for the press release in case his book was awarded the Prize."

The photograph showed that Compton was fortyish, trim, and handsome in a way. He was smiling at something or someone and not looking directly out of the picture. He wore an open-collared white shirt. In the background was either a lake or a river. I liked his face. Maybe I'd like his books. I doubted it. Atherton and his selection committee wouldn't have liked the kinds of books this man looked like he ought to have written.

I put the sheet and photograph down and asked Atherton, "What exactly are you hiring me to do, Mr. Atherton? To find him and report his whereabouts? To find him and carry a message? What?"

Atherton shrugged expansively. "To find him, Mr. Hanrahan, and to ask him what are his intentions. That's all. I've reached the point where I don't care where he is or what he intends. I just want to know what he has to say." He paused. "And, of course, it must be understood that your task remain unknown to the press. The Granville Prize is not some kind of lottery winning. Can you assure me of discretion?"

"Sure," I said. I'd made up my mind. "Okay. I'll look for Compton. But on this condition: if I find him, and if he doesn't want the Prize or if he wants it but no further publicity and no interviews, his wishes must be respected."

"Of course, Mr. Hanrahan. I can agree to that. Shall we discuss your fee?"

Atherton not quite stammered in surprise at my rates. Apparently he thought good detectives were glutting the market. I gave him a contract to sign, then the carbon of it, and kept the original and the retainer check he'd also signed. When we were through with that business, I finally asked, "What made you think of hiring a detective to look for a missing author?"

"It wasn't *my* idea, Mr. Hanrahan. An interested party suggested the idea, and also suggested that we use your services." Atherton grinned sheepishly. "It wouldn't have occurred to me at all."

I stood up, put on my overcoat, and glanced around the room. It was a nice office, with oak-paneled walls and high ceilings. Solid, airtight construction that did not need any cork soundproofing. "Think you'll have to give some thought to finding new space for the Foundation soon?"

Atherton wrinkled his brow. "Excuse me?"

I nodded to the wide, double-paned window behind him. "You can't hear it, but the area's being built up and this building is probably just part of a parcel on your block. It's only a matter of time."

Atherton beamed proudly. "We're not worried about that, Mr. Hanrahan. The Granville Foundation has occupied this building since it was built almost fifty years ago. We'll be here another fifty. The Foundation owns it."

2

I agreed to look for Gregory Compton not so much because I was interested in Compton, but because I was curious about publishing. The case gave me an excuse to peek behind the magic curtain that seemed to veil the business. I had much the same attitude toward book publishing that I once had toward philosophy and academia: it gave me the impression that it was not run by earthlings and that whoever or whatever did run it seemed to pick the most cynical and dreariest people as its champions. It was as though the brains behind the kinds of books you saw in bookstores today were mortal enemies of men and that if they couldn't conquer the race with zap guns and flying saucers, they'd try with boredom and despair and artful filth.

I walked a few blocks from the Granville building to a bookstore on Fifth Avenue and went in past the window displaying covers of *Walk Around the Sun* with a placard that read, WINNER OF THE GRANVILLE PRIZE FOR FICTION. The store was fresh out of stock of the book. I tried another store a few blocks down; it was out of stock, too. Well, I thought, maybe I'll be able to pick up a free copy from Gussie Spendler.

Gussie Spendler, according to the sheet Atherton had given me, was Gregory Compton's literary agent. Her office was on Madison, too, but way down in the mid-Forties. I checked my watch; it was almost eleven. I hopped over a lake of slush and hailed a cab.

Spendler had an office in one of the smaller buildings near Forty-fourth. The lobby directory said that it was on the penthouse floor. The elevator went only to eleven and I had to walk up a flight of stairs to reach the top floor. At one end of a short corridor of six other offices was an opaque glass door that bore the painted sign, AUGUSTA SPENDLER AGENCY, in fancy script.

As I approached the door, I heard voices in argument. I knocked on the glass. No one answered. I knocked again. The voices continued, oblivious to my knocks. I turned the knob, went in, and found myself in an empty office. Empty of its occupant, who'd obviously stepped out while the people in the adjacent room finished their argument.

"Oh, you're just jealous, Gussie!" said a man's voice. "You know damned well that none of your mainstream hacks would ever win the Granville! Grow up, will you?"

Gussie Spendler shot back, "In twenty years of agenting, Earl, I never expected any of *my* angels to be taken 'seriously'—and excuse the euphemism! By the same token, I never expected any of your touchy, off-the-wall literary cripples to be eclectic enough to make the Granville or any other league, either!"

I sat down at the vacant desk, leaned back, and listened. I'd no scruples when it came to free information. None at all.

"Look who's being so damned critical! The exclusive agent for Ralph Goff, the proud author of *Girder!*—with an exclamation point, no less! Disaster on the construction site! Danger! Sex! Burly, earthy hardhats! Sensitive fire-fighters! Confused crane operators! Freudian pile drivers!

The pregnant riveter! *Ke-rist!* And I happen to know that Ralph Goff is the pen name for Marilyn Coates, a housewife with three kids in Howard Beach!" Earl laughed.

Gussie Spendler retaliated. "*You're* one to talk about trash, Earl! What senior editor predicted in an interview in *Editors Weekly* that Marvin Schiff's *My Regards to Posterity*—a lead Pericles title—would be a literary staple for the next twenty years, but then was unavailable for comment when said 'masterpiece' broke all speed records getting to the remainder tables? Who, Earl? Tell me who!"

"Its original title was *The Backside of a Saint*, Gussie. If we'd stuck with that . . . who knows? Anyway, that was Corry's idea—the title change *and* the interview. I don't run the show over there."

Spendler laughed out loud. "'Another memory hole punched into a wall that's already about to collapse!'"

"Huh?"

"Orwell, Earl. *Nineteen Eighty-Four?* Remember that one? The classic which *you* fortunately never handled?"

"All right, all right! You expect me to catch every hyperbole you throw at me?" Earl paused. "But let's put the axes away for a while, Gussie. Okay? Answer me this: *Why* didn't you tell me you'd submitted William Grackle's book to the Granville jury? *Why*??"

"Why didn't *you* tell me you'd submitted Compton's book?"

"I asked first! I asked first about twenty minutes ago!"

Before I could stand up and play innocent, the glass door opened and a young woman walked in, partly out of breath from climbing the stairs. When she saw me at the desk she slammed the door behind her and asked angrily, "Can I help you?"

"I don't think so," I said, standing up. "I'm waiting to see Gussie Spendler."

The oak door of the adjacent office opened then and a thin, pinched-face guy of perhaps sixty came out. "She isn't in," he growled, looking me over.

The young woman plunked her purse on the desk I was at in a display of ownership. I moved away from it, saying, "Yes, she is. And I don't think the other title would have helped Schiff's book, either. It stank."

He was about to reply in an ungentlemanlike manner when Spendler called out, "Let him in, Earl."

Earl stood aside and I saw Gussie Spendler sitting behind a desk in an office that was only a little larger than my kitchen. She looked like a bulldog and was pushing or past sixty, too. Her desk was piled with manuscripts, and there were stacks of books and manuscripts on the floor and on top of file cabinets. There were framed photographs of faces on the walls, a calendar, and a caricature of herself, which emphasized her saucer eyes and a permanent wave hairstyle of thirty years ago.

"I'm Augusta Spendler," she said. "What can I do for you?"

"I'm Chess Hanrahan, a private investigator. I'm here to talk to you about Gregory Compton."

"He was sitting here listening to you and Mr. Teague talk, Miss Spendler," said the young woman behind me. "At my desk." She went in and put a take-out bag from a coffee shop on her boss's desk.

"Thank you, Pauline," said Spendler. Pauline walked out, her nose in the air.

Earl Teague glared at me. "Where is he?" he demanded.

"Mr. Hanrahan," said Spendler, taking a plastic cup out of the bag, "I'd like you to meet Earl Teague, Mr. Compton's editor at Pericles Press. Mr. Teague's next bestseller is rumored to be a book on manners."

We nodded to each other, then Teague scowled at the agent.

Spendler asked, "You're a private investigator, Mr. Hanrahan?"

"That's right." I took out my wallet and showed her my license. She glanced at it dubiously. I put it back.

"Earl, I have a visitor," suggested the agent. "Would you mind?"

Teague grumbled and reached for his coat that was on a chair by the door. "I have to get back to the office anyway. Will you be wanting to see me, Mr. Hanrahan?"

"As soon as I'm finished here," I said. "I know where your office is."

"Great. I'm practically right across the street." Teague slipped into his coat. "Gussie, we'll pick up where we left off later." Then he left, slamming the front office door behind himself.

I unbuttoned my own coat and sat down in the leather chair in front of Gussie Spendler's desk after closing her door again.

"Would you like coffee, Mr. Hanrahan?" she asked, taking another cup out of the bag. "This one was meant for Earl."

"Thanks," I said, pulling the cup close to me and taking off the lid. "Actually, wasn't it really meant to get Pauline out of the office while you two went for a couple of rounds?"

"How much did you hear?"

"I'm not saying," I grinned. "But I'll tell you this much: you two ought to get married. You'd make a great couple. I'd invite you to all my parties."

Gussie Spendler put her cup down and roared with laughter. When she'd gotten a hold on herself, she said, "I'm sure you have great parties, Mr. Hanrahan, and I'd love to be invited to them, but not at the price of marrying Earl."

"Well, you'd do in a pinch if I couldn't get Coward and Lawrence."

"Goodness, our ages must be showing," mused Spendler. "*He's* Compton's editor at Pericles?"

"Sadly," sighed the agent. "What made you say that about Schiff's book?"

I shrugged. "I made it up. I've never heard of Marvin

Schiff. I just wanted your friend to know that I knew you were in. But it doesn't sound like a book I'd bother with."

"Well," said the agent, taking out a cigarette, putting it in a holder, and lighting it, "if you've come to ask me if I know where Greg is, I'm afraid I can't tell you. I don't know, either."

"Why do you think I want to know where he is?"

"Doesn't everybody? For instance, if Earl knew where to find him, he'd go there and wring Greg's neck. So might I if I knew." Gussie paused and then continued, "I suppose the Granville people hired you to look for him."

I just smiled. "How long have you represented Compton?"

"Going on five years, Mr. Hanrahan. I submitted his first book for three years before it was accepted, unfortunately by a publisher who refused to do any more printings and allowed the book to go out of print. He ought to change his tune now."

"And you sold *Walk* to Pericles?"

"A year and a half ago."

"And you're William Grackle's agent, too."

Spendler chuckled. "You heard quite a lot, didn't you? Yes, I am. Why do you ask?"

"Which book of his did you submit to Granville?"

"*Partly Cloudy Over Kansas*," said the agent. "Have you read it?"

I nodded. "I tried to. I thought the tornado at the end should have struck in the first chapter."

"Why, Mr. Hanrahan," replied the agent, wrinkling her brow in a shock I couldn't decide was feigned or not, "have you no taste? That book was written and is viewed by the critical establishment not only as an answer to Baum's *The Wizard of Oz*, but as the ultimate commentary on the American condition."

"Are you pulling my leg?"

"Mr. Grackle's original title was *Green Skies Over Wichita*."

I shook my head. "I don't think that title would've helped much, either."

I thought I detected secret pleasure in Gussie Spendler's expression. I asked, "How did Teague know that you'd submitted Grackle's book?"

"Actually, *I* didn't submit the book," she said. "I persuaded his editor at Bonaventure Books to. All the houses that submitted books to the Granville Foundation received a list of winners and runners-up. If Greg's book hadn't won, Grackle's would have."

"So why is Teague upset?"

"Because he'd like to publish Grackle and plans to." The agent paused. "I placed Greg's second book, which was *Walk*, or I was about to place it, because I agreed to a trade with Earl. He would publish *Walk* and Greg's short story and novella collection if I agreed to become Mr. Grackle's agent. Grackle submitted his novel to Pericles without benefit of an agent. Earl wanted to publish it, but the executive editor at Pericles, Charles Corry—Earl's only a senior editor—did not because he doubted its commercial possibilities. Earl asked me to give him a first look at Mr. Grackle's next novel if I managed to sell his first and if it proved itself."

"And why was he upset with you?"

"Because I neglected to tell him what I did. And I neglected to because he isn't Mr. Grackle's publisher."

"And he likes Compton, too?"

Gussie Spendler frowned. "Have you read any of Greg's books, Mr. Hanrahan?"

"No, not yet."

"Earl *despises* Greg *and* his books. He'd have to tell you why himself. When I submitted *Walk Around the Sun* to him the first time, he sent it back with disparaging remarks. I called him and told him he was a damned fool. A while later he asked me to lunch and he proposed the trade. He gave me Mr. Grackle's manuscript of *Partly*

Cloudy at the same time." The agent paused. "He virtually drooled over it."

"I guess Teague's changed his tune now about Compton, too."

The agent shook her head. "Oh, no, Mr. Hanrahan. Not at all. Of course he's pleased that Pericles has published a prizewinning novel, but it could have been a comic book for all he cared. Anything but a book by Gregory Compton." She reached up to a shelf above her and took down three books. "Here are Greg's books. I hope you have time to read them. But I want them *back*."

"Sure," I said, knowing that she meant it. I put them on the rug beside my chair. "Why didn't Teague try to market Grackle's book himself?"

"Editors can't sell to *rival* houses, Mr. Hanrahan," scoffed Gussie Spendler. "Where's your sense?" Then she chuckled. "Besides, Earl could offer someone the Bible, and nobody'd be interested."

"Not even after Compton's success?"

The agent sighed. "Greg's success is arguable. Of course his books sell, but not as well as they should. Clarity Press, his first publisher, won't go into a third printing, and Earl won't, either. Nor has either firm marketed the books as they should be marketed. That'll all change now, of course."

I picked up the books again and studied the jacket. *Walk* had been published by Pericles Press, and *Lake Anglique* by Clarity. The third Compton book, *A Select Circle of Friends*, the title of the novella with the short stories, was also published by Pericles.

Gussie Spendler said, "*Circle* hasn't even had a second printing. Damn Earl! And I know for a fact that bookstores have received countless queries about Greg's first two titles. But both publishers ignore them and plead lack of money."

"Are his books any good?"

"Judge for yourself, Mr. Hanrahan."

I glanced around and noted multiple copies of other published books on her shelves, among them *Girder!*, *Braid*, *Next-of-Kin*, *The Coffee Shop Kid*, *Color Me Blind*, and others I'd either read and didn't care for or had flipped through in bookstores and hadn't been tempted to buy. "You sold these, too?" I asked, nodding.

"I did," said Gussie Spendler, not quite hiding the defensiveness in her voice.

And I didn't quite manage to hide what I thought of the books in the expression on my face.

She saw that and said, "Look, what I manage to sell makes it possible for me to represent writers like Greg for years without seeing a penny. So don't give me any sermons on literature."

I hadn't planned to anyway, but if she was that sensitive about it, she might be an ally. I guess I looked baffled then, but Gussie Spendler made no effort to elaborate. I didn't ask her to, and she didn't.

"Do you think Teague might know where Compton is?"

"Earl would be the last person on earth Greg would confide anything to. He thinks less of Earl than I do."

"Where do *you* think he might have gone?"

"I couldn't say, Mr. Hanrahan. He severed his ties years ago with whatever family he had back in Michigan, so it's not likely he's gone there. You might check with his employment agency. He had to work, you know. It's a long time between royalty checks and those checks have been none too grand. He has one close friend I know of. Geoffrey Sayres, a playwright. I think he lives in the Village. I met him only once, at lunch with Greg about a year ago. He's a younger, moodier version of Greg. You have Greg's address?"

"Yes. What about girlfriends?"

"I'm not aware of any. I just told you as much about his private life as I know."

"Is he emotional, high-strung, depressed? Likely to overreact or fly off the handle?"

"Greg?" chuckled the agent. "You must be joking. He's the most stable man I've ever known. Intense, but stable. Catastrophes roll off his back. He doesn't use drugs, doesn't drink, except socially, and then he'd nurse the same glass of bourbon all New Year's Eve." Gussie Spendler laughed. "Greg is as likely to go on a bender as I am to propose to Earl."

We both laughed. That seemed to break the ice that had formed for a while. I collected the books she'd loaned me and stood up. "Look, we'll have lunch together some time soon, whether I find Compton or not. Thanks for the tip on this Geoffrey Sayres. I'll find him."

Gussie Spendler leaned back in her chair. "Would it be good manners to ask who's hired you to look for Greg?"

"It's natural curiosity," I said, shrugging my shoulders. "You've already guessed it."

"Good hunting, Mr. Hanrahan," said the agent. "And don't forget who loaned you those books."

"I won't."

3

Out on the street I became aware that I was carrying three hardback books and a leather portfolio stuffed with my notebook and random paperwork. The books would grow heavy. I went into a Lamston's and talked a salesgirl out of a plastic bag and put the books in it. It was twelve-thirty and the sidewalks were swarming with midtown lunchtimers.

Earl Teague had a strange notion of proximity. Pericles Press was across the street, all right, but down Park Avenue South about ten blocks. That part of the avenue, between Twenty-third and Thirty-second, was seedy and ill-kempt. It housed marginally successful importing companies, Armenian rug dealers, a thousand and one charities and obscure foundations, stark-looking coffee shops and Greek restaurants, and the Traffic Violations Bureau. Nearer to the great insurance towers and castles bordering Madison Square Park were a few publishers. At night the area was deserted for a full hour before the prostitutes, pimps, and other fringe people came out.

Pericles Press's front office, on the tenth floor of a building that had been new when Wilson was in Paris being disillusioned by the League of Nations, was probably the focus of whatever luxury spending the firm had indulged in three or four years previously. A few wall cases displayed upended copies of Pericles's best-selling titles. A couple of crudely patched-over black leather divans and a scratched glass table sat in the middle of a balding rug. And the receptionist chewed gum, a pastime I had always thought was a substitute for cogitation. I told her who I was and why I was here. She called a number somewhere in the back offices. Before I could sit down Teague came bustling out.

"Ah, Mr. Hanrahan," he said expansively. "Glad you could come. Come on back."

That was a change of tune. I followed him. The rug ended just beyond the door behind the receptionist's desk and a cheap-looking partition. The floor was vinyl tile that would soon have to be pulled up and replaced. The row of desks we passed on the way to his office was ready for donation to some charity. The people sitting at them didn't look too swift, either. A mailboy in a dirty gray smock pushed a wire cart before him and dumped loads of letters and heavy brown envelopes on each desk and almost ran over my toe.

Teague's office was a re-creation of Gussie Spendler's, except that it was twice as big. His desk had a name plate and one of those YOU WANT IT WHEN?? cartoon signs with a figure doubled up in laughter. On one wall was a Zen calendar surrounded by photographs of faces I supposed belonged to authors and on another was a poster of some abstract artwork from the Munich Exhibition, whatever that was. This was my first behind-the-scenes view of publishing. I was a little disappointed.

"Now, Mr. Hanrahan," said Teague after he'd closed the door of his office and settled comfortably at his desk, "how can I help you?"

I sat down. "By giving me information that might help me find Gregory Compton."

"What did Gussie tell you?"

"Whatever she told me is confidential. And of no use to me, either."

"Hmmm. Well, if *I* knew where he was. . . . Well, you probably know what I'd like to do to him."

I unbuttoned my coat. "Did you let Miss Spendler and Compton know that you'd submitted *Walk Around the Sun* to the Granville Foundation?"

Teague looked at me shrewdly, probably wondering how much I'd heard from outside the agent's door or what the agent had told me. He decided on the right thing and told me the truth. "No, I didn't."

"Why not?"

"Because I wanted to surprise them, if the book won, that's why not. I wanted *Walk* to win. And another reason why I didn't tell either of them was because I couldn't predict how Compton might've reacted. The damned fool might have sued to stop me from submitting the book."

"Why might he have done that?" I asked.

"Because writers are crazy, that's why. Compton's no exception. All locked away in some little closed universe of his own and you never know what's inhabiting it or what his rules are. Just because someone's written a good book doesn't mean he's sane. Compton is typical. Fought us on every page, every comma had a meaning, every sentence had to remain untouched. Had to wring every permutation out of every excess restatement of his theme, which I doubt anybody else but he understood. I think I managed to get him to drop one line of dialogue from *Walk*. And that's all."

I didn't think he had answered my question. So I asked another. "Why did you publish *Walk Around the Sun?*"

Teague studied me again. And this time he said the wrong thing. "Because I thought it was a great statement about the life of a sensitive artist in a society that's been so commercialized and systematized. The story is about a symphony composer who's discovered at the last minute, just before he cracks up, and then he's two-timed by his new wife and his best friend who's a pianist." Teague shook his head. "Melodramatic, of course, nothing original, and you didn't have to tell me that *Walk* was just an allegory about publishing. Christ, no other house would have thought of considering the book, so I've heard. But Pericles specializes in books that are critical of the culture, of the status quo. That's how new talent is discovered, and we discover a big proportion of it."

Great statement? Now, either Teague or Gussie Spendler had lied. It was tempting to not believe Teague. Spendler, after all, had admitted to selling garbage. But here was Teague behaving like a bag lady who was claiming to have invented the adjustable shower head. "Did you like him because you liked *Lake Anglique*?" I asked.

"More or less," said the editor after a considered pause. "Christ, even the villains in *that* one are angels." His phone rang then. He let it ring until somebody outside picked it up. Then his buzzer brayed. He picked up the receiver, listened, then said, "Tell him I'm in a meeting, Carol, and won't be free until late afternoon. And take messages for me for a while. I've got company. Thanks."

Teague put the receiver back. "Where was I? Oh, yeah, *Lake Anglique*. Well, there's no depth to it at all. Not an iota of cranial input, I mean, not a twitch of *energy*. *Walk* has a bit of that, but not *Anglique*. Everyone and everything is so squeaky clean it's nauseating. Compton's reluctant to address the little things in life, the *important* things, and that's one of his writing's liabilities. *Walk* is better in that respect, but it still leaves a shovel sticking up in ground of truth. The kinds of people he creates don't exist, they're all in his simplistic head." Teague paused. "Have you read any of his books, Mr. Hanrahan?"

"Not yet," I said, lighting a cigarette.

"Well, take *Walk*, for example. It's all about this composer who makes it after twenty years, falls for the wrong woman he paints as an opportunistic, flashy, sleep-around bitch. Yet *I* found *her* to be the most sympathetic character in the story. I mean, I *know* people like that, and they're not bad people at all. I mean, who else is there? By Compton's ethics she gets hers in the end, but in *my* hands she'd have had a chance to show the composer just how naive and rosy-eyed and rigidly judgmental he really was. So what if he'd stuck to his ideals all those years? First of all, it isn't plausible, and second, well, so do a lot of other people. I'm reading a manuscript now"—he slapped the top of a bundle of paper that was four inches high sitting on his desk—"about this woman who wants to cross the country on a skateboard. That goal isn't any more idiosyncratic than the hero's in Compton's book. It's a difference of *scale,* and the fact is that it's the skateboard-level people who populate the earth, not Compton's heroes. Writers should focus on *tangible* dreams and conflicts and struggles—which, fortunately, many writers do."

I made him pause by threatening to tap my ashes into his coffee cup, which had smutty blue silhouettes of couples ringing it. He brought out an ashtray from under some paperwork. There was a mountain of butts and pistachio shells in it.

"Another example," said Teague. "A big point in Compton's book is how all the composer's contemporaries zoomed ahead because they weren't so picky about how they got ahead, leaving poor lonely Stridivant behind to wash dishes and his questionably triumphant compositions unread and unheard. He reaches the age of forty, he's in the middle of his worst crisis, he's on his knees from worry about whether he'll ever live to hear his stuff played by an orchestra. He's exhausted, he's gathering strength to get back up and face the hostility and indifference and rejection for the umpteenth time—and then he's discovered!

"You feel like kicking his teeth in. He's so good about all the abuse and neglect he's put up with, he hasn't even the time or the good sense to realize that it was just dumb luck that someone read his sheet music, and that his music won't make a damned bit of difference in the world, people are just going to go on being grasping and petty and venal and just plain human. In Greg's stories the world looks good and habitable even after all the pain, but it's a fairy tale, I tell you, the whole approach is an escapist roundtrip flight between fantasy and reality."

I blinked once, then fixed my glance on a dying plant on his windowsill. Teague had published Compton. I'd like to have heard what the editors who had *rejected* Compton thought of him. I looked back at Teague and asked, "So why did you think his book had a chance for the Granville and why did you submit it?"

The editor narrowed his eyes. "Why do you ask that?"

I shrugged my shoulders. "I don't know anything about the Prize, what kinds of writers have won it, or who decides what book gets it. I'd like to know, that's all."

Teague leaned back in his chair. "Well, I got an invitation to submit one book—most publishers get them—I looked over what we had, and I picked *Walk*. Then it was cleared with the permanent sitting committee at the Granville Foundation, and they passed it on to a jury. I also had to send them a bio of Compton, and copies of all the reviews the book had since its publication date. A couple of months later they notified me that *Walk* was with the jury and that it was okay for me to cross my fingers." Then he stopped rocking back and forth. "And on Friday afternoon, just as I was going to lunch, the letter came from Atherton, who's president of the Foundation, telling us that Compton's book had won."

He didn't sound too excited by it. I wouldn't have understood why not if Gussie Spendler hadn't told me the story behind *Walk's* publication. I asked, "How did you feel about Grackle's book coming in second?"

"How . . . oh," said Teague. "Gussie must've told you about our trade."

"I guess she did."

"Well, I was glad it got *some* recognition. Grackle will

get another shot at first place with his other books. Read *Kansas* yet?"

"No, not yet," I lied.

"*Wonderful* story," smiled Teague. "Set during the last recession. This boy, Bud, sitting in a roadside diner, in the middle of nowhere in Kansas, listening to the radio the cook's got going, and you know Kansas, it's all horizon and blue sky. Grackle's a bright and prolific kid, he can really set a mood. Bud's young and unemployed, no home, no ties, no commitments, so he drives off in any direction, and he learns five-hundred-and-forty-eight pages later that everything's the same everywhere, that the horizon's just an illusion, that no matter where he goes, all he'll find is the same nausea, the same kinds of people, the same self-loathing and pretensions and phoniness, even in his hero, this hard-living, womanizing truck driver. The blue sky, it's always there, he gets so he hates it. And in the end he winds up back at the crossroads, and while he's listening to the same old weather report, a tornado drops down out of the sky and he stands right in its path, welcoming the destruction it brings."

Teague nodded his head in appreciation, ignoring my stifled yawn. "This Grackle," he continued, "he's a master of words and moods. Bet you anything it gets optioned by Hollywood. God, that boy's got a career in front of him! And I'm going to be a part of it, you wait and see!"

I wasn't going to wait and see, but didn't say so. I put my cigarette out and asked, "Have you ever met Geoffrey Sayres?"

"Sayres? Sayres? The name rings a bell. Yeah, I've heard of him. Never met him. He writes plays, I think."

"Does Compton have any other friends you might know about?"

"None that I know of." Then Teague leaned forward and said, "The only person who could probably help you—she won't help *me*, damn her—is Rhea Hamilton. You've heard of her, haven't you?"

"No."

"She and Compton are like *that*," said the editor, holding up a hand with two fingers crossed suggestively. "Have been for quite a while."

"Why should I have heard of her?"

"She's the daughter of Wallace Conover, the shipping king. He builds these container ships. Has yards up and down the East Coast and one in California."

Wallace Conover I had heard about. His Polaris Steamship Company made the financial sections of most papers every other week. He'd not only developed the "break-apart," modular container, which expedited shipments of merchandise, helped shippers cut storage and transport costs, and put a dent in pilferage, but had designed new freighters to handle the containers he leased to shippers. For the last three months the papers and the trade were speculating on a radically different kind of freighter Conover's engineers were designing. These hydrofoil models would be faster than any Coast Guard cutter and powered by Conover patented supercharged diesel engines that could devastate air cargo lines and revolutionize ocean transport. I'd have bought Polaris stock long ago except that there wasn't much of it on the market.

But what Teague had just told me contradicted what I'd been told by Gussie Spendler. If Compton wasn't disposed to talk about his private life—whether from habit or from secretiveness—how would Teague know about his connection with the daughter of a billionaire and not the agent? So I asked, "How do you know she and Compton are lovers?"

Teague shrugged. "Read about it in a gossip column somewhere. And word gets around. She's filthy rich herself. Could probably buy Compton a publisher if he'd let her."

"Why wouldn't he let her?"

"He has strange ideas of success. Says it has to be 'real,' whatever that means."

"Ever talk to her?"

"Once. On Tuesday, when nobody'd heard from Compton. She wouldn't admit that she knew where he was. I called her, was civil as hell, but she's as cold and stuck-up as they come."

I tried to imagine Teague being civil and found myself thinking of someone devoid of personality. I asked, "Why don't you promote Compton's books more?"

Teague barked a laugh. "Gussie complained to you about that, eh? Well, I've already told her too many times. *I* don't think that would increase sales. At least I didn't think it would. The Granville changes everything, of course. I've ordered our publicity department to crank out a new ad campaign."

"Why couldn't you have taken Compton's books without making a deal with her over Grackle?"

Teague frowned, then chuckled. "Gussie must have unloaded her soul to you. You can tell her that *I* didn't think he was good enough to take on. But I wanted Grackle—and I'll land him sooner or later—and I had her in a corner. We made a deal. You tell her that, Mr. Hanrahan. And you can also tell her that I might hold up publication of his next book until she gets Grackle over to this house." The editor paused. "What've your questions got to do with Compton anyway?"

What was the matter with this guy, I thought. Did he think he was talking to somebody who had the retentive powers of a crow? At the same time, I was fascinated, too, by the effortlessness of his patter. He was used to talking to people that way. You could be an idiot or his confessor. It didn't seem to matter. I said, "You know, what you just said contradicts what you said earlier, about how you thought Compton's book was a great statement."

Teague sniffed. "No, it doesn't," he said. "Where's your sophistication, boy? People who take words literally tend to be written off as retarded, or pushovers."

I smiled. "Spendler's thinking of getting Compton a new publisher."

The editor's face grew livid. "Like hell, she is! Compton owes Pericles one more book. I'll bet she didn't tell you *that*, did she? Compton signed a contract committing him to three books. We'll do his next one and then he can go where he damned pleases!"

I looked away once, then shook my head. "If you think so little of Compton's books, why did you bother with them at all?"

Teague leaned forward sharply and pointed a finger at me. "Look, mister, just find the sonofabitch so we can all get on with living. That's all you need to know."

"Strange attitude," I remarked as I stood up.

"It's *mine*," said Teague. "And if you find Compton, you tell him that if he pulls a stunt like not accepting the Granville, he can throw away his typewriter, because he'll be finished in this business. For good. We'll stop production of his books, and no other house'll take him."

"Why is that?"

"No one likes a sore *winner*," said Teague. "You tell him that."

4

$\mathbf{I}$ walked back to my office on
Thirty-fourth and Madison. Earl Teague didn't just leave a
bad taste in my mouth; if he had slipped on the ice on the
sidewalk I wouldn't have offered to help him to his feet
again. And there was either something very wrong with the
way Compton's books were published, or I didn't know
enough about the business yet. But I couldn't believe the
book industry was populated by the likes of Teague. And I
wondered why he'd volunteered the tidbit about Rhea
Hamilton.

The wind was bitter and gusty and the temperature
dropping. The slush in the street was beginning to freeze
over. A particularly strong breeze blew some snow off a
coffee shop's canopy and into my face. I went into the
restaurant for some lunch, gave my order to the waitress,
and opened *Walk Around the Sun*.

The voices and clatter faded away, ceasing to be even
distractions. Other customers passed by me, creating drafts
and brushing my elbows with the coats they were putting
on or taking off. My coffee grew cold and the cigarette I had
lit burned down to the filter after only one drag. And when

the waitress said "Excuse me" I looked up with resentment that she had brought my order so quickly.

It began with a wineglass dropped onto a tile floor by Stridivant, a dishwasher in an exclusive restaurant. And from there I had to read the next sentence, and the next, and by the time my burger came I was on page twenty. I ate that burger almost as ravenously as I read the book. I smiled at how Stridivant the lowly dishwasher handled the petty power-game players in the restaurant kitchen. And I followed him home on a near-empty subway train and through the rotting neighborhoods to his one room in a noisy, vermin-infested building. And that's where I learned that he was the composer.

I paid my bill, left a big tip for the waitress who'd kept refilling my coffee cup, and went up to my office around the corner. It was nearly two o'clock.

By four I was almost three-quarters finished with *Walk*, and might have even finished it if it hadn't been for some phone calls and the time I took to trace Geoffrey Sayres in the phone book and through the operator. There was no listing of him anywhere.

I'd never consumed a book as fast as I did Compton's. He didn't sweep you into the story at all; he simply opened each chapter with an innocuous statement about something and then built each subsequent paragraph on it and on each other, and before you knew it, and whether you liked the story or not, you were into it and *had* to finish it. There was some kind of geometry at work in his writing style that was the root of the hypnotic effect he created in his method. You read on just to see what was going to happen next.

And I *liked* the story, and that made reading the book thrilling. Half of Stridivant's world I knew, the other half I didn't. I knew something about integrity, something about vision, something about determination. But the poverty, the menial jobs, the deprivation, the squalor, and the hopelessness of the other half of his world were alien to me. I'd never had to experience any of those things—until now.

I shivered in his unheated room. I counted my coins to buy groceries. I brought nobility to the job of sweeping floors. I felt the sting of hot, greasy water and watched the skin of my hands grow pulpy under streams of suds. I woke up in the middle of the night—sometimes to jump out of bed to write down a score on some sheet music by the light of a cracked desk lamp, and sometimes to wonder where my life was going.

And I went through years of that. Years. Stridivant was so real to me that I almost felt I could reach out and touch him—and everything else in the story. I'd read other books in which the same kind of character turned out to be a maniac. Stridivant was a maniac, too, but a maniac who was portrayed as normal, as human, and who made all other kinds of normalcy and humanity look slothfully obscene, because he had a *purpose*. When he'd wake up in the middle of the night to write down a new idea, you could feel the cold on his busy hand and hear the quiet of the deserted street beyond the smears of his taped-up window, and you knew, like Stridivant, that nothing else mattered then, not even the possibility of success . . .

And by four o'clock I'd forgotten that I'd been hired to look for Gregory Compton. And I was only reminded of it by the call I took then and whose ring on the phone made me curse once and pick up the receiver to say, "What??"

The voice on the other end was taken aback by the irritation in my own. It asked, tentatively, "Mr. Chess Hanrahan?"

"Yes?"

"This is Sandra Mead, secretary to Wallace Conover. Mr. Conover would like to know if you could see him tonight. If you're not busy."

The frown vanished from my brow and I put the book aside. "No," I said, "I'm not busy tonight. May I ask what in reference to?"

"I don't know, Mr. Hanrahan. He's asked me to invite

you to his residence in Tarrytown. May I give you the address?"

She certainly could. I drew a pad and pencil to me. "Shoot." When I'd written it down, I asked, "What time?" Seven o'clock.

"Have you a tux?" asked the secretary. "There will be cocktails and dinner."

"Yes, I have one," I said. "Will there be other guests?"

"Yes, Mr. Hanrahan. Fine, I'll tell Mr. Conover that you'll be there."

"Thanks," I said. "Sorry if I sounded a little nasty when I answered. I was in the middle of a good book."

"That's all right, Mr. Hanrahan. Good day."

I put the receiver back and sat and thought for a moment. Wallace Conover? What could he want with me? I didn't know him, and he certainly didn't know me. And I couldn't for a moment believe that Earl Teague knew him at all. But then Atherton had alluded to someone whom I was not likely to know, and Wallace Conover certainly fit that bill.

I squeezed in the last two pages of the chapter I was finishing, then got busy. I took the books and portfolio downstairs, hailed a cab to my place, showered, changed into the tux, and fed Walker. I put Compton's book on my reading chair, then took the elevator to the garage, picked up my car, and headed for Flushing, which was where Compton lived. I was lucky and beat the beginning of the rush-hour traffic jams by about two minutes.

It was an isolated, dismal section of Queens, on the most eastward fringe, hemmed in by expressways and boulevards. There were single-family houses cornered by wire fences, minuscule, weed-grown front lawns, and narrow, rutted driveways. The gutters were choked with months old leaves and refuse. The houses themselves were either nondescript and dingy, or gaudily overdone with cheap, cracked materials bought in five-and-dimes. Neglected cars and vans lined the sidewalks on one side and on the other were bare old trees whose giant roots were buckling the concrete and disintegrating the pavement into undulating hills and valleys. I had to watch where I stepped every few feet; dogs had been everywhere. Not even the snowfall had prettied up the area. It had only made it look more apathetic.

The house Compton lived in was no different from the others. A Mercedes, a ten-year-old, four-door model, sat in the driveway near the house's backyard. I walked up the asphalt slope and looked it over. Other than a missing hood ornament and a rear hubcap, it was in good shape. The radiator grill was a bit banged up, and I'd have given it a new paint job just to protect the metal, but the machine was no piece of junk. It didn't belong in this neighborhood. I looked at the yellow registration sticker on the windshield over the steering wheel.

"It's not for sale."

I turned to the voice. It was a fellow in his late twenties with a lean, sharp face that was wary and hostile. He carried a briefcase in one hand and his other arm was loaded with a bag of groceries. His overcoat needed replacement, not repair. There was a hole in two of the fingers of his gloves. But the fellow was no piece of junk, either. There was pride and strength in his carriage. If I had been a car thief, he would have dropped those groceries and tried to beat the hell out of me.

I took out my license and showed it to him. "I'm looking for Gregory Compton. You know him?"

"I know him," said the stranger. "What do you want with him?"

"Some people want to know where he is. Who are you?"

"A neighbor of his. Geoffrey Sayres." He paused to get a better grip on his bag. "I live across the street. Who hired you?"

"I can't say." I put my wallet back. "I guess you don't live in the Village anymore."

"I just moved here." Sayres studied me for a while

longer, apparently making up his mind about something. Then he gestured with his head. "Come on up for a coffee. I'm just getting home from work. I'd like to know where he is, too."

"You're a playwright, aren't you?" I asked as we walked.

"A dramatist," said Sayres, still not sounding very friendly. "If I ever develop a sense of humor, which isn't damned likely, then I'll be a playwright." We stopped at the gate to his house. "How did you know?"

I shrugged. "Somebody mentioned your name."

"Who?"

"Can't say," I smiled. "What made you move from the Village?"

We went through the gate and up the steps of his house. Sayres kicked some soggy newspapers out of the way, collected his mail from a box that was hanging from the brick, and unlocked the front door. "Greg learned about a vacancy here, and told me about it. It's cheaper and a lot quieter. Sometimes too quiet. Most of the people who live around here lock themselves in and don't come out unless they have to." We were in a short hallway that stank of cats and some foul-smelling soup being brewed by the sole ground-floor occupant. Sayres produced another key and unlocked yet another door at the end and led the way upstairs to his place, which was two rooms—a kitchen, a bath—and clean. "But at least I don't have to listen to other people's noise and run into creeps and dope pushers everywhere I go."

"How long have you known Compton?" I asked, taking off my overcoat in the kitchen and draping it over a chair.

Sayres eyed my tux incredulously, then turned to unpacking his groceries. "About four years. We met on a temp job." He filled a kettle with water and put it on a burner.

"A what?"

"A temporary job," he said. "We were both working for this same big agency and were sent to the same company one week to type invoices." Sayres pulled down two cups from a shelf and measured out some instant coffee. "Greg's still working temps. Last week it was a real estate company, this week it was a cosmetics firm. I think he's going back there next week." The dramatist paused. "Why were you looking over his car?"

"I didn't know it was his," I said. "If he had gone somewhere out of the city he would have taken it. Do you know where he is?"

"No." Sayres sat down at the table and cleared some books and papers out of the way. "I don't think anybody knows where he's gone to."

"Nice car on temporary wages," I remarked.

Sayres laughed ironically. "No. He didn't buy it. *She* gave it to him. Rhea Hamilton. She spotted it in one of those used-car lots on Queens Boulevard and bought it then and there. He doesn't use it much, though. He can't afford auto insurance and gas is expensive."

"You know her?"

"We've met. But I don't much like her and she doesn't care for me. I think we've exchanged a total of about thirty words."

There was jealousy in his eyes and a hate that wanted to be love, too. I noticed an ashtray piled with extinguished cigarettes, so I lit one up. So did Sayres. I looked around the place, then asked, "You live alone?"

"I get more work done that way."

"When did you last see Compton?"

"Saturday afternoon. Last Saturday, that is."

"Did he say where he was going?"

"No. I hadn't any idea he was going anywhere. He's on an assignment somewhere with another agency, and they're a little upset that he hasn't called in or asked for a replacement. I called the agency on Tuesday to ask if they'd heard from him. They hadn't."

"Where are you working now?"

"I've got a permanent job with an ad agency. I write copy—for the time being."

"Ever have one of your plays produced?"

Sayres shook his head. "My stuff has gone only as far as readings. Once a director wanted to do my third play, but the producer talked him out of it." He paused. "It's a tougher business than Greg's. The market's smaller and the money's tighter." The kettle began shrieking then and he got up to pour our cups.

There was an unrelieved tension in Sayres, tension and pent-up anger. I couldn't pinpoint its source. I asked, "What did you and Compton talk about Saturday afternoon?"

Sayres brought the coffee to the table and put out some cream and sugar. Then he sat down. "About the Granville Prize," he said. "You must have something to do with it."

"Maybe. I know that he won it."

"Ever read any of his books?"

"I'm reading one now."

"Think he should have won the Granville?"

"I don't know. Should he have?"

"No."

I took a sip of my coffee. "Why not?"

Sayres did the same with his. "He got the notice in the mail Friday. It was there when he got home from work. He must have stayed up all night thinking about it. Then the next day he came over. I'd just come back from the cleaners and had picked up a Saturday paper and we noticed the Granville story on the front page. We talked about it for a while. We couldn't make sense of it. He didn't think he should've won it, either."

"Why did he think that?"

"How many people have you sent to prison, Mr. Hanrahan?"

"Dozens," I said, wondering what he was leading to.

"Did they ever form an association and give you a silver

medal for your work in law and order? Or a gold-plated cell lock?" Sayres snorted and answered his own question. "No? Well, that's why Greg shouldn't have won the Granville." He paused. "He hadn't even a suspicion that he was a candidate for it. His publisher never told him. And Greg didn't want it. Had no use for it. He thought it would be a detriment to his career. He despised the kinds of authors who'd won it in the past and the kinds of people who were responsible for awarding it." Sayres lit another cigarette. "What Greg finally decided was to turn it down."

The thought had occurred to me, too, in Atherton's office, but my speculation didn't have the emotion behind it that I saw in Sayres. "He told you that?"

"He typed up a draft of a letter he was going to send to the Foundation, and he wanted me to read it to see if it was cordial enough. He was furious. Seething. I told him one doesn't turn down something like the Granville and not expect consequences. That would've made as big a headline as the original announcement. But he was determined, and he needed me to make sure that he'd said the right thing. And he had. I can quote it for you, it was so short. 'Gentlemen: I cannot in good conscience accept the Granville Prize for Fiction, and would be grateful if it were withdrawn. Sincerely, Gregory Compton.'"

"And he mailed it Saturday?"

"That's what he said he would do, once he typed up a clean copy of it."

"But you're not certain that he mailed it?"

"I didn't actually see him put it into a mailbox."

I narrowed my eyes. "Why do you doubt it?"

Sayres's eyes bored into me. "I don't doubt it," he said. "I mean, if he'd mailed that letter, wouldn't we have heard about it in the news already?"

He had a point. If Compton had mailed that letter, Atherton would have had it and known about it. And *I* was being suckered for some reason. And wouldn't he have informed Gussie Spendler and Teague about his decision?

But now I thought I knew what was bothering Sayres. His hero or friend might have let him down.

"Did you see Compton after that?"

"I saw him go out about an hour later. My study is in the living room, and I can see everything that goes on out on the street. Which isn't much. It was about two o'clock."

"Did he use his car?"

"He got in and drove off."

"And you've no idea of where he might have gone?"

"He probably went to see her. Rhea Hamilton, I mean. But he could have gone anywhere. Or just for a drive. I . . . didn't envy him for the decision he had to make." Sayres paused. "He has a family back in Michigan, but he broke off with it ages ago."

"Did you see him come back?"

"No. On Sunday morning I noticed his car in the driveway, just where you found it, and assumed he was back. I went over and knocked on his door, but there was no answer. I asked his landlord, who lives on the ground floor, if he'd seen him. He said Greg wasn't up there, he'd just come down from fixing a leak in the kitchen faucet Greg had told him about."

I sipped my coffee. "How did he and Rhea Hamilton meet?"

"In a restaurant where he was working as a waiter. That was about two years ago. When he wanted to save up enough money so that he could work on a book without interruption, he'd get a job as a waiter in a five-star restaurant. He'd make a fortune in tips, then quit. That's how he finished *Walk Around the Sun*."

"Interesting," I remarked.

"She's a magnificent-looking woman. She's the kind you think ought to be waiting for you when you've come off the desert, when you've fought all your battles and won a great victory. A prize in and of itself, one that somehow matches what you've endured and fought for." Sayres closed his eyes for a moment, then continued. "Well, I don't blame Greg for having fallen for her. He'd put up with a lot, denied himself a lot. If anyone had the right to be a cynic, he had. But it doesn't show up in his writing, and to look at him you wouldn't suspect the hell he'd gone through. Perhaps he's decided that if he's going to know some joy in his life, it might be a small price to pay to be domesticated, especially if you don't have to wait on tables and when your kennel is a six-room luxury apartment on Fifth Avenue." Sayres finished his coffee, then shrugged. "And perhaps he's decided to accept the Granville, too." Suddenly he flung the cup to the floor and it exploded into a hundred pieces. "Well, why shouldn't he, goddamn it!! Why shouldn't he!!"

Sayres jumped up and went to the window to stare out.

I waited a moment, then asked, "How could it have hurt him to accept the Granville, Sayres?"

He didn't answer. I checked my watch. It was fifteen after six. Tarrytown was a long drive ahead even without bad roads and traffic. I stood up and put on my coat. He turned and watched me. I said, "We'll talk again soon."

He nodded and saw me to the door without further word.

5

As I drove, Sayres's behavior—his entire character—was on my mind. Gussie Spendler said that he was a moodier version of Compton. What I'd just witnessed wasn't moodiness; it was pure, unchanneled anger. With a little desperate, repressed self-pity mixed in. It would have been pointless to ask him more questions even if I had the time. He'd simply clammed up. We'd have another session.

What actually piqued my interest now was the possibility that Compton had turned the Granville Prize down. Sayres apparently was the only one who knew that. If Compton had mailed that letter, why would Atherton have hired me to look for him? And if he hadn't mailed the letter, why hadn't he? Did he change his mind? Was he talked out of it by Rhea Hamilton or by somebody I didn't know existed yet? And why would Compton turn down the prize? I had a glimmer of an idea of why, but I had to finish his books before I tackled it.

When I reached Tarrytown it was seven-thirty, and I discovered three gas stations later that Wallace Conover's place was not in the village of Tarrytown, but a bit north of it. I drove cautiously by some of the biggest estates to be found anywhere, where the only sign of habitation was a stone or wooden wall broken every quarter mile by a gate. I found the road, and then the number, turned into a paved driveway that was better lit than the county road, and at eight I pulled up in front of Conover's mansion. There were a dozen other cars and limousines parked out in front of the brilliantly lit house. I parked mine near the frozen fountain, got out, and went up the granite steps.

A servant met me at the door. I gave him my name, he took my coat and scarf, then led me down a rich carpet through a spacious hallway in the direction of the music and voices. We ran into a crowd of guests moving from one big room into another. I'd made it in time for dinner. All the men were in tuxes, and the women in gowns. The servant left me for a moment and disappeared into the one room, and came back with a rugged-looking man with a clean, compact face and wavy, pepper-gray hair. He was in his early sixties and looked tennis court-fit.

"Mr. Hanrahan," he said, offering his hand and an inquisitive smile, "I was afraid you wouldn't make it. I'm Wallace Conover."

"Hi," I said, shaking his hand. "Sorry I'm late. I got lost."

"I should have asked Sandra to give you more specific directions. My apologies. We're just sitting down to dinner, but you must still be cold and in need of a drink. What can I get you?"

"A dry sherry, thanks."

I followed Conover to a bar in the vacated room. A caterer's crew was already cleaning the place in preparation for the after-dinner social. He found a bottle, two glasses, and poured the drinks. After I'd tasted mine, he said, "You're probably wondering what this is all about, Mr. Hanrahan."

"The dinner *and* my being here, yes."

"The dinner is to celebrate the twentieth anniversary of Polaris Shipping. Most of my executives and top technical men are here tonight. I started out working for a firm that bought old freighters for scrap. Now I'm building new ones."

I smiled. "And designing a few that'll skim the oceans."

He grinned in surprise. "Only in calm waters, Mr. Hanrahan. How did you know that?"

"I'm always looking for a good home for my money. Not all detectives wear used shoelace."

Conover studied me with interest for a moment, then said, "As for your being here, well, I understand that you're looking for Gregory Compton."

"Per your suggestion," I said. "I came highly recommended by the party that hired me." I paused. "He didn't mention your name."

Conover grunted. "I am impressed," he said. "How on earth did you piece that together?"

"I'm a detective," I smiled.

Conover shook his head in appreciation. "I suggested you to Atherton at the Granville Foundation for two reasons. I liked the way you exposed that kidnapping hoax last week. Also, Sloane University is my alma mater. You were given quite a write-up in the alumni newsletter over that Walsh Hall murder. What made you leave East Auberley?"

"My universe got bigger."

"Excuse me?" smiled Conover.

"It's a long story." When I left East Auberley, Massachusetts, I left behind a neatly wrapped package, a lot of friends and memories. Sometimes I yearned to go back to the town, just for a visit, to relive those memories *in situ*. I felt the same thing for the school and town as I did some of my favorite boyhood haunts.

"You must tell me that story sometime," said Conover. He finished his sherry. "I think I should rejoin my guests now, Mr. Hanrahan. Oh, there's one more thing before we go in. My sister arranged the seating and I wasn't able to put you at my elbow. You'll be sitting among strangers. May I ask a favor of you?"

"Of course."

"If anyone asks what you're doing here, please don't mention Gregory Compton. Invent some vague story no one would be likely to pursue. I'll explain why later, when we're alone. Then I'd like you to meet my daughter, Rhea." Conover paused. "Have you made any progress in finding him?"

I shook my head. "I've met some interesting people who know him, that's all." I finished my sherry. "He'll turn up. Do you think your daughter knows?"

Conover sighed. "I wish I could say, Mr. Hanrahan. She says she doesn't, but she may be lying to protect him." Then his face brightened and also grew red. "How did you learn *that*?"

"People talk."

"Too damned much," sighed Conover. He put his glass down. "We'd better go in now. No one will touch his soup until I do."

If it was a pleasant dinner, I didn't notice. I ate, I listened to a short speech by Conover's vice president of research, I introduced myself and got caught up in small talk not one word of which I would ever remember again, and I had too much coffee. The small talk especially got on my nerves because I had to sit with my elbows on the damask and pretend I was interested in what someone was saying, when all I wanted to do was sit and watch Rhea Hamilton.

There were several attractive women at the long table of perhaps thirty people, and a few who were beautiful. Rhea Hamilton was beautiful, was graceful without being delicate, had poise that was not acquired in any finishing school, and a presence that was powerful but unconscious. And if it were conscious, it would have wilted most of the men at the table and made them wish she were indifferent. She was indifferent, and I could see how it was a strain on the guests around her. She wore a red gown that left her back bare, and droplet earrings, and her brown hair swept up from her bare neck and ears and curved sleekly to curl arrogantly over her forehead.

It was her face I wanted to watch. It set her apart. It was indifferent and painfully courteous and scornfully inexpressive and that made it the most animated face at the table. And yet those same things could express greed and lust and passion, and I could think of few men who could withstand being their object. Sayres had said Rhea Hamilton was magnificent. She was. But she was no prize to be given. She was something that would be waiting for you of her own accord when you came out of the desert from all your battles. You had to be a prize yourself before you could want her. And to want her you had to be able to grasp that bare neck and stare into that scorn and stab her lips to let her know that your battles weren't over and would never be because she was a prize you wanted to earn over and over again.

She turned her head suddenly and saw me watching her. She held my glance for a moment, then frowned. I loved what that did to her hazel eyes. She knew it and her frown became stressed. Then she turned to speak with her father next to her at the head of the table. I reached for a bottle of white wine and poured myself a glass.

Perhaps I'd been away from women too long, I thought. I doubted it. Most of them simply baffled me. Six months ago Helen Nash had broken off our affair because she said I was too serious. She enjoyed everything I had to offer and, I, everything she had to offer. But one evening she came in without notice and when I didn't want to go to a concert because I was near the end of reading a riveting espionage novel and wanted to finish it, she took affront at my choice, screamed at me, accused me of seeing other women, of not wanting to go anywhere with her, and then she walked out. The closeness I thought I'd shared with her about some very important things simply vanished and left me cold. She was intelligent and was an executive with a local broadcasting company. She should have wanted me to finish the book. One of the last things she accused me of was taking books too seriously. It was the one accusation of hers I couldn't deny. Why should I have?

So I didn't think it was hunger or loneliness that was coloring my reaction to Rhea Hamilton. It was simply the natural desire for a great woman.

Dinner ended and I drifted back with the other guests into the other room, which was probably also Conover's study or library. I avoided talk and looked over the titles on the shelves instead. I found his fiction shelf and recognized a lot of new friends, then spotted Compton's three books. I took down his copy of *Walk* and saw that it was autographed. Maybe when this was all over I'd have my copies autographed, too.

"Rhea's engaged to him, you know," said a woman's voice brightly.

I turned to the voice and recognized the wife of one of the younger executives. "I can understand that," I remarked.

"Oh?" she said brightly. "Why?"

"Ever read his books?"

"I read the one you have in your hand, just to see what kind of man it was she was interested in *this* time. I can't say I liked it. And I couldn't stand that hero of his, Stridivant. Makes the rest of us look like we all ought to be locked up or something. His minor characters were more real to me."

"Such as the villains," I suggested.

The woman smiled. "That's right, you know! Now why couldn't he have made Stridivant that way?"

"Stridivant's the most authentic character in the story. It's his minor characters I find almost implausible. I guess that's because there are more of them in the real world." Before she could think that over, I asked, "What did you mean, 'this time'?"

"She's been married before," said the woman. "What was his name? Bernard Hamilton. It was a post-college marriage. He was some kind of engineer and pretty loaded, too. I think he drifted into government construction programs and drink, and it broke up. Then she began running around with writers and clothes designers and actors, but none of them lasted for more than a month. Compton's the latest and he's lasted two years. I think they're serious."

"I think so, too."

"They say *Walk's* his best book," said the woman. "I don't wonder, not with the time she can give him."

"How do you mean?"

"What was it Mencken said about artists?" The woman took a sip of her brandy and looked up at the ceiling. "Oh, yes. 'The best and clearest thinking'—ah—'and the finest art is produced'—ah, yes—'not by men who are hungry, ragged and harassed, but who are well-fed, warm and easy in mind.'"

She was quoting from Mencken's *Prejudices*, and in all fairness to him that wasn't exactly what he'd said. I'd read Mencken, too, and that particular essay of his I thought was one of his most dismal. If you believed everything he said in it, you may as well shoot yourself or go to Tibet. "That's not necessarily true," I said. "Think of all the well-fed, warm, and easy-minded authors who turn out garbage."

"I *won't* hear anything against Ч. L.," said the woman in mock reprimand. "He's my mentor."

"The problem with a first-rate iconoclast is that he may be too good. A culture that doesn't produce a first-rate champion tends to appoint the iconoclast its fount of wisdom, and that gives most people an excuse to destroy everything, good with bad." I paused. "But, then again, a culture that appoints one as its high priest is in serious trouble anyway. It means that it's ready to die."

The woman furled her brow. "Did *he* say that?" she asked, surprised. "Where?"

I should have felt flattered that she thought I was quoting her mentor. "No, *I* said it," I smiled. "Just now."

"Oh . . ." smiled the woman vaguely. "What a cynical thing to say. Well, I must join my husband. It's been nice talking with you." She turned and walked away.

She hadn't even been curious enough to ask my name. I suppose she thought that since she didn't recognize me as an authority, what I'd said couldn't be true. Maybe I'd struck her secret chord and caused her to realize a truth about herself. Or maybe she was too embarrassed.

But I stopped thinking about her because I saw Rhea Hamilton moving among the guests. She moved from group to group with a detached grace, almost as though she were a school teacher moving among her students in a classroom. Her beauty and manner and ease of conversation brought unanimous smiles to the guests, but when she moved on she left behind a pond of frozen silence that took a few minutes to thaw. She glanced in my direction a few times, a shadow of anger in her eyes, but didn't approach me. I think she knew that we would meet eventually, and so was in no hurry. Neither was I. It would happen.

I did not join any of the conversations, but wandered around the room studying Conover's book titles and admiring some of his artwork. One of the executives cornered me, though, and halfway into a discussion about the stock market, Conover came up. "Excuse us, Gerry," he said to the man, "but I must speak with Mr. Hanrahan."

I waved to the executive and followed the shipbuilder through the crowd to another, smaller room. He closed the door, then lit up a cheroot. I lit a cigarette. He gestured to one of the three armchairs in the room and we sat down.

Conover sighed. "I think I'm safe for a few minutes. By the way, June Goddard asked me who you were. You seemed to have upset her somehow. She was telling me that you must be a friend of Gregory Compton. I said no, you weren't, that you were a detective and an old chum of mine. She couldn't quite digest that. What did you say to her?"

I repeated my conversation with the woman.

Conover laughed when I finished. "It would appear that you really don't wear used shoelace." He studied his cheroot in silence, then said, "Before Rhea comes in, I'd like to explain my interest in Greg—Gregory Compton. Have you read any of his books?"

"I'm only just finishing *Walk Around the Sun.*"

"What prompted you to start reading him?"

"Things people have been saying about him and about his books."

"I see. He and my daughter are engaged," said Conover. "Perhaps you've already learned that, too. Well, what I want to say is this: of all the men in my daughter's life, I'd like her to settle on Greg. I'd like him to be the last. I want that for my own sake as well as hers, because I admire him and we share the same perspective and I wouldn't mind having him as a son-in-law. When she brought him home for dinner one evening, I thought he would be just another of her artsy boyfriends, the kind that bears a grudge against the world and is always lambasting the kind of people we are and the way we live. She was married once, soon after she left college, to a fellow who was brilliant and showed much promise. But . . . he sort of fell to pieces. A few federal and state pork-barrel projects came his way, and he became addicted to them, he began drinking and using drugs, and she divorced him. That was about five years ago."

"She kept his name, though."

"Yes. She keeps it as a reminder, she says. So since her divorce she's gone through a lot of personal trouble. Greg's ended that, brought her back to her old self—and back to me. Anyway, she brought Greg home one evening, and for once I liked her choice. He was raw—not vulgar, mind you—not crude or anything like that. He was independent, indifferent to most human attachments you or I might need or place some value on, or grow to need. He's dedicated to his writing, devoted to it, in a way I've never imagined possible for anyone but which I accept because, well, it's what I am to my containers and ships. It's a clean, unsoured passion. I've seen the same look on his face—the times he's stayed here with us—when he has some idea, as I've seen on some of my engineers down in the design yards. He's raw, but oddly enough the most civil and gracious person his age I know. Often times, when I'm with him, I get this feeling that I'm the least important thing on his mind, then or at any time, because he's thinking of something else. And I don't mind it, because I know there's something great about to be born, something wonderful he's incubating in that stubborn head of his. I feel honored that he takes me for granted." Conover paused. "Do you understand any of this, Mr. Hanrahan?"

I nodded.

"And of his books," the shipbuilder said, smiling, "they're so beautifully written. They're clean, too. And you read them, and you get the sense of reading a story set in the past, or written in the past, but you look up out your window and see the things present in his novels. His stories are set in a different world, one resembling our own, but one without the nonsense, the mockery, the comfortably damning self-appraisal. . . . And they're marvellous books, too, because you can read them over and over again and find new insights and notice new meanings in observations and in the dialogue. He's offered to let me see the first chapters of the new one he's working on, but I said no, I want the chance to sit down and read the entire book from end to end."

"From what I've read so far, Mr. Conover, I'm sure I'll share your estimation."

Conover spread his hands. "So where is he, damn it! No one's seen him since Saturday. He and my daughter were together that evening, but she won't tell me what they talked about. Naturally, I'm worried. I can't imagine winning the Granville has affected him any, it would never have swelled his head, he's too solid for that. He's worked so hard for what he wants, I'm happy that he won the damned Prize. He couldn't write about the things he does—the enforced obscurity, the torture of it, the dedication, the triumph—unless he'd known those things intimately himself.

"And in *Lake Anglique* you can see what else is inside him, a self-contained innocence, one that sees corruption but refuses to be dulled by it. . . . Well, all his writing is governed by that. Do you know the story of Francesca da Rimini, the one in which the beautiful woman is sent to hell for rejecting her ugly husband? Well, Greg's life has been just the opposite, he's been to hell for rejecting the ugly, but he's convinced Lucifer that God has his admission requirements backwards and persuaded him to lay siege to heaven."

I smiled. "I like that."

"Don't credit me. It's from *Lake Anglique*," chuckled Conover.

"Have you or your daughter ever offered him money or help of any kind?"

"We have, but he won't take it. He wants to be on a steadier footing with his books before he'll even move in with Rhea. She bought him a used car, and some clothes, but that's all, and he accepted those things because they were from her. Why do you ask?"

"I'm trying to find a motive for why he's being silent."

"I don't think we could have offended him that way," said Conover. "Rhea has her own money, Mr. Hanrahan. My wife was an heiress and she left Rhea the bulk of her assets. My daughter owns an advertising agency, an investment advisory service, real estate, and I've forgotten what else." He shook his head. "I don't thi ' she would have forced anything on him, Mr. Hanrahan. We both know better than that."

"She asked me about you, Mr. Hanrahan," continued Conover. "She didn't recognize you and I hadn't warned her that you would be here tonight."

That was one way of putting it, I thought. For a while I'd

suspected that she'd asked her father to kick me out of the house. "Does she live here?"

"No. She has a place of her own in Manhattan, and a place in the Berkshires for when she gets tired of the city—"

The door opened then. My back was to it, but when Conover smiled I knew it was Rhea Hamilton. All I was aware of was a chill on my back, her perfume, and the rustle of her silk.

6

"Your guests are beginning to miss you, Father," she said, "and Aunt Peggy is beginning to tell convent jokes. You know how quietly they thud."

Conover put his cheroot out and stood up. "All right," he sighed.

I rose, turned, and he introduced me to his daughter. "Rhea, this is Chess Hanrahan. Mr. Hanrahan, my daughter."

We couldn't shake hands, as she was holding a tray with a bottle of French brandy and two goblets. I nodded, and she gave me a frosty smile.

"Mr. Hanrahan might be able to help us, darling," said Conover. "Please answer his questions."

"If I can," she replied, promising nothing.

Conover gave me an encouraging grin and went out.

Rhea Hamilton crossed the room and put the tray down on a table. "I brought something for you to drink, Mr. Hanrahan. I know how being a booze hound is so intrinsic to a detective's mystique." She picked up the bottle, then paused. "Or is brandy too rich for you? I'm sure Father has some cheaper liquor in the basement. Would you prefer that?"

So that was how it was going to be. "Brandy, please," I said. Her eyebrows went up in mock astonishment, then she came over with the goblets and handed me one. "And to forestall further comment on my alleged mystique, you should know that I own this tux and another like it, contributed to a chair of philosophy at your father's alma mater, and while I think that the bouquet of this particular brandy is indifferent, your own is not. Quite the contrary."

The hazel eyes flared briefly in anger. I loved that reaction, too, and answered her anger with a smile. Then the anger receded, reflecting her realization that I wasn't to be toyed with and that if she could get personal, so could I.

With a final glance of cast-off defiance, Rhea Hamilton moved away from me. "I suppose Father's told you that I'm opposed to anyone looking for Greg."

"No, he hadn't told me." I sat down. "He did tell me that he isn't sure you aren't lying when you claim you don't know where he is."

A small, warm smile bent her lips. "I don't mean for him to take it that way, but I can't help him. I won't help you."

"*Do* you know where Compton is?"

"No, Mr. Hanrahan. I don't. And if I did, I wouldn't tell you."

"Why not?"

"I said I didn't want anybody looking for him. I don't want anybody to find him."

"And you haven't heard from him or seen him since Saturday night?"

"No."

"Aren't you worried about him? Your father is. So are other people."

"Of course I'm worried about him. *I'd* like to know where he is. But I want people to leave him alone. He'll come back when he's good and ready, damn you all."

She said it with a quiet resolve I knew I'd never budge or weaken. "Why don't you want him found?"

She turned her back on me and stood at the fireplace in the center of the room. I could see her face in the mirror above it. "I don't want him subjected to the fawning he'll get, now that he's won the Granville. He isn't used to it and he detests it. He's so used to being hated—worse, being ignored—that I don't think he could handle it. He's used to opposition, to resistance, to doors being slammed in his face. Suddenly, there's no resistance, and not only that, but he's practically yanked inside the literary establishment by the very people who had been opposing him. I don't think he can comprehend the enormity of the victory he's won. It wasn't a victory he sought. Well, if he chooses to behave strangely now, can anyone blame him? They're not recognizing Gregory Compton, they're humiliating him. He wasn't happy with winning that Prize, Mr. Hanrahan. He said it was like being nominated to have his likeness installed in a wax museum of horrors."

"Did you know that he wrote a letter to the Foundation, asking them to withdraw the Prize?"

She looked at me in the mirror. "No, I didn't," she said carefully. "Have you asked my father?"

"No. Did he see Compton on Saturday?"

"I believe he called Greg that morning to congratulate him. They talked, and Father said he sounded odd."

I took a sip of my brandy, then said, "I'm being paid to find Compton, Miss Hamilton. If I find him, I don't think your father would tell the world. I think he wants to know just for his own peace of mind. He holds Compton in very high esteem, probably as high as he holds you."

"Thank you for not telling my father. He wouldn't have understood the matter." Rhea studied me in the mirror. "Don't you think it's a paradox, Mr. Hanrahan? Greg not wanting the Granville, that is?"

I leaned back in the armchair and studied her back. "Paradoxes are my specialty. They don't exist in nature, so I don't think they should exist in people's minds, either. They cause too much pain and misery. And they can be solved."

She turned to me, a hint of a smile on her lips. "I agree. So would Greg. Why didn't you let me know earlier that you were . . . this way?"

"You slammed a door in my face." I smiled. "So I picked the lock."

"You place a great value on certainty, don't you?"

"It's a goal of my profession."

"What's another?"

"Justice. They make each other possible. One without the other is either nonsense, or tragedy."

She came closer and sat on the arm of the other armchair. "You're beginning to make me wish I could tell you where Greg is, Mr. Hanrahan." She glanced away nervously. "I think you would . . . like each other."

"Is he anything like his stories? I like what I've read of *Walk*."

"Better than his stories." Rhea Hamilton paused. "He makes his stories plausible, credible. If he weren't that way, he'd present another paradox."

"How did you meet? And when?"

"About two years ago. I went to dinner with someone—I forget his name now—we went to a restaurant in Manhattan, Greco's, I think, and our waiter was Greg. He was so good at being a waiter, and there was something about him I noticed and couldn't stop watching. It was his indifference to the fact that he was waiting on people. In most other waiters, no matter how good they are, you can still see the contempt and envy in their faces. But that was absent in Greg's. He'd reversed the roles, and I almost expected him to upbraid one of us for using a wrong knife or for having one side dish before another. My date was conscious of it, too, and stumbled over the wine order. I tried to break that palace-guard attitude of Greg's and get him into an argument. I said, 'This coffee is cold, and the wine tastes as though it had been uncorked yesterday. What do you intend to do about it?' And Greg said, 'Replace both the coffee and the wine and deduct them from your bill, madam.' And I said, 'Suppose I'd found something wrong with everything on this table?' And without missing a beat, Greg said, 'Credit you and your companion with a free meal and recommend to my employer that neither of you ever be admitted to this restaurant again, madam.'"

Rhea Hamilton paused. "My companion swore never to return to the restaurant. But I did return, the next night, alone. That's how we met."

"Did you know then he was a published author?"

"No. But I knew that some quality about him couldn't permit him to be just a waiter. No job shames him, Mr. Hanrahan, and he shames no job."

I lit a cigarette.

"May I have one?" asked Rhea Hamilton. I rose, gave her one and a light from my lighter. I went back to my chair. "Why do you think he hasn't contacted *you*, at least?"

She shook her head. "He's a very private person. Unpredictably private, sometimes. It's hard to get him to share things that ought to be shared. But when he smiles at you, it's an intimacy you wouldn't trade for anything else in the world. Just to have him smile at you. You'd have to be something before he'd smile at you, and if you ever doubted what you were, or wouldn't acknowledge it, he'd smile and release something in you because he knew it was there if you didn't. You spoke of justice, and certainty. In his presence you can't doubt those things."

"Ever meet Geoffrey Sayres?"

Rhea Hamilton frowned. "Once."

"What about Compton's agent?"

"What's-her-name, Spendler? No."

"Earl Teague, his editor?"

"I've spoken with him. He called me the other day, wanting to know about Greg."

"I'd like to get into his apartment," I said. "There may be a clue there to where he's gone. Have you a key to it?"

She nodded. "But you can't have it. And I'd rather you didn't try to find him."

"But I must. It's what I'm being paid to do."

Rhea Hamilton rose and paced back and forth for a moment. Then she turned to me and said, "My father's paying you to look for him, isn't he?"

"No," I said. "The Foundation is. He asked them to hire me."

She looked startled, paced some more, then said, "Whomever. I'll pay you *not* to look for him, Mr. Hanrahan."

This time I frowned.

That only made her go on. "I'm serious. I'll double whatever it is they're paying you."

Her offer only intrigued me, but I shook my head. "I'm sorry."

She put out her cigarette in the ashtray by the chair. "I must rejoin my father, Mr. Hanrahan. It's been pleasant speaking with you."

I wasn't going to argue with her. I stood up and watched her go to the door. She put a hand on the knob, and turned a last time. "You're sure you won't consider my offer?"

"I'm sure."

"Would you do it for nothing—as a favor to me?"

"That's a cheaper shot than the one about the brandy."

"It wasn't meant to be." She smiled. "You looked just like him then, Mr. Hanrahan."

"How?"

"Judgmental. Critical. Unassailable."

"I wasn't aware of it."

"Greg's like that. He rarely knows what expression is on his own face, he's so literal about things and people. It's made him a lot of enemies."

"I'll take it as a compliment, then," I said.

"It's all I can ever offer you."

"It's enough."

Rhea Hamilton made to open the door, then paused, and

without looking at me, said, "If you find him, Mr. Hanrahan, please tell him I'm sorry."

Before I could ask her for what, she was gone.

I stood thinking for a minute, then helped myself to another brandy. Her goblet was sitting on the tray, and instead of pouring more into my own from the bottle, I finished what was left of hers. It was all she could offer me. That much I'd suspected. There was lipstick on one side of the goblet. I flicked a finger against the rim and listened with satisfaction to the ring. A pure, magnificent ring.

Conover came in then. I shook my head in answer to his silent question. "I don't think she knows, Mr. Conover. But just to be thorough, have you thought of her Berkshires place?"

Conover nodded. "I sent one of my people up there yesterday. The place is closed up and snowbound."

"Okay." I asked for the addresses of her Manhattan apartment and the retreat, too, and wrote them down in a pocket notebook. Then I asked, "Did they ever argue?"

Conover studied me for a while. "Not that I'm aware of. I can't conceive of them arguing. Did she say that they had?"

"Not in so many words." I glanced at my watch. "I'm going to follow up a thought, so I'll be leaving now. Thanks for the invitation."

"You're welcome, Mr. Hanrahan."

"May I keep this?" I held up her goblet.

"Of course. But whatever on earth for?"

"A souvenir," I said.

7

I'd driven a mile until I realized that it had grown noticeably warmer. I turned on my car radio and flicked the dial to an all-news-all-the-time station to catch a weather report. Temperatures in the forties and fifties with a ninety percent chance of rain. That meant a fast melt and seas of slush. I crossed the county to get to the Hutchinson River Parkway that would take me to the Whitestone Bridge and Queens. It was almost eleven o'clock, but, key or no key, I was going to look over Compton's apartment. If there was a clue to the writer's whereabouts, it would probably be there.

As I drove, I thought of the people I'd met so far and who'd known Compton. There was Atherton, aristocrat and Foundation president; Spendler, feisty literary agent; Teague, editor and conscientious cretin; Sayres, angry, watchful playwright—excuse me, dramatist; Conover, the only university graduate I knew personally who'd made his own billion; and Rhea, the enchanting, lovely, stimulating, and puzzling heiress. She was on my mind so much that I ran a red light near the Parkway. I'd been thinking of her back and of the shadows it made when it moved, of her graceful neck, of her hair, of the intense look in her eyes and the angle of her profile and the parted lips. I loved watching her. I was happy about that. It didn't matter that I hadn't a chance to hold those shoulders. . . . I was simply happy that someone like that could exist and that I had seen her.

And I wondered what she had to be sorry about. The kinds of people she could cause pain to she would never meet or never have anything to do with.

I wondered, too, if Compton ever felt depressed when he came back to Flushing from 26 Pheasant Road, Tarry-town. I was as I threaded through its streets, but I didn't feel that way for myself because I didn't have to live here. He did. The closest space to his house was a block away. I parked my car there and walked. The air was warmer and the only sounds I heard were a few barking dogs and the patter of snow melting from the roofs and awnings. As I approached the driveway I glanced across the street to Sayres's window; it was lit but he wasn't at his desk.

The Mercedes was still parked in the rear and hadn't been moved. I stood for a while and considered my next move. I could either knock on the ground floor occupant's door on the probablity that he was the landlord and ask to see Compton's place, or I could let myself in. I had the keys for that in my coat pocket. It was a little past eleven-thirty and the ground floor was dark. That decided me.

I walked up to the front door, kicked some soggy newspapers out of the way, took out a ring of skeleton keys, and a minute later found myself in a hallway that was a duplicate of Sayres's, even to a lingering odor of a dinner. I stopped to listen at the ground floor door. They'd either gone out or retired early. Not a sound. On a stand in front of Compton's door was a pile of mail. I glanced through it, then put it under my arm and used the keys again. The latch snapped, the door opened, and I closed it gently behind me as I felt for a switch and turned on the lights. Then I climbed the stairs.

Compton wasn't home, of course, and hadn't been for a while. The place looked exactly like that of a man who'd rushed out in a hurry one day and never came back—an unmade bed, dishes in the sink, a stuffed laundry bag and a box of detergent together at the top of the well-worn stairs. In his study, which also overlooked the street, were shelves of books, a television, stereo, a desk, a few chairs, and an electric typewriter. On the desk was a stack of wire-ring notebooks and a pile of manuscript paper. The top sheet read, "Defender of the Realm, by Gregory Compton." This was probably the novel he owed Teague. I looked at the last sheet; it read, "The End." So he'd finished it.

I searched for, but did not find, a copy of the letter of refusal to the Granville Foundation that Sayres had told me about. There was nothing in his study waste can but discarded sheets of manuscript, some balled up, others torn up. Those and junk-mail envelopes he hadn't bothered to open and ripped open ones from the telephone and utilities companies.

There was a framed color photograph of Compton and Rhea on the wall by the desk, of them sitting together on the bow of a sailboat, he in poplin walking shorts and a rugby shirt, she in a bikini that made me sigh. They were looking neither at the camera, nor at each other. Compton was glancing away from Rhea off into the distance. Rhea was looking at him covetously, her eyes two pools of ownership, worship, and contentment. They looked happy together. Rhea's expression struck me suddenly with an odd loneliness. No woman I'd ever known had ever looked at me that way. There'd been no one like that waiting for me after my desert battles. They'd wanted to be wanted, not earned, and for no good reason. Sayres had a point.

I snapped out of it and reached down for the waste can again, dumped its contents on the rug, and searched again just to be sure. Nothing. Then I went to the kitchen and searched through the trash can there. Minutes later I found the draft, the one Sayres said Compton had asked him to read. Compton had typed it on the back of some company's letterhead—Tyle Properties—had balled it up and tossed it into a soup can in the trash near the sink.

It read exactly as Sayres said it did. After I dabbed off the soup with a paper towel, I folded the draft up and put it in my jacket. Tyle Properties, I thought. Well, Sayres said Compton had "temped" at a real estate company.

In the background of my reverie I'd heard the roar of an engine out on the street and only made the connection when I heard the front door downstairs slam shut, then quick, impatient footsteps in the hallway, and finally the door at the bottom of the stairs open and shut. I stood in the kitchen and watched through the banister spools to see whose head emerged. Someone rushed up the stairs.

It was Rhea Hamilton. When she saw me she whirled into the kitchen. "Is he here?" she asked, breathlessly.

I shook my head. "No. I don't think he's been here for days."

"Then please leave. You have no right to be here."

"Legally, no, I haven't," I said. "But I am looking for him and I'm here."

"I don't want you here!" she said. "I want you to stop prying! I want you to leave him alone! Why should you care? What difference can it make to you?"

I put on my overcoat. "Maybe I'd like to see you happy. Besides, I shame no job." I stopped to smile, then asked, "Was Compton going to turn down the Granville Prize? I know that he was thinking of it, at least."

She didn't answer for a while. She just stood there glaring at me. Finally she said, "I'm under no obligation to answer any of your questions, Mr. Hanrahan. What was discussed between Greg and me is a private matter."

"True. But it's a position you may come to regret."

"Why?"

"Tell me if Compton intends to turn the Prize down and I'll tell you."

"What makes you think he would want to turn it down? Who put that notion into your head?"

I smiled. "A sharp ear and my own literary sensibilities." I stood there for a moment, soaking up her regal scrutiny. "Still want me to tell him you're sorry?"

Rhea looked away and I saw the tears in her eyes that she wouldn't let out.

"Sorry for what, Miss Hamilton?"

"That's a private matter, too, Mr. Hanrahan," she said. "Forget that I said it."

I gave her the benefit of the doubt. I'm so used to having my presence anywhere objected to—especially because it's a prying presence—that I occasionally forget there may be genuine reasons for the objection. She'd raced up those stairs expecting to find Compton, but she found me instead. I said, "I'll be speaking with you again soon, Miss Hamilton." And then I left.

She'd parked her car, a silver Porsche, in the driveway. The make of the car pleased me. It was her kind of car: fast, efficient, and a no-nonsense contender in city traffic. I glanced up at Sayres's window. He was there this time, watching either me or Rhea up in Compton's place. I waved to him; he raised a hand in recognition, then moved from the window.

I drove back to Manhattan, trying to think of where else I could look for Compton. His apartment seemed to be a dead end.

In the city, the sidewalks were already bare of snow and dried out. I stopped by a newsstand and picked up the next day's *Times*, then drove home. Walker gave me one of his "Where have you been all night?" looks, then led me to the kitchen and his dish. I fed him, changed into something more comfortable, and made myself a coffee. I half expected to see front-page speculation on Compton's whereabouts, but there was nothing in the paper about him. Out of curiosity I turned to the arts section and the book review page. And struck gold.

Well, not exactly gold. Nickel-plated copper, maybe. Oliver Gullum, senior book reviewer for the *Times*, was somebody I'd stopped reading months ago simply because I could never understand or care about what he wrote about. He threw literary acid on even his favorite writers, and his favorites were esthetic lepers anyway, novelists like Grackle who were always bemoaning, parodying, or belittling life. I'd read Grackle's *Partly Cloudy Over Kansas* chiefly because I couldn't believe the story as Gullum had related it, and also because I'd wanted to see something he'd liked. He'd insulted Grackle only twice in the entire review, and his peak of praise had been something to the effect that the novelist "did some interesting things with commas and ellipses." What, I never found out.

His article, entitled "Major New Mythmaker," occupied a quarter of the page and was all about Gregory Compton. After announcing that *Walk Around the Sun* had won the Granville Prize, and that there was some dissent in literary circles about it—in fact, not only dissent, but outrage— Gullum's next paragraph read: "Now *Walk Around* is emphatically *not* a parable for our time. A parable, for those readers who may be scratching their heads in vague recollection, is a short fictitious work with a moral point (usually, but not necessarily, attached to a religious context). *Walk Around* has neither brevity nor point, moral or otherwise. Nor is it even a stab at contemporary relevancy."

My God, I thought to myself, he was being clear for once. You usually had to wade through to the next-to-the-last paragraph to learn what he actually felt.

"These days myths and gods and most things sublime are being shattered, if not retired to the attic or donated to thrift shops. This is a good practice, for it proves the maturity of a culture. No, say rather of a society, since a culture suggests some kind of sacred repository frequented by Maypole elitists in pure white togas and with garlands in their hair. I have not personally encountered an elitist since the Truman administration, and may have missed the obituary of the last surviving one. And, anyway, there is nothing sacred left to sigh about. By now it should be clear to anyone that there is nothing that was ever sacred."

That was more like it, I thought. Gullum devoted two more paragraphs to that theme, then discussed Compton's book.

"But mythmakers still occasionally emerge in our maturing society and turn many heads. The phenomenon, like the beaching of pilot whales, cannot be explained. Compton, as mythmaker, would have us believe that life can be simple and grand and tally-ho heroic. Stridivant, the composer-hero in *Walk Around* and who apparently was given no first name by his parents, is a larger-than-life repository of these notions, and has all the charm of a drop hammer. He meets all challenges of a personal, professional, and abstract nature and in the end triumphs over everything and everybody, including that sneaky, conniving little concertmaster who torpedoes Stridivant's every rehearsal. Compton's grip on the composer's perspective is unrelenting. He asks us to feel anger, outrage, hopelessness, and joy about Stridivant's progress and victory. At least that is what I think he is asking us to do. I could be right. But while I felt nothing for Stridivant and doubt that he will ever qualify for inclusion in Sandletter's *Dictionary of Literary Characters*, the one scene in which he did get a rise out of me—in fact, scared the wits out of me—is the last one of the book, in which he raises his baton in the air and whips it down like a cavalry saber. This is the sole imagery of note in the story, but one hardly worthy of modern appreciation. It is a gesture of hate, a peculiar hate sustained through 584 pages of perverse melodramatics featuring a regiment of characters as pat as chess pieces."

I smiled. If I hadn't started Compton's book already, Gullum would have only got me interested in reading it. It might have been better if he'd kept his mouth shut. I put my paper down and thought about it for a while. That *would* have been the better tactic. I wondered if Gullum had written anything about Compton in the past, on *Lake Anglique* or on *Walk* when it was first published. If he hadn't, why was he writing about it now? I made a mental note to look into that later, then read on.

A few paragraphs later Gullum got nasty, not with Compton, but with the novelist's readers. "Compton's books appear to be popular with those who wish to escape from the burdens of the real world for a while and through this respite return to it fresh, invigorated, and ready to take on a bunch of the big boys at the Porte de Nesle, to paraphrase a certain long-nosed swashbuckler with similarly ludicrous and juvenile headiness. Even a colleague of mine (who shall remain nameless for I wouldn't want to embarrass him) once said that Compton's books didn't abuse one's sense of self as most others went out of their way to do. Well, if enlightenment is abuse, then I guess each of us deserves a breather and a swig of our favorite soft drink now and then."

Keep it up, Gullum, I thought. You're only encouraging me. I'd like to have known who the colleague was. He had a point. I poured myself another coffee, lit a cigarette, and finished the article.

"Returning to Stridivant's threatening baton, it can be seen as a symbol of Compton's literary sin. He is guilty of moral imperialism. He hasn't the sense to realize that it is heinous presumptuousness to judge people by their quirks, flaws, failings, or shortfalls. Nor does he seem to care. Compton only seems to be daring. He has thrown down, not his gauntlet, but his pen. He poses as a rebel, as a champion of the sublime, a defender of the myth. But in fact Compton's mythmaking is as old-hat as the stovepipes of yore. Both the pen and the baton are a wasted gesture, for no critic who takes himself seriously will pick either up or engage in any such machismo antics. Compton expects us to rush his encampment and be cut down by ordered volleys from his neat British squares. But the more sensitive reader will realize that he, too, is capable of a gesture, and will turn his back and *walk away*. (This is an epistle, mind you, not a parable.) Victory, while itself an obscene concept, can be had by the nominally—endowed in the tested strategem of literary pacifism."

And you're no Fuzzy Wuzzy, I commented mentally to Gullum, recalling Kipling's tribute to courage. Following the reviewer's last words there was a solid line and then in the same border a postscript in italics by the page editor: "Mr. Gullum has been appointed Distinguished Louis Olcutt Professor of American Literature at Regina University, Virginia, and so his column will appear on these pages less frequently."

That will be a relief, I thought. Maybe I'd start reading the book review page again. Walker jumped up onto the paper, which I'd put on my lap. "No, no," I warned him, picking him up and removing the paper. "You might get your paws infected." I dropped the paper and let him snuggle down, then began massaging his neck. He started purring instantly.

It struck me that Gullum and the waiter in the all-night diner had a lot in common. The one refused to acknowledge what was bad, and the other refused to acknowledge what was good. But they shared something, and even though I couldn't put a finger on it now, I knew it couldn't be very pretty. Whatever it was, Gullum had said it in so many words. I thought the waiter had been smarter; he couldn't be quoted.

So where could I go from here? The one person who knew where Compton might be wouldn't talk. I believed Rhea when she said she didn't know, but there had to be more to his disappearance. But the more I thought about it, the more I waded deeper into a puzzle of incidentals. I woke Walker up with a pet on his jaw, then put him down, fixed myself a final coffee, then went to the living room to finish *Walk Around the Sun*.

At a few minutes to four in the morning I finished it.

Gullum was wrong, about everything. Stridivant triumphed, not because he conquered, not because he manipulated people, and not because he had any help. He triumphed because for as long as he kept his vision, he had to triumph. The facades of all his enemies peeled away one by one. He was alone in the end, but that was what he had been throughout the entire story. He could bear it. But you felt like keeping him company anyway. And you also felt that if you were in the least bit anything like Stridivant, you had company, too. You had to be able to identify with him.

And now I understood why Gullum took the raised baton the way he did. Compton hadn't mentioned anything about sabers in his last sentence. He'd written: "And with a downward slash of the baton, he sent the first notes of his symphony rocketing to the sky." But Oliver Gullum had nothing in common with Stridivant, so I could understand his reaction to it. It was the cringe of a coward in the face of a rebuke. But punishment wasn't what Compton was offering the world.

Through the story of Stridivant, I understood Compton much more. I began to be convinced that Rhea was right. I wanted him left alone, too, even if he never produced another book. I stood up and went to the bookcase where I'd put her goblet and twirled the thin glass stem in my fingers, thinking. Maybe I wouldn't look for Gregory Compton. Maybe I'd stop looking just as a favor to her.

I smoked a last cigarette and stood at my window watching the sleeping city. I set my clock for nine, and went to bed.

In the morning, as I was fixing breakfast, I heard on the radio that Gregory Compton had been found. Dead.

8

He'd been found by the Suffolk County police on a bad stretch of road near Little Port, out on the Island, a hit-and-run victim. That was on the North Shore, on the Sound, and I knew how treacherous the roads were around there, all hills and steep grades and sudden turns that could leave a driver smashed across the pavement or on the ocean rocks if he wasn't careful. In fact, Compton's body was found because another accident had happened. A limousine had turned a corner and run head-on into a truck hauling about a thousand gallons of spring water only fifty yards from where the body lay on a slope near some bushes. And if the rain and warm ocean breezes hadn't helped melt the snow, it might not have been found for another week. He'd already been dead for nearly a week—or at least since Saturday.

I didn't have time to ponder that. My office phone was ringing as I unlocked the door. I put down my wet paper and portfolio and answered it. It was Edgar Atherton's secretary, requesting that I come up to the Foundation immediately. No, Mr. Atherton could not speak to me over the phone.

I suspected what it was he wanted and cursed him for his phone shyness. At the Foundation I was ushered into his office almost as soon as I stepped off the elevator.

"Good morning, Mr. Hanrahan," he said, rising. "Thank you for coming on such short notice."

We sat down. I said, "It's about Compton."

He nodded. "Yes. You're no doubt aware that he . . . has been found."

"It explains why he didn't claim the Prize."

"So it does. I feel foolish for having said the things I did about him." Atherton sighed. "Such a tragedy. So young. I travel that very road every day, and so I know what it's like."

"I wrapped up my last case not five miles from that spot," I said. "You live near there?"

"Warm Springs Harbor," said the president, flashing a brief smile. He paused. "Of course, the Foundation has no further use of your services, Mr. Hanrahan."

"I expected as much."

"There is the matter of your retainer. I feel that as you put in less than twenty-four hours work on the Foundation's account, at least three-quarters of it should be returned to us."

I shook my head. "The contract specifies that I keep all of it. It also specifies that I can charge my daily fee over and above that, contingent upon circumstances. Actually, the Foundation owes me, Mr. Atherton, but under these circumstances I'll waive it."

Atherton grew red in the face. He yanked open a desk drawer, took out his copy of the contract, and read it over, which was what he didn't do yesterday. Finally he dropped it disgustedly on the blotter in front of him.

I said, "I explained it all before you signed it."

"So you did, Mr. Hanrahan. So you did." Atherton stood up. "Well, it's been nice doing so little business with you. If it weren't for the fact that you were hired on the advice of someone whom I don't wish to offend, this agreement would be forwarded to the Foundation's legal staff. Good day, Mr. Hanrahan."

Hell, all his legal staff could have done was tell him that he signed a contract and was bound to its terms. He was no semiliterate ninny I'd duped. But he was taking me for one. I'd been prepared to return the retainer. The check he gave me was still in my portfolio. I didn't need it; I'd gained more in the last twenty-four hours than the amount could ever buy me. I rose and put on my coat. "See you around," I said to him, then I walked out.

As his secretary escorted me through the quiet offices to the foyer, I asked, "What will happen to the Prize now that Compton can't claim it?"

"Excuse me, Mr. Hanrahan?"

"The Granville Prize," I said. "Will the check and paperweight go to his next-of-kin, or will the Foundation keep them?"

Only then did she understand me. I'd assumed that she knew why Atherton had hired me. She was the one who called me on both occasions. "Oh!" she exclaimed. "What will happen to them? Well, I'm not really quite sure. Why would you wish to know?"

She still hadn't understood me. "I was hired to find Gregory Compton." I'd just been fired, too, but she didn't have to know that.

"Oh," she said, studying me. "I see now. Well, I couldn't answer your question, but I'm sure Mr. Neary could. I'll take you to him."

"Who's he?" I asked as we took a detour. The place was a rabbit warren.

"He's chairman of the permanent sitting Prize committee, Mr. Hanrahan. He oversees the whole Prize process, from appointing the Prize jury to the selecting of the books that are considered. He's done that for years."

"Guess he has nothing to do now," I said.

The secretary chuckled. "No, he hasn't. But he's leaving us and going downstairs next week. He was promoted to vice president of our fellowship program. We'll miss Mr. Neary."

"Like hell we will," piped a voice from one of the cubicles we passed.

I grinned, but the secretary scowled. "Who was that?" I asked.

"Adele, one of our malcontents," said the secretary sweetly. "This is the accounting department." She said it as though the accounting department was only a rung above the mailroom, or the janitor's slop sink.

At last we stopped by an office and she introduced me to Mr. Neary, an earnest-looking, portly old fellow of Atherton's age. The secretary repeated my question, and he turned to me and asked, "Are you a relative of Mr. Compton's?"

"No, I—"

"He found Mr. Compton," prompted the secretary. "Mr. Atherton hired him yesterday to look for him." She still had it wrong.

Neary shrugged. "I see. His next-of-kin may claim both the check and the scribe piece. If there is no next-of-kin, then they may be claimed by the publisher."

"If no next-of-kin claims the Prize, could it go to the author's fiancée?"

Neary's brow smoothed in response to that, and I saw a little fire in his otherwise cold eyes. "That would be up to the publisher, Mr. Hanrahan." He paused. "When did you say you were hired to look for Mr. Compton?"

"Yesterday morning," I said. "Why do you ask?"

"I wasn't advised of the matter, that's all, Mr. Hanrahan." Neary gave me a frigid smile. "Have a pleasant day."

Office politics, I thought.

A branch of my bank was on the next block down from the Foundation. I deposited the check there, then stood in the lobby to watch the drizzle outside, and decided on my next step. I hailed a cab and told the driver to take me to Wall Street.

The offices of Polaris Shipping down near the Battery were also quiet, but with a difference: the thinking going on beyond the receptionist's desk was almost tangible. I had a peek of busy drafting tables down one long corridor and a glimpse of some engineers in an off-lobby conference room discussing an enormous blueprint that was taped to the wall over a blackboard. Messenger boys kept coming and going, delivering and taking long tubes of what I guessed were also blueprints, and also large, thick envelopes that were probably specifications. The receptionist's phone never quit ringing and some brisk lad raced through the lobby twice pushing a mail cart while I waited. Conover was in, but the receptionist said that he was just coming out of a meeting. I looked at the paintings of Conover's various container port operations and studied the glass-enclosed models of freighters in the visitors' lounge area. I felt good here. I'd forgotten what energy people could make you feel just by being energetic themselves. It was contagious.

In about ten minutes a young woman came out and took me back to Conover's office. It was about half the size of Atherton's, with a jumble of technical books and blueprints and extra work tables, and a wide window with a view of the New York harbor. And on the richest Oriental rug I'd ever seen was spread a six-by-three-foot ozalid print held down on three corners by piles of books and on the fourth by a miniature reproduction of Nike.

Conover was in his shirtsleeves, which were rolled up, and he'd tucked his silk tie inside his shirt. He finished writing something on a yellow note pad, then dropped the pencil, and lit a cigarette. "Thank you for coming, Mr. Hanrahan," he said after a moment. "I half expected you."

I sat down in a leather chair near his desk. I smiled. "I half expected you to say that," I said. He didn't have to ask why I was here. And I didn't want to cheapen our understanding by saying the obvious.

"Rhea's . . . taking it very hard," he said after a moment of staring into space. "We drove out to the morgue in Little Port this morning. I refused to let her identify the body. He'd been dead for a while. I didn't want that to be her last . . . sight of him."

I nodded once.

"Careless, drunken sonofabitch," said Conover quietly after another moment.

"There's a good chance those county cops will find whoever it was," I said, lighting a cigarette. "That's not a major road and only local residents are likely to use it. It might take time, but they'll narrow it down."

Conover glanced at me with a silent question.

I shook my head. "No. The police are better equipped to hunt for that driver than I am, Mr. Conover." I paused. "Could you tell me what he might have been doing out there?"

Conover sighed. "Sometimes he would walk miles when he had an idea. He did that up in Tarrytown."

It was a long way from Flushing to Little Port, Long Island, but I wasn't going to bother him with my ideas now. I said, "Atherton called me and gave me notice."

"Did he give you any trouble over your fee?"

"No. I gave him trouble."

"Useless man," said Conover with a grimace. Then his expression changed and he leaned forward. "Would you do me a favor and talk to Rhea, Mr. Hanrahan? She's keeping it all bottled up, and she's being quiet, and I'm afraid for her. Nothing I say seems to reach her, and she refuses to talk to anyone else. You touched her somehow last night."

"I'll talk with her. I'll try to see her tonight."

"Thank you. If you don't make a dent, I'll understand."

"Don't tell her I'm coming, though."

"Let me know what happens. I'll be leaving here shortly and will be home the rest of the day and this evening."

"All right."

I went home, took out a map of Long Island, located Little Port, and then Freehold Road. I munched on a sandwich, did some thinking, then took my car out of the garage, and headed for the Queensboro Bridge.

I didn't know the area as well as I thought I did, even though I'd driven through the area a few times two weeks ago. Twice I took a wrong turn and found myself at the wrong crossroads. The area reminded me a lot of Tarrytown, but when I was looking for Conover's place I had the excuse of darkness.

I found Freehold Road and drove up and down its winding length twice, looking for the accident site. But it must have been cleaned up damned fast for I didn't see a single piece of broken glass on the paved surface. Little Port's town center was a railroad station, a post office, a grocery store, and a police station tucked in between two heavily wooded hills.

There were only three men in the town's police force, and one of them was the captain. His name was Farrell and he was a rustic sixty years old. I introduced myself, said I was working for Wallace Conover, and asked him to show me where Compton's body had been found. He had nothing else to do and said yes. We drove up to the site in his private Cadillac because it had a police radio.

"So you're working for that fellow Conover," he said as he drove.

"That's right."

"Nice fellow. Nice daughter. They were here around eight o'clock this morning, you know. That's the earliest I've ever been up in years."

"Guess not much happens around here," I said, trying to make the best of his conversation.

"No, nothing at all. Just an accident or two once a month. Usually on Freehold. Last year 'bout this time a carload of kids went through the railing and onto the rocks on the Sound side. They didn't collect the last body 'til a week later. Tide kept movin' it around."

"You have a morgue in town?"

Farrell shook his head. "Nah. No use for one. There's one

in Middleport. That's where the county cops took this Compton fellow and the chauffeur. They do all that kind of work around here."

"The chauffeur?"

"The fellow who was driving that limousine. Don Brooks. Ran smack into that truck and got flattened. The truck's cab was sittin' right on top of him. Made too wide a turn."

"What time did this happen?" Farrell drove quickly but confidently around the bends and turns, which were making me as a passenger hold on to the armrest.

"About four this morning. He worked for the Hurst family up on Hidden Haven Trail. No one else was in the limousine. No one knew what he was doing out with it at all. The Hursts are out of town for a while. I think he was using the limousine to make some extra cash, picking up fares from the airports. Lots of these chauffeurs around here do that on the sly."

"I guess Little Port's pretty heavily salted," I remarked.

Farrell glanced at me with a mysterious grin. *"Only* wealthy people, Mr. Hanrahan. Voted themselves out of Middleport when the town raised its taxes. Incorporated themselves into Little Port, and that called for a police force. I was fresh out of the Army then, just back from Korea, a patrolman on Middleport's force. They asked me to start on here. So I did." He slowed down, pulled over onto the gravel on the side, and stopped. "Here's where they found that other fellow."

We got out and I buttoned up my coat against the wind. Farrell did the same and moseyed to the guardrail. It started where we had stopped and continued on for about a hundred yards to disappear around a turn that looked like a perfect right angle. Across the road, creating that blind spot, was a hill and a split-level castle I could see through the bare trees. On our side, beyond the rail, was a steep slope of grass, bushes and rock outcropping, with patches of snow clinging to the ground here and there. At the bottom began another stand of trees that rose with another hill. Somewhere in the distance waves broke on the jagged coastline of the North Shore.

Farrell raised an arm and pointed to a spot about thirty feet from where we stood. "Down there, that's where they found him. This was all snow-covered last night, and you can't see that spot from a car. Right there, behind that outcrop. Folks across the street would've seen him, snow or no snow, but they're all in Florida right now."

I stepped over the rail and went down to the spot Farrell had pointed out. Except for a lot of footprints caused by the authorities and crushed grass there was no sign that anyone had been here. I looked up at Farrell. "Did they find anything of his?"

Farrell shook his head. "No. Everything that was his was still on him. Wallet, house keys, watch, couple of pens, pocket change, stuff like that."

"That's strange," I said, climbing back up the slope.

"What?"

"He must have been hit pretty hard." I'd reached the top again and rested a foot on the guardrail.

"His kneecaps were crushed," said Farrell. "His hands were scraped, because he wasn't wearing gloves. County detective said he was facing whoever hit him."

"Wouldn't you think that someone hit that hard by a car—probably a pretty fast-moving one, to have thrown him so far—would have lost anything loose in his pockets, or his shoes, or *something*?"

Farrell thought about it. "Sure. But it isn't necessary. I mean, I saw guys in Korea blown six feet in the air by mines, but they still had a cigarette in their mouth or food in their hand or glasses on their head. They were dead, but they didn't lose anything."

"And the coroner's sure it was hit-and-run?"

Farrell shook his head again. "Medical examiner. He's sure."

I sighed and began roaming around the Cadillac. "They didn't find anything out here on the road?"

"Not a thing."

I stepped onto the pavement. "These skid marks," I said, pointing to a faint pair of tracks leading off the gravel and onto the cement. "They must have been caused by he driver."

"Probably," said Farrell, shrugging. "But they're too faint, you see. The road was wet and covered with slush. Tires don't make that much of a mark on it. They might be anyone's. Or just old."

I turned around and looked down the rise of the road, then started walking that way. Farrell followed. About a hundred feet later I stopped at a point where I saw the vague impression of tracks leading onto the gravel. They didn't just veer gradually onto the dirt, but jerked over suddenly. I squinted my eyes at that. The tracks swerved just as suddenly back onto the road up where Compton had been hit.

Farrell had been studying me for a while, then he said something interesting. "The county fellows chewed over it the same way you are, Mr. Hanrahan. They're writing it off to a drunk or someone who was dozing at the wheel."

I looked at the captain.

He continued. "Wouldn't be the first time. I've seen it often enough. But it's risky driving along here even when you're sober and alert, especially at night. I've hit my share of squirrels and raccoons and dogs. Suddenly they're just there, and that's that. I hurt my chest once on the steering wheel one night. Kid on a bike farther up the road. Suddenly he was there. I stopped just in time."

"Anybody in town see him that night?"

"No."

"What time does the medical examiner say he died?"

"Somewhere near midnight on Saturday. He wouldn't swear to it, though."

"Anybody think to question what he was doing out here that time of night?"

"No. Lots of strangers and hikers pass through here."

"Okay," I said. "I've seen enough. Do you have a report I can read?"

"Not yet. County detective said he'd send me a copy for my files."

We walked back to his car and drove back to the station. I asked Farrell if he'd let me look at the County report when he got it.

"I'm afraid I couldn't do that," he said.

"I was with the homicide division in New York for ten years," I said. "And I was a chief of police up in Massachusetts. I think I'd be able to read it."

"Oh."

After I recapped some of my career high points, Farrell agreed to call me when the report came in.

I drove back up to Freehold and spent an hour scouring the roadside and slope for something the county cops might have overlooked, but there wasn't even a candy wrapper or a beer can. I drove over the skid marks a couple of times and tried picturing Compton "suddenly" being there in my lights one miserable evening. It wasn't adding up. And I'd gone and told Conover that the authorities here were on top of it.

But why should the police here suspect murder? I knew more about Compton, and wasn't entirely convinced of it myself. I puttered around the area just to acquaint myself with it. Middleport was bigger than Little Port by four buildings, which included a seafood restaurant. I drove to the far end of Freehold Road where it skirted the cliff and stopped by the spot where Farrell said a carload of people sailed off the pavement to the boulders below.

No, I wasn't entirely convinced Compton had been murdered. But the suspicion was there. I wondered what it would take to convince me. Or to dissuade me. I was, however, going to give it my best. It was the least I owed him.

9

As I drove back to the city, my reaction caught up with me. I'd been moving and acting on the emergency drive that's in all of us and which can let you think clearly instead of running around in a panic. Damn it, I'd no sooner discovered something than it was gone. Compton's books would always be there, and his new one would be published someday. But it wasn't the same. The source of something wonderful had been snuffed out, extinguished. Killed. Whether by design or accident, it didn't matter. The manuscript on his desk in Flushing could have been his last, or he might have turned out masterpiece after masterpiece for the next twenty years. Those things didn't matter, either. What had happened to him was wrong. *Wrong.*

I pounded my steering wheel once in anger and hit the horn instead, startling the driver ahead of me. Damn it, it was wrong. And it was wrong for me to be feeling this way. *Wrong*, I kept thinking. *Wrong.* Why was it bothering me this way? If I'd never been involved in the matter, if I'd simply opened the later edition of the *Times* this morning and read about the hit-and-run, I'd have thought nothing of it and planned to see a movie tonight, or called Helen Nash to see whether she was still angry. I might have even gone out and bought the prizewinning novel by the late novelist, and thought it good, and thought no more about the author. I would have gone on living.

Accidents are neutral. In the long run you can't feel anything personal about them. You can feel murderously angry with the stupidity, negligence, or carelessness that can cause accidents. What's missing from them is design, or intent, consciousness. And I had no reason to think that Compton had been murdered. So why did I feel that it was so wrong that he was dead? Something in my mind was causing that feeling. What?

I kept dismissing the fact that Compton the writer had lived in a culture inimical to both him and the kinds of novels he wrote. That could have nothing to do with the possibility of his murder, I told myself over and over. But I couldn't get the notion out of my head. It popped back into my thoughts whenever I reviewed the things I had learned or been told by people so far. And then there were the people themselves. Earl Teague was actually hostile to his best author. Gussie Spendler represented Compton more from hopeless affection than from conviction. Geoffrey Sayres was angry, I gathered, at the possibility that success might have corrupted his idol and good friend. Edgar Atherton didn't seem to particularly care that Compton had won the Granville. And neither Rhea Hamilton nor Wallace Conover seemed to care, either. No, I corrected myself: they didn't seem to *mind* it, in the same way that you don't mind getting a piece of junk mail that claims you've won a chance at a billion dollars if you subscribe to six magazines. So far I'd met no one who was wildly enthusiastic that Gregory Compton had won the Granville Prize. In fact, I'd met no one who would have been offended if he *hadn't* won it.

And that led me back to my own evaluation: should Compton have been awarded the Granville? Ought he to have even been a candidate for it? No, not from what I knew about literature. I didn't write books, didn't review them, didn't hand out paperweights and tax-free checks. I was only on the receiving end of the business. I had my favorite books and authors, and none of them had ever been offered the purple. The ones who usually won it abused me and my sensibilities, as Oliver Gullum's colleague might have put it. I'd read one of those books and to wash out the taste of jaded contempt it would leave in my mind I'd pick up a good clean Western. Or a book by Gregory Compton. From my perspective his being awarded the Granville made as much sense as my being offered a dollar by a bum. Or, as Sayres had put it, a gold-plated padlock by all the criminals I'd sent up in the past.

There *was* something wrong with that, but could it have had anything to do with his death? On the face of it, the idea was ludicrous. And not a little paranoid. Or at least it seemed that way. If Compton hadn't won the Granville, would he have ever gone wandering around the North Shore? How did he get there? His car was in Flushing, and Sayres said that Compton had driven it away Saturday afternoon, and that it was back in the driveway the next morning. If Compton couldn't have driven it back—because he was dead and buried beneath a snowfall—who had? Had he mailed that letter of refusal? Was Sayres telling the truth? Rhea? Conover? Compton's agent? Teague was hiding something, I was certain of that. But was it anything relevant to Compton's death?

I needed to discover a reason for murdering Compton. A reason revolving around that car. Sayres could have told me as much of the truth as he knew of it; then again, he might have told me only half of it, or none of it. That reasoning applied to everyone I'd met so far.

I pulled off the Parkway and ten minutes later was back in Compton's neighborhood. It was four-thirty.

I parked, walked up the driveway, and looked at Compton's Mercedes again. I studied what was left of the stem of the missing hood ornament. It was jagged, as though it had been snapped off. I looked over the hood, grill, fender, and headlights. There were bumps and hollows over everything, but nothing suspicious, nothing dramatic. I stood against the grill and saw where my knees touched it. At one point in the latticework I saw two little indented pockets. I stooped down to examine them for fibers that might have come off the trousers of a man struck by the grill. Nothing. If there had been any they were washed away by the melting snow.

I stepped away from the Mercedes and examined the fender. There were two little pockets on it, too, in a line with the ones on the grill. There were irregular pairs of them all around the fender, but that pair was the neatest.

Now what? I asked myself. I remembered Farrell saying that Compton's hands had been scraped. If his hands could be scraped by the impact, so could have been the hood's finish. But it was clean.

Well, I could make a fool of myself and call the Suffolk County police and tell them I probably had a murder weapon for them. But there wasn't anything on the car that could prove it had killed Compton. I doubted now that even a microscopic examination of it would turn up anything.

But whoever drove it back might have left traces of himself inside. I looked inside the window on the driver's side. There were no keys in the ignition. Incredibly, there was a paperback dictionary on the dashboard, under the windshield. Couldn't get away from the books. Otherwise, the car was clean, front and back. It hadn't accumulated the odds and ends people usually stash in the back seat or on the floormats. Sayres said that Compton hadn't used the car much. I believed it now.

I pondered for a moment whether or not to force the door open and get a closer look inside, and decided against it. I had a friend in the New York police who could do a better job of it for me and dust for prints, too.

90 · EDWARD CLINE

That was that, I thought. Time to get home. I glanced across the street, remembering Sayres again. His windows were dark. I wondered how much copy he was able to write today.

At home I had a snack, fed Walker, then sat down at my desk for a while and wrote out a plan of how I was going to tackle this case.

At six-fifteen I picked up the phone and dialed a number Wallace Conover had given me. It was an unlisted number. After a few burrs a soft, distant voice answered, "Yes?"

"Rhea? This is Chess Hanrahan."

After a moment of silence, she said, "Oh, yes. How do you do, Mr. Hanrahan?"

She sounded mechanical and far away. I said, "I'm calling to offer my help and understanding."

After another moment, she asked, "How would you be able to help, Mr. Hanrahan? Or understand?"

"I've . . . seen more death than I hope you ever will, Miss Hamilton."

"Are you beating your chest about it?"

"No. But it's a fact."

"I . . . don't know," she said.

"I do," I said, deciding for her. "I'll be over in an hour."

Then there was a silence, too long a one. "Hello? Rhea?"

"Who did you say you were?" she asked me, this time in a firm angry voice.

"Chess—"

Then she disconnected the line.

I blinked once. Perhaps Conover had overestimated me. Maybe I hadn't touched her. Well, I was going at seven anyway. I reached for Compton's *Lake Anglique*, took it to my reading chair, and read the first two chapters.

Rhea lived across town from me, in one of the older, Art Deco buildings. It had a doorman and a garage attendant for its residents. As I was about to get out of the cab in the half-moon driveway, the attendant roared up to the front entrance in a silver Porsche, jumped out, and held the door for Rhea Hamilton, who darted from the building's lobby. Before I could climb completely out and shout to her, she took the wheel of the Porsche, slammed her door, and tore out of the driveway, her tires screeching. I ducked back inside the cab and told the driver to follow her and not to lose her.

Who did I say I was? Chess Hanrahan, I mused as we weaved in and out of the traffic in pursuit of her. Remember, the fellow you had a brandy with last night? No, I couldn't be too harsh on her. Not when I knew what she must be going through.

She led us up and down Manhattan and across it twice. My driver didn't mind. He was having fun and running up a stiff meter. I thought the chase was finally over when Rhea abruptly stopped and parked on Twenty-third Street, a block west of Fifth and the Flatiron Building. She got out and walked west. I told the driver to follow her discreetly. Rhea was in slacks and a hooded mink coat.

The driver asked, "The lady ran out on you, mister. Sure you can pay the meter?"

"I can buy this cab *and* the medallion," I remarked with a serious grin.

Rhea crossed Sixth Avenue, walking furiously. When she reached the other side, she stopped, looked at all the people ahead of her on the sidewalk, then turned, and recrossed Sixth. The driver waited for a moment, then he did a U-turn and followed her back east to Fifth Avenue. I sighed and wondered when and where this would end. So did the driver.

When she reached her car, she unlocked it, swung in, and shot out in a wide arc, going into the westbound traffic lane for a hundred feet before jerking back into the eastbound, then ran the red light at Fifth and turned onto the Avenue and drove south. Luckily Twenty-third was virtually empty, and luckily for me the light turned green and we were able to follow her.

She did the same thing again on Fourteenth Street—parked the Porsche, walked swiftly for a block and a half, then went back to her car. Her face was in shadow under the hood. At eight-thirty Rhea Hamilton came to a complete stop. She parked on Eleventh Avenue and walked up to Little West Twelfth Street and disappeared into a bar. I gave the driver a twenty-dollar bill through the screen. He looked at me curiously as he gave me my change back.

"Sure you want to go in after her in *there*?" he asked.

I slid my tip through the screen. "Death in the family," I said. "She doesn't know what she's doing."

The driver shook his head. "You watch yourself around here, mister, or there'll be another death in the family."

"I know," I smiled. "Thanks."

"Want me to wait?"

"No. She'll give me a ride."

The driver sighed wisely. "Like I said . . ." but he didn't bother to finish. I climbed out and shut the door.

Of course I knew about the area. It hadn't changed in all the years I'd been away. This was where people came to be pointless, to lose their minds, to contact the parasites of their sick souls, to face what they called reality. You could be killed around here, or maimed, or seduced, or you could patronize any of its bars and just sit and weep. The area didn't even have a name. In back of me, across the wide, busy Avenue, were the long, rotting sheds and docks of the Port Authority reaching into the Hudson. The sky above New Jersey was black and clear and I could even see a few stars. Around me were old warehouses and factory buildings. And up and down the sidewalk were furtive pools of red and blue neon lights, almost afraid to advertise themselves. Slicked-up men stood beneath most of them. A few looked at me expectantly. I walked past them unconcernedly to the doors beneath the black and white neon sign that read, THE COAL PIT.

It was an appropriate name. The din of the howling voice

and bass guitar and drumbeat was louder than a battery of coal crushing machines going full blast. It was solid pain and it hurt my ears and my head, thumping incessantly, trying to beat my consciousness into a pulp. I saw people in the dim light dancing to it. I say people because I couldn't be sure of their genders; "persons" would have been too specific. Knots of men in leather jackets and studded SS caps wore black bug-eyed sunglasses in a place you could barely see a lit match, and if you could, the flame was green. Smoke and jasmine perfume lay thick in the air, along with other smells I didn't care to identify. The place wasn't crowded, though. There were a few empty tables along the bare brick wall, with menus laid out and their obscenely shaped candles flickering alone. Even the bar was half empty; most of its occupants glanced speculatively at me. I guessed that by ten o'clock you wouldn't be able to shoulder your way through the crowd, though.

"Madison Avenue's that way, man," said a girl near me, sitting by herself at a table. Her glossy leather jacket opened to reveal a T-shirt and the twin facts that she was a girl. And her spray-painted green hair and earrings looked like the sawed-off ends of screwdrivers.

Somebody moved at the bar and I saw Rhea poised on a barstool at the far end. The bartender took a tall empty glass away from her and gave her another. She took the glass and drank half its contents, then put it down and bent her head, but not so quickly that I couldn't see a single tear roll down her cheek. I walked over and stood next to her and asked her above the racket if we could go outside. She glanced at me without recognition and then back at her drink. I asked her again. She couldn't hear me. I literally couldn't even hear myself. Then she raised her head to squint at me, and shook her head. I took her elbow, nodded my head. There was a ten-dollar bill and change on the place mat in front of her; the bartender could keep it. Rhea allowed me to lead her out.

The Thing with Green Hair rose from her table and

stood in our way. She shouted, "Where you goin' with *her*, man? You goddamned *man!*"

I braced myself to push her out of the way, flat on her back, if necessary. But suddenly Rhea brought up the toe of one of her calfskin boots and lashed out at the girl, hitting her where it's supposed to hurt a man more. Green Hair screamed in pain and surprise, but it was lost in the noise. She staggered backwards and sat on the floor beneath someone's table. I grabbed Rhea's elbow again and hustled her out of there.

She walked quietly beside me the long block to her car. My mind still ached; the thumping wouldn't quit. When we reached the Porsche, I turned to Rhea and said, "Keys. I'm driving."

She said simply, "It's not locked. They're in the ignition."

My mouth opened to reply automatically, but I stopped myself. Instead, I opened the passenger side for her, let her get in, then closed the door and went around to the other door. When I was behind the wheel, she'd already lit a cigarette and was staring into space. I clasped my hands over my ears and shook my head a few times to clear my mind of the pulverizing hammer blows that were still echoing within the walls of my skull. It didn't work. I turned the engine over and drove away, not caring where I went just as long as I left that sound behind me.

"What were you drinking in there?" I asked after we'd reached Twenty-third again.

Rhea glanced at me. "Bourbon, in there," she said. "At home, Scotch. Why do you ask?"

"I want to know what I'm up against." I stopped for a red light. "Why *that* place?"

"You don't approve of places like that?"

"Not even in daylight. We're both lucky the rough customers hadn't shown up yet." I was angry. "You know what kind of place that is? That's where people go to surrender to their neuroses, to have their minds and identities numbed so that they don't have to think. That and a thousand places like it around town. You don't belong in any of them."

"It was the best place I could find to forget Greg. You can't help but forget. It won't let you remember anything, it just lets you see what's sitting in front of you." Rhea paused. "It's for people who have no future, and no present."

"You'll never forget Compton," I said. "Not even with help like that."

The light changed and I turned right on Twenty-third. There were all-night places between Ninth and Eighth where I could pour coffee into Rhea and aspirin into myself.

She asked, "Haven't you ever been tempted to surrender, Mr. Hanrahan? To grief, to fatalism? To loss?"

I sighed. "I tried running once. I got bored. I liked living."

"But you can still lose, even for facing life. Greg did. As no other man I've ever known." Rhea paused. "It's . . . no use, though. No use. It can't last."

"Best to die on one's feet, than on one's knees," I said.

Rhea looked at me, frowning.

"Aeschylus," I added. Then I shook my head. "But one needn't die at all. Or surrender. Look at Compton. *He* didn't surrender. He fought his way up his own Mount Subarachi and raised his flag. To hell with fatalism."

"How did you know I was there? In that place, I mean? Did it have a name?"

I saw a coffee shop on Ninth and a parking spot close to it. I said as I maneuvered the Porsche into the space, "Look, when you've had a quart of coffee, I'll answer any question you ask. Not until then."

And the only thing I said to her half an hour later, at a table in the crowded shop and after she'd had a carafe of black coffee, was, "Let's go."

10

$\mathbf{R}$hea sat on the broad sill of my living room window, profiled against the brilliant lights of my city, a tigress in repose. She wore black slacks and a white sweater. She was wide-eyed sober now and placidly conscious of my presence, leaning against the side of the frame, her boots drawn up and crossed. I'd put on a tape of Renaissance dance music rendered by a harpist. The soft, courtly music matched her and how she sat there, lending an almost fairy-tale air to her and to the city beyond. She looked like the apex of an elegance of a long-ago culture, or the proper beginning of a new one. I couldn't decide whether she evoked a sad dignity, or an exquisite prelude to a magnificent adventure. I sat stretched out on the couch a distance from her, a drink in my hand, watching her, not in much of a hurry to decide which she was.

She turned from gazing out the window. "That's enchanting music. Do you listen to it often?"

"When I read. Or when I need an antidote."

"Why did you come after me?"

"I promised your father I'd see you. He was worried."

"Is that the only reason?"

I smiled. She understood and glanced away. I asked, "Where did you learn to kick like that?"

"Then and there," said Rhea. "She was ugly and evil, and a . . . man-hater. God knows what her conception of a man was. She looked as though she loved pain, though, so I hurt her. I was ashamed of myself afterward." She paused. "Must we discuss that?"

"No."

"You're not at all my idea of a detective, Mr. Hanrahan."

"What is your idea of a detective?"

"Someone who's hard, cruel, cynical, indifferent. Grasping." Rhea paused. "I didn't think I'd ever meet one who listened to the harp. Or who could quote Aeschylus."

I smiled, "It was only a month ago that I learned to speak whole sentences."

Rhea laughed, in spite of herself. "Why are you so different?"

I shrugged lightly. "How do I strike you?"

"I look at your face and seem to see everything you've seen, everything that ought to make you what I think you should be. But instead you're like a man being reborn, a man in the process of putting all those things aside."

I was so struck by the accuracy of her description that I simply stared at her with that special undisguised admiration you reserve for the woman you ask to step out of a line of women, and for whom you'd tell the rest that the job was taken. If my life was important to me, then this was the woman I'd want to walk shoulder-to-shoulder through it with me, because she'd go anywhere and do anything—not to contain your life, but to help you live it.

Rhea must have known what I was thinking. And while she seemed surprised to have said what she said, the rightness of her words held her glance uncontrollably on mine in mutual understanding. Her lips parted in some unspoken thought, and for a moment, between us, there was no Gregory Compton, no sadness, no outstanding problems to resolve—just her, myself, and the city beyond the window.

Then memory of why she was here in my apartment came back to both of us, and she broke the connection by glancing away. "Is your headache gone?" she asked.

"The aspirin helped," I said. "There's still a ringing in my ears but it's fading."

Rhea looked out the window. "Greg was a real man, too," she said. "Real . . . real. . . ." Then she shivered once, bent her head to her knees, and began sobbing.

I got up and crouched beside her. "You should stay with your father for a while, Rhea. You need him right now as much as he needs you."

She looked up at me.

"It's a loss for him, too."

"What am I to do?"

"Recover, and go on living," I said. I smiled wisely, because then I had a brilliant idea. "Make sure his last book is published."

She nodded once, faintly.

I called Conover at his Manhattan apartment, and told him to come and pick his daughter up. He was there fifteen minutes later, thanked me silently, and went out the door, an arm around her shoulders. I followed them out, retrieved Rhea's Porsche from a parking space near my building, and drove it back to her garage near Sutton Place.

When I got back to my apartment I collapsed on the couch, exhausted. Which was worse, I asked myself: seeing someone you cared for in grief for yourself, or in grief for another man? I knew the answer and all its implications, and that knowledge had caught up with me, too. It was becoming a strain on me. Well, I could deal with it. I would just have to put it aside for a while. I had work to do.

By four o'clock in the morning I had finished Gregory Compton's *Lake Anglique*. It was lightweight, bubbly, happy, and short. Too damned short, I thought. I thought so simply because I didn't encounter that kind of story very often. Teague was right about *Lake Anglique*: even the villains were angels. In fact, the only characters in the story one couldn't possibly feel empathy with were characters who reminded me of Teague. Compton had used them as mere foils. No wonder Teague hadn't thought the book very "deep." Everything he was and wanted didn't matter in the story. His crotchety view of life got left behind.

That was Teague, I thought. And I thought of the resistance this book must have met even before Compton had found a friend in Gussie Spendler, his agent.

I had quite a lot of work to do if I was ever going to understand that. I turned off my reading light, put Walker on the floor, then set my clock for eight o'clock, and fell gratefully into bed.

11

A couple of years ago I would have looked in the mirror and laughed at myself and at the idea that I could take on the literary establishment. After all, I was just a simpleminded, literal fellow who'd been successfully scarecrowed from those Elysian haunts. Like most honest, normal people, I'd bought the notion that its sacred soil was too good for me to tread, and that if I did happen to trespass, what sense could *I* hope to make of anything?

But unlike most other honest, normal people, I didn't accept the pronouncements of the literati as the final word. I wondered quietly, almost incidentally, why the preponderance of verbiage in literature was so overwhelmingly weighted in favor of the discouraging, the perverse, the satirical, the unattractive, the undistinguished. There was a chasm between it and myself, one I didn't care to bridge. I'd never been able to fathom its purpose. And the last people on earth who would claim that the dozenth study of the subtle effects on his prose of an author's clinically defined emotional disturbances, or the alleged universal significance of trailer-park incest among functional illiterates, would ever drive anyone to climb mountains, re-invent the wheel, write a great symphony, or welcome the sunrise, were those very same people, the ones who wrote the stuff and the ones who knighted it. They'd deny it with an emphatic smirk.

There were stars in the sky, and beacons in the night, and paths of glowing gems and jewels that led one to thrilling, glorious unknowns. There were also asteroid belts and smoldering city dumps and shortcuts through vacant city lots. So why were all the telescopes focused on the asteroids and the swarms of scavenging seagulls? I didn't know the answer. Not yet. And I was afraid of the answer. Not for myself. But for Gregory Compton.

No, I couldn't scare that easily anymore. The only mental license I needed to look into the literati was the one signed by Chess Hanrahan.

If my goal was to discover why Compton ought, or ought not to have won the Granville Prize, then the best place to start was at the beginning. So I hunted up the copy of the *Times* from that Friday night and read the front page article I'd been too bored to finish. And grinned when, on the inside page, near the end of the article, I saw a list of the Granville jurors. Well, that saved me the task of bribing someone at the Foundation.

In smaller print, following a list of the winners and their publishers, were the names of the people who voted. Victor Neary, chairman of the permanent sitting committee for the Prize. Three permanent committee members: Shelby Roth, Sean O'Scully, and Lisa Yeager. And the guest jurors: Hector Chamblee, professor of American literature at Packerd University and distinguished critic; Evelyn Zirbel, syndicated book review columnist and publisher of *New Leaves* magazine, which published short, experimental fiction; Jerome Hixon, critic and arts editor for the *Manhattan Chronicle*; Ruth Marchessini, professor of English literature at Worthing College of the Humanities. And Oliver Gullum, senior critic for the *Times*.

I laughed when I saw his name. No wonder he'd been so hard on Compton; he wanted everyone to be certain of which way *he* voted.

Jerome Hixon's was the only other name I recognized. The *Chronicle* was a daily, too, though Hixon's page covered a lot less of the arts than did the *Times*, and it appeared only four times a week and Hixon didn't have a regular column. He reported on only those books he thought worth mentioning. I liked him, principally because he said the right things about the right books, and said it in a quarter of the space that Gullum would use. But if he'd written anything about Compton, I'd missed it.

One of the things I was curious about was the margin by which Compton had won. It couldn't have been a unanimous vote, not with Gullum. Rhea said that Compton had been "yanked inside" by the very people who had been keeping him out. Well, were these the same people? I went to the public library's Main Branch to find out. I was there when the doors opened at ten o'clock.

At two o'clock I rubbed my eyes and broke for lunch. I made two calls first, one to Tyle Properties and one to Gussie Spendler. The agent sounded like a ghost on the phone, but she agreed to meet me at the Lantern restaurant around the corner from her office and only a block away from the library. At Tyle Properties a secretary told me that, yes, Gregory Compton had indeed "temped" there, but that the office manager, William Leif, was the only one there who could tell me anything about him, and he would be out of town until next Monday. I gave her my home and message numbers and asked that Leif return my call. I could wait. All I was after was feedback about Compton from someone who wasn't personally connected with him.

Gussie Spendler beat me to the Lantern and was in one of the back booths. As I expected, she was in a much less talkative mood than she had been two days ago. Her mind seemed adrift.

"Sorry you had to lose him," I said.

Gussie nodded once, then narrowed her eyes. "Now that he's dead, my phone won't stop ringing. Everybody wants to know about his last book, and whether I can get out of that damned contract with Pericles. I was supposed to be having lunch with some eager beaver from Penmaster Press right now, but I canceled out after you called because you're handsome and would never make me gag."

"Can you get out of it?"

"I've a mind not to try, just to spite those goddamned vultures," said the agent. "But I think I can. It depends on how much another publisher is willing to pay to buy out the contract."

"He finished it," I said. "I guess you knew that."

"He was supposed to give it to me today." Gussie paused and stared at me, her eyes watery. "This was supposed to be *his* lunch." She glanced away and lit a cigarette. "How did *you* know he'd finished it?"

"I saw it, at his place."

The waitress came and took our orders. Gussie said, "His brother in Michigan traced me through Pericles. He'll be here tomorrow. Greg's parents are dead and George—that's his brother—is his nearest surviving relative."

"Know if Compton left a will?"

Gussie shook her head. "I wish I did."

"What's his brother like?"

"He was just a voice on the phone, Mr. Hanrahan. He owns a garage. I think he's older."

The waitress came with our cocktails. "I'll bet Teague's all broken up," I remarked half seriously.

"Earl?" scoffed Gussie. "He's worried that George Compton won't let him go ahead with *Defender*, that's how broken up he is! Bastard won't even be in town next week."

"Oh? Why not?"

"Would you believe he's going to start a writers' colony? Somewhere in Pennsylvania, just across from New Jersey. A hundred acres of wooded land and babbling brooks. And some log cabins some developer never finished."

I chuckled. "How much do you want to bet he calls it 'The Babbling Brooks Writers' Retreat'?"

Gussie looked at me in amazement. "That's *exactly* what he plans to call it, Mr. Hanrahan. Did he tell you?"

"I was trying to be funny," I said, shaking my head.

"I laughed, too," said Gussie. "But Earl said, 'Just you wait, it'll be famous someday. Some great books are going to come out of there.'"

"Or a lot of tornados." I paused to sip my drink. "But how can Teague afford to buy so much land? Pericles can't be paying him that much."

"I don't know. He said the land was pretty cheap."

"What exactly is a writers' colony? I mean, what's wrong with Manhattan?"

"It's a place where writers go to write, in peace and quiet. Many writers can't produce anything in the city. Or they want an inexpensive place to go to get away from families."

Gussie said nothing else until our lunches came. I ate my London broil while she picked at her super salad. After a while, she asked, "Why are you still asking questions about Greg, Mr. Hanrahan? Are you still working for the Foundation?"

"No," I said. "The Foundation let me go yesterday."

"I don't understand, then. There's no one to look for now."

"Yes, there is, Gussie. I'm looking for the emperor who gave Compton a twenty-year sentence of obscurity in a room full of hacks, mediocrities, and lepers. Or, better yet, in the arena of the Roman Coliseum, except that there were no lions, no gladiators, not even a crowd. Just a tiny indistinct figure in the emperor's box gesturing thumbs down, chanting *vox populi, vox callidus.*"

"Come again?"

I didn't answer her. I just went on. "Except that Compton wasn't executed. He wasn't even martyred, or crucified. The emperor just left him locked up in that damned arena. And he had to stay there and listen to the roar of the crowds *outside* of the Coliseum. That's where the action was. Ever listen to a crowd roar in a stadium that's a half-mile away? It can be thrilling, or it can be frightening. It depends on what the spectacle is. It could mean a winning touchdown or it could mean a Nuremberg rally. Compton wasn't allowed to know. He wasn't even allowed to see who was pronouncing judgment on his life. Well, Gussie, *I* want to get a good look at that emperor, and hang a bell on him."

The agent looked at me curiously. "Finish your salad," I said. "And no questions."

Gussie shook her head. "You don't know what you're getting into, Mr. Hanrahan—"

"Chess," I said.

"—Chess. You're too nice a man. Clean. Intelligent. Rational. And honest. You'll never make any progress. You'll never find that emperor. I've been in publishing one way or another for thirty-five years, and I *know*." She paused. "*Vox callidus?*"

"The experts," I said. "My high school Latin comes in handy now and then." Then it was my turn to shake my head. "You're wrong, though. I'm halfway there."

"Halfway to where?"

I didn't say. I didn't give her a hint. "Do me a favor," I said.

"If I can."

"Don't tell Teague I'm still looking for Compton."

"If I told him that he'd think you were crazy."

"Don't tell him anything."

"Why have you told me?"

I smiled. "I haven't told you anything. You're a nice lady and I promised you lunch. You haven't seen the last of me."

I left her in front of the restaurant, mystified but back to her old scrappy self. And I went back to the library.

I'd forgotten how much work it was to do research, and how tiring it could be. But by closing time I'd filled about a quarter of my new notebook and spent about ten dollars on photocopies. I was still in the main reading room, alone at one of the long tables.

Apparently none of the Granville people had written anything. There was nothing in the card catalog or indexes about Victor Neary, Shelby Roth, Lisa Yeager, or Sean O'Scully.

Jerome Hixon, on the other hand, while he hadn't written anything about *Walk Around the Sun*, had reviewed both *Lake Anglique* and *A Select Circle of Friends*. *Lake Anglique*, he wrote, was "magical and spellbinding. Imagine this story line in the hands of another contemporary author: a weekend house party in a lovely mansion on the shore of a placid lake, held hostage by a not-so-desperate gang of extortionists, whose leader, with the reputation of being a *gallant*, has his bluff called by the heroine, who promises to marry him if he'll go straight and make a fortune on the stock market. On second thought, don't imagine what another would do with it. Buy the book. Read it. When you finish it you won't believe that the story was set in the present. But, then again, maybe you will. *Lake Anglique* is as invigorating as a day in a pure oxygen chamber." That was three years ago, in the *Chronicle*. Six months ago he'd written of *A Select Circle of Friends*, the short story collection, "Gregory Compton is not a combative novelist. That is, his stories are set in a world where the heroic is the norm, even among the less-than-admirable. There are no strictly defined 'good guys' or 'bad guys' in either these stories or in his novel, although there is conflict, and conflict such as none of us ever thought possible to human beings. Compton is not concerned with the sick and the lame and the halt, nor even with the fiend next door. All these get left behind on a flat bottom boat in the middle of a sluggish river. Titans rule Compton's stories, and they never abdicate, not even in defeat."

So I was certain of which way Hixon had voted.

Evelyn Zirbel, the syndicated columnist and publisher of

New Leaves, could also have voted for Compton. Or for Grackle. Or even for Daffy Duck. She reviewed new poetry and experimental fiction, and also wrote a lot of it herself. Ten years ago she'd been awarded a minor poetry prize for having invented something called "free-flow phonetics." I read a few reviews of her work by others, but exactly what she had accomplished defied my comprehension. Her latest innovation was "proportional poetry," in which content and clarity were secondary to print density and "margin imagery." I checked out her famous *Escape 68,* which consisted of four, almost infinitely repeated words— "no," "maybe," "stop," and "yes"—which were purported to simulate the sound and "psychic feel" of waves rolling in on the Maine coastline. There were a hundred and fifty-eight pages of that in *Escape 68.* I held the book up and let the pages fan down, thinking that perhaps that was how one was supposed to read Zirbel's opus. But all I got from that exercise was some very curious looks from people at the other tables. I concluded that the only way you could get anything from *Escape 68* was if you were brimming with dope. I put a question mark after Zirbel's name in my notebook, and massaged my chin. She was definitely unglued. She'd never reviewed either Compton's or Grackle's book.

Hector Chamblee, the professor of American literature and another distinguished critic, was an import, a Frenchman but now a U.S. citizen. His specialty, according to his essays and interviews, was everyone's condition. He was the author of two seminal critiques of American culture, *The Shoes We Wear* and *On the Edge of the Glacier.* Neither of them was in the library's stacks, but one reading of a few of his essays and interviews convinced me that I'd never fill out a reserve card for Chamblee's books. "Freedom is dangerous, and man is never so dangerous as when he is free," he'd written for the *Times* a few years back in a retrospective on modern literary trends. "Man is larger than life, more animated than existence. I do not, however, fall in with those who claim that man's ambition and vanity are natural vices, or that they are the polluting sins of megalomania. No, these are merely aspects of his nature, as morally neutral as antlers on a deer, as claws on a tiger. My quarrel has always been with those who would perform the Procrustean task of ordering, regimenting, or otherwise homogenizing man while neglecting his most vital aspect: his psyche. It is not his physical appendages which must be altered or abbreviated so that he might be fitted into a shrunken universe or a secure society. Ignorance or indifference to this fact has been the cause of so many brutal and terrible tyrannies. Misery is mental, as is elation. A diminished psyche will forget, or never discover, what these things are, or what they might be."

Chamblee, I concluded after half an hour of that, could not have voted for Gregory Compton. Stridivant would not have appealed to him at all. Zirbel the Unglued I could laugh at. Chamblee left me depressed.

Ruth Marchessini, the professor of English literature at Worthing College, was hard to pin down. She'd written dozens of articles, but all of them seemed to be on Elizabethan literature or Shakespeare. I read a few of them, and none of them told me where her tastes in modern literature might have run. Her two big books were *Accidental Judgments*, *Casual Slaughters*, a study of Shakespeare's tragedies, and *The Engine of Language*, an analysis of the impact of William Caxton and his printing press in the fifteenth century. Marchessini seemed to be a reputable and respected author. None of the reviews I found of her books sunk to the level of Gullum or Chamblee. No barbs, no venom, just straight-to-the-point appreciation.

I drew my notebook closer and studied my list of jurors for a moment, and decided that Marchessini, along with Hixon, most certainly had to have voted for Compton. His worst margin of course would have been five to four. And if all the permanent committee members had voted for him, while Gullum, Chamblee, and Zirbel—assuming that she wasn't as loony as her work suggested—voted for Grackle, then his margin would have been six to three, counting in Hixon and Marchessini.

Zirbel had never mentioned Compton or Grackle in her reviews. Neither had Chamblee in his. Hixon had reviewed Compton's first two books, but had said nothing about the prizewinning novel. My betting was that he couldn't ethically say anything about it while he was a Granville juror. Gullum, though, hadn't wasted any time. He was the only juror to have written about both authors.

Oliver Gullum. I wanted to talk with him. But not now. I simply wondered what he looked like, what he was like in person. And I had to know how the Granville people had voted.

"Excuse me, sir, but we're closing."

I looked up and saw a library guard. He and I were the only two souls left in the reading room. The clock on the wall said six o'clock. I rose and stuffed all my paperwork into the portfolio, then left and hailed a cab outside on Fifth.

At home I looked up Worthing College of the Humanities on a map. It was in Haverford, a small town on the other side of the Hudson, about thirty miles north of Tarrytown. From the operator I got Ruth Marchessini's home number. She lived in Kisco, another town not far from Haverford. I dialed her number.

When she answered, I suddenly panicked. All I wanted to ask her was how she'd voted, and whether she could tell me how the others had voted. But people had strange ideas about voting. Most claim they'd rather endure torture than say how they'd voted in an election, or simply say that it was no one else's business how they'd voted. Suppose Marchessini, Elizabethan literature scholar, was the same way?

I cursed silently and pressed the button, disconnecting the line. Well, what about Jerome Hixon, the critic? I got the *Manhattan Chronicle*'s number, dialed it, and asked for him. After a few runarounds and misroutings, I got someone on the arts page. No, Mr. Hixon was not in and would not be back for a week. He'd just flown out to San Francisco to attend an international book fair.

Damn it. The only juror I could probably be honest with was out of town. I sat and thought for a moment, then dialed Marchessini again.

"Hello?" answered a gentle voice.

"May I speak with Ruth Marchessini, please?"

"This is she."

"Hi. My name is Chess Hanrahan. I write for the . . . *San Francisco Profile*, and I'm in New York on a sort of working vacation, and I was wondering if I could see you some time soon."

"Oh. Well, I don't know," said Marchessini. "What is the *Profile*?"

"It's a weekly cultural magazine," I said. "Just a year old."

"I see. You must be calling about my new book. I'm afraid it isn't due out for a few months, Mr. Hanrahan."

New book? I asked myself. I said, "Well, we plan articles months in advance, and this article will be about both you and the book." I scratched my head. "I really enjoyed *The Engine of Language*. I won't take up much of your time."

"I can't come to New York, I'm afraid," said the woman. "I'm much too busy. But, if you'd like, we could have lunch tomorrow, right here at home."

"That would be wonderful," I said. "What's your address?"

Marchessini gave me her address, then we agreed on a time. Twelve noon. I said thanks, and Ruth Marchessini hung up first.

I felt a little ashamed of myself. Just a little. I was after the truth.

12

I spent the rest of Friday evening in Queens. I met Jack Bartlett at a diner on Queens Boulevard in Forest Hills where I bought him dinner. Since I wasn't hungry yet, I had a few coffees while we talked about my problem. Bartlett had been an occasional stakeout partner of mine when I was on the force. Shortly before I resigned he transferred to the Auto Theft Division. He was still there when I came back to the city, and still a sergeant. And still a friend. On one of our last jobs together a couple of thugs had tried to mug him with razor blades. I'd shot both of the bastards. After I'd filled him in on what I was doing now, he asked, "So why don't you lean on this girlfriend of Compton's? Or on her father?"

I shrugged. "I'm not in your shoes anymore, Jack."

Bartlett waved to the waitress and asked for a beer. The place was packed with moviegoers from the Midway just up the boulevard. He said, "I guess it makes a difference, not carrying a *real* badge," he grinned.

"You bet it does," I conceded. "You have the power of the courts behind you. I don't. If somebody lies to you—even if he's not guilty of anything—he'll still be in trouble. You have fear on your side. I don't. You can be lied to, but only at risk."

"Then why *don't* you get the police in on it?"

"How can I?" The waitress came then with Jack's beer and I waited until she was gone. "I'm not even certain a murder was committed, Jack. Manslaughter, maybe, but not murder. If you were the DA of Suffolk County, and looking at the cold facts, would *you* order an investigation?"

Bartlett thought about it for a moment, then shook his head. "No, I guess I wouldn't. I'd just see a hit-and-run."

I smiled. "And *then* suppose someone came to you with a story about a missing letter, a lost Mercedes mascot, and a treatise on modern literature?"

Jack gave that a moment of thought, then laughed. "Throw the nut out. Threaten to have the jerk's license revoked." He sipped his beer. "But we get lied to, Chess. All the time. You know that. Just last week we nailed a guy who reported his car stolen. When we found the car, we learned that it wasn't his anyway. *He'd* stolen it three years ago." He paused. "Say, Chess, you still got that cat you found on one of our jobs? Where are you living now?"

We sat for an hour while I told Jack my life story.

In Flushing, he looked over the Mercedes as thoroughly as I had. He nodded to me after he inspected the hood. "Yeah, that ornament was definitely broken off, Chess, not sawn off. Grill's all nicked up, but if this is a second- or third-hand car, that's not surprising. These grills are tough, only a tank could dent them. Let's take a look inside."

He produced a ring of keys—master keys to almost every line of domestic and foreign car sold in the country—and opened the door on the driver's side. I took the front, and he the back. Then we switched, and went over the car again.

Aside from Compton's dictionary, the only other things in the car were maps of New York, New Jersey, Pennsylvania, and Connecticut. The car was otherwise clean. There was some dirt on the mat beneath the pedals, and some dirt and leaf fragments on the floor in back, but that was all. There was no key in the ignition or anywhere in the car.

Bartlett shut the door and we checked the trunk. There was nothing in it but a spare tire and the tools needed to change a flat. "If this was a murder weapon, Chess," he said, slamming the trunk shut, "you'd have a hard time convincing me of it."

I grinned. "See what I mean?" I nodded to the hood. "You don't think a shop inspection would turn up anything on the grill or headlight . . . ?"

"Nawh," scoffed Bartlett. "Those bumps and nicks could've been made by anything, Chess. And if there *were* any threads or skin left on the car from a hit-and-run, they'd have been washed off by now. We had that snowstorm, you know, and then that fast melt. I mean, even if you could match the paint on the hood with paint you might find on this guy's clothes, it wouldn't prove *this* car hit him. There are thousands of Mercedes of this model in this area alone, driven by some pretty wealthy lunatics, all with the same paint and polish." Bartlett paused. "Maybe his girlfriend did it with her car," he suggested.

"It's possible," I said, lighting a cigarette. "And maybe her father did it. Or his best friend. Or his agent. Or his editor. Anybody could have done it."

"Or a complete stranger," suggested Bartlett as tactfully as he could.

"True," I conceded.

Bartlett dropped me off in front of my apartment building. I said thanks again and told him to call me anytime for a return favor.

By now I was hungry. I fixed myself a late dinner, went over my library notes and read some of the photocopied articles and reviews I hadn't had time to read earlier. I wondered if I'd ever hear from Farrell in Little Port, and made a mental note to call him tomorrow morning before I left for Haverford.

I gave some thought to Edgar Atherton and his story that Eunice Davies-Granville had died of consumption—or tuberculosis. Oh, she'd died of "consumption," all right— of cocaine, liquor, and men. According to the microfilm of the *Times* news stories of the period, she'd committed suicide in a women's residence. According to the news stories of the long-defunct *Courier-Post*, it was more like she'd overdosed in some fleabag hotel on the West Side. There were six major dailies in New York in that era, and only the *Times* had tried to pretty up the scandal. Cosmetic journalism. I speculated on the reason her parents had established a foundation in Eunice's name. Penance? Whitewash? People with money could behave in the strangest ways. Especially about their children.

As I sat on the couch and watched Walker on the windowsill peer at the traffic below as though it were a parade of bugs, I thought about Rhea and her strange behavior. But then I checked my thinking about that, telling myself again that I'd only known her for a very short while and that she had been in a state of crisis. I wanted to see her again, if only to just console her. After all, not many women these days fall in love with heroes. They want the nice, solid, practical fellows with secure futures and respectable potential. There was too much risk in a hero; no guaranteed victories, no steady income. They accepted the lunacy in today's world as the norm but sought security against it. Women as rich as Rhea, of course, could become addicted to lunacy—or they could afford to fall in love with someone who wasn't practical. But should the money make any difference to either party? I asked myself.

I was beginning to feel bitter—and envious of Compton—when I thought of Hector Chamblee and what he'd written about diminished psyches. He wasn't writing about some terrible, social-engineered future; he was writing about today. That's what had depressed me about him in the library. I recognized the world he was describing. Chamblee, Gullum, and Zirbel. If it were possible to Compton, then it was possible to me. But I recognized those diminished psyches.

I shook my head once and rubbed my eyes. I was tired and my mind was beginning to spin its wheels. It was only ten o'clock. It wasn't the full day's research that had exhausted me. It was the discovery of a truth. Or a handful of truths. Suspicion of truth is one thing, much like a captivating Spanish melody on guitar. Confirmation of it is an orchestration of that same melody, intense, violent, and thrilling on one hand, frightening and numbing on another. Someone had once told me what an awful burden and responsibility it was to know the truth about the world, and how tempting it was to believe that ignorance was bliss. He'd said that I'd reach a point when I'd envy the ignorant. I understood the burden and responsibility; I didn't completely agree with him about the envy.

I took a shower, set my clock for six, and went to bed. I fell asleep fast enough, but had a fitful sleep and a recurring dream about Hector Chamblee, who had my head in a vise, while Oliver Gullum laughed in my face and Evelyn Zirbel tatooed my chest with a poem that looked like a crossword puzzle. I think I was tied to a stake, too, and a crowd of people from "The Coal Pit" was dancing around a bonfire to the beat of a pile driver. The man-hater was there, too, and kept leaving the silhouetted dancers to kick me in the knees. Each time she did, Chamblee would tighten the vise and sigh something in French. Rhea was off to the side, sobbing, and I yelled to her over and over again not to cry, that I wouldn't tell anyone where Compton was. When I saw what it was they were fueling the bonfire with—boxes of Compton's books—I woke up with a start that sent Walker flying off the covers. I sat there for a moment, trying to remember if I'd had anything rich to eat. No, I decided, it wasn't what I'd eaten today; it was what I'd read. I went to the kitchen, warmed up a pan of milk, drank it, and went back to bed.

* * *

Farrell said that the county report had come in and I could drop over anytime to read it. I asked him over the phone to read me the items that had been found on Compton's body. I wrote it down as he read off the list: one wallet with identification and fifty-two dollars in bills; twenty-seven cents in change; three subway tokens; a silver Franklin half-dollar; a leather key case from Saks Fifth Avenue, containing six keys but no car keys; a gold Dunhill pen; a pack of cigarettes; a pocket notebook; a handkerchief.

"No car keys?" I asked.

"No, Mr. Hanrahan," said Farrell.

"What about a lighter or matches?"

"None at all."

"No letters or envelopes?"

"Sorry, Mr. Hanrahan. That was everything."

"Okay, thanks. I'll drop by sometime next week."

Walker jumped up onto the stand and inspected the phone. "No key, Walker," I said to him. His ears perked up, as though I'd just mentioned a new line of catfood. "No lighter. And no letter. See you tonight, kid."

An hour and a half later I drove into Haverford, a picturesque little town north of West Point. I drove past the Worthing College campus. It wasn't as big as Sloane's up in Massachusetts, but it took me back in time and made me smile. Kisco was west of it. Ruth Marchessini lived in a one-story stone house near a stream.

Marchessini was a trim, tall, white-haired woman of perhaps sixty with bright round eyes and big dimples. I'd expected her to offer me tea but she offered me a choice of drinks. I picked a cream sherry and she looked at me with approval. "We're having lamb," she said, sitting down opposite me in an armchair. "My lunch is my dinner, I'm afraid. I didn't want to baffle you with that idiosyncrasy of mine and neglected to ask you yesterday what you'd like."

"Sounds fine," I said.

"First we'll have Greek lemon soup and then the main

course." She paused. "Mr. Hanrahan, where is your tape recorder? And your notebook?"

I reached inside my jacket and took out my pocket notebook. "I'm ready."

"You know, I called your magazine yesterday after we talked. Your editor spoke very highly of you."

I blinked once, then must have blushed as deep a red as some of the bindings of her books on the shelves around us. Ruth Marchessini burst out laughing. "Really, Mr. Hanrahan," she said, "you ought to be ashamed of yourself! Trying to deceive someone like that! If you had stated your purpose, I'd never have questioned your desire for an interview."

I smiled. "Guess the joke's on me."

"It most certainly is. Of course I recognized your name. Don't you realize how famous you are in academia? And your name appeared in our town paper recently, in connection with some kidnapping prank you'd uncovered."

"It was more like a scam than a prank," I said. "I'm glad you're not angry with me."

"Well, I'm not. Now tell me: what did you really want to see me about?"

"The Granville Prize," I said.

"I see," said the scholar. "Oh, yes. That poor young man." She frowned. "Was he *murdered*?"

I shrugged dubiously. "I'm not certain yet. Evidence is pretty scarce."

"Why would you even suspect he was murdered?"

I put my glass down and leaned forward. "I don't think he should have won that Prize, Miss Marchessini."

"Oh? Why not?"

"Let's just say that I think he was too good to win it and let it go at that. It's my major premise and no one's going to shake me of it." I paused. "You were on the Granville jury. How did you vote?"

"I don't mind telling you, Mr. Hanrahan. For Gregory Compton's book."

"I thought so."

"Oh? Why?"

"I read some of your articles. I can't quite put my finger on it but you and Compton seemed to share the same perspective on life. I mean, that it could be . . . bigger than life. And plotted by people's premises, flaws, and strengths." I shook my head. "I just couldn't imagine you voting for Grackle."

"Neither could I, Mr. Hanrahan. William Henry Grackle is such a pretentious, self-pitying bumpkin." Marchessini paused. "Thank you for the compliment, by the way. That isn't the only reason I chose Mr. Compton's novel, however. There was the beauty of the language. And the power. I know of few other authors who can pack as much drama into so few words. Are you familiar with Shakespeare, Mr. Hanrahan?"

I smiled. I knew the difference between a folio and a quarto, and not much more. But I was familiar with Shakespeare. "I read him in high school."

"Then you can appreciate why I put so much stress on language." Marchessini rose. "Excuse me for a moment. I must check the oven."

While she was gone I took out my clipping from the paper and scanned it again. I'd been right about her, but something still didn't make sense. There was an ashtray on the coffee table, so I lit a cigarette and had another sip of the sherry. Marchessini bustled back. "Another ten minutes, Mr. Hanrahan."

"How did you vote in the other categories?" I asked. "For the drama and poetry and criticism Prizes, I mean?"

The scholar shook her head. "I didn't, Mr. Hanrahan. There were juries for each of those categories. I was on the novel jury."

Light seemed to flood my mind. "That's strange," I said. "I got the impression that there was only one jury."

"The Granville Prize for novels *is* the more famous, I suppose," said Marchessini. "I was happy to be invited to be a juror. Surprised, but happy. It was a convenient way of catching up on my reading. And it was an ideal opportunity to get closer to the Jupiters of literature, so to speak."

"Why were you surprised?"

Marchessini shrugged. "I'm not that well-known," she smiled. "Nor would I ever want to be. Tudor studies is not the glamour business that newspaper criticism is, that is, it's not as visible to the general public. I expect to be drawn into the controversy over the relative merits and flaws of the Oxford and Arden editions of Shakespeare, and look forward to some vigorous correspondence between myself and my colleagues around the world over my new book for a year or so. But I hardly expect to be deluged by offers to appear on television talk shows."

"Then why do you think you were chosen to be a juror?"

"Why? Well, Mr. Hanrahan, look at the composition of the jury: two famous critics, one deep-thinking literary Frenchman, and one poor imitation Gertrude Stein. I think Hector and I were chosen to lend respectability to the thing." Marchessini paused, then grinned. "This is so exciting! I've always wanted to be part of a mystery."

I smiled sadly. "Or a tragedy?"

"Oh, yes. Did you know Mr. Compton?"

"I wish I had."

The scholar glanced at a clock that was on a shelf beneath a print of Elizabeth I. "Well, shall we eat here or in the dining room?"

We ate in the dining room. Over a delicious roast lamb I learned that this charming lady's new book, *Around the Globe*, was on the Tudor era perspectives of politics, philosophy, and existence as expressed in its literature and drama. Aside from teaching Shakespeare at Worthing College, she was often called in as a consultant by theater companies putting on the Bard's plays, and had even gone to Hollywood to serve as a script consultant. At the moment, her biggest project was a monograph on Elizabethan loanwords. "Did you know that the English language grew the most between 1575 and 1580, Mr. Hanrahan? At least, that is the accepted time period. I'd put it back a bit, say, starting in 1570, but standardized usage could with some argument be pinpointed to those five short years. And it was the drama that fueled the change, mostly. Everybody went to plays in that era, and that's where people learned the language, the new uses of French and Latin words. Old English grammar was perfectly suited to absorb new words, and even the grammatical rules of other languages to some extent." The scholar helped herself to another slice of lamb, and asked me if I'd read any Shakespeare since high school.

"I've scheduled *Twelfth Night* for next month," I said.

"Ah! Remember then what I told you about 'you' and 'thou.' Pay *particular* attention to Toby's advice to Andrew, and you'll see what I mean!"

When I finished the peach melba dessert, I asked, as she poured our coffees, "Can you tell me how the others voted, Miss Marchessini?"

"Not entirely, Mr. Hanrahan. That is, I can tell you how the other guest jurors voted, but as to how the Granville jurors voted, I'm afraid I'm ignorant."

I sipped the coffee. "Didn't you all meet in a conference room and decide by a show of hands or sealed envelopes?"

"Oh, no, that's not how it was done at all! Each of us mailed his vote in to the Foundation, along with a critique of his favorite book and a ranking of the other nine. In fact, the envelopes Granville supplied us with were addressed to the Foundation's accounting firm for secret tabulation. What was that firm's name, now? Oh, yes! It was Grainer, Patrick, Drake, and Bookman."

The look of disappointment must have shown on my face.

"I'm sorry, Mr. Hanrahan," said Marchessini. "We never met as a group, not even for the award ceremony. It was hardly feasible. Evelyn Zirbel lives and works in Boston,

Mr. Chamblee teaches at Packerd down in North Carolina, and dear Jerome is traveling about the country too much."

I looked up. "You know Hixon?"

The scholar beamed. "We're old friends. I taught him what little Shakespeare he knows. That was ages ago, when he was a student at Norwood University and I was an assistant lecturer. We had quite a lengthy telephone conversation about the vote after the papers published the results."

I sat forward expectantly.

Marchessini laughed. "You look so predatory, Mr. Hanrahan! So wolfishly single-minded! Well, let's see. Evelyn Zirbel called me to ask how in heaven's name could I have voted for Compton, didn't I have enough taste? Hector called to tell me that he'd never read another book of mine, wasn't it an injustice that Grackle had lost? Jerome invited me to dinner sometime soon, he was happy that Compton had won and we were thinking of inviting him to our little feast."

"What about Oliver Gullum?" I asked. "You or Hixon have any idea of how he voted?"

"Why, for Grackle, of course, though that's just speculation on our part. He's been a juror in a number of prize contests and he *never* discusses how he votes. At least, that's what Jerome says."

Something about what she said bothered me, but I couldn't identify it. I asked, "Any ideas on how the Granville people voted?"

"None at all, Mr. Hanrahan. They're not permitted to discuss the matter in public or even with other jurors."

"But you or Hixon must have some idea. I mean, they're complete unknowns outside the Foundation. Why are their votes given equal weight?"

"Because they are employed by the Foundation, Mr. Hanrahan. I understand that each has a doctorate in some aspect of the humanities." Marchessini paused, then said, "Confidentially, my opinion of *those* four is that they are typical failed academics who could not sustain themselves even minimally in their chosen fields of expertise. There are so many of them and they usually wind up in foundations."

"Academicians," I smiled, just to tease her.

"Just for that little reprimand, you shall have another slice of my melba," said Marchessini, reaching for the pan.

I smiled. "Unusual punishment, but not cruel."

13

Ruth Marchessini was wrong about one thing: Oliver Gullum *had* discussed how he'd voted, in the Thursday *Times*. She'd seen the critic's latest diatribe and reached the same conclusion as I had about its purpose: it let everyone know where he stood.

I emerged from her little stone house with my head stuffed to capacity with loanwords and Shakespeare. I'd tackle her books someday. She was a wise lady and had been of far more help than I'd expected her to be. "I hope you're wrong about Gregory Compton," she said to me at the door. "I mean, about his being murdered. That *would* be a tragedy."

"I hope I'm wrong, too."

"If it *is* true, I'm sure it couldn't have anything to do with the Granville Foundation," she said. "I haven't much use for what those people do. Even if I wished the pox on them, though, I can't see how they could be responsible."

"We'll see," I'd said. I waved good-bye and got into my car.

I had an open road all the way down to Nyack and the Tappan Zee Bridge, and I hit Tarrytown around two-thirty.

Why not drop in on Conover? I asked myself. I was there and I wanted to see how he and Rhea were doing. I pulled off on the nearest exit and backtracked up the Hudson.

I didn't get lost this time, though it was still a trick to find Pheasant Road. The area was just as hilly and the roads as winding as in Little Port. In fact, the only difference between it and the Long Island town was the Sound. I half expected to see the Connecticut shore across the water every time I topped a hill.

Again there were several cars parked in front of Conover's place, including Rhea's Porsche and, to my surprise, Compton's Mercedes. Before I went to the front door, I looked it over, then went up the great steps. I asked the butler for Conover, and he let me wait in the hall while he went to announce me. Conover came out a minute later, dressed in slacks and a pullover sweater.

"This is a pleasant surprise, Mr. Hanrahan," he said, shaking my hand. "What brings you here?"

"Thought I'd drop by and see how you and Rhea were doing."

"All the way from Manhattan?" he chuckled.

"I had business up this way," I said.

Conover walked me to his study. Without all the people in it, this time it looked as spacious as J. P. Morgan's library. Some of the furniture had been pushed aside on the rug to make room for several blueprints of the new container ship. "Still at it?" I remarked.

"Yes," said Conover. "We're having problems with the hydraulic motors that control the hydrofoil struts. They're compartmentalized inside some of the bulkheads and the heat they generate is so great that we may have to give them more space. That means sealing problems." Conover studied the blueprint directly beneath him abstractly for a moment, then turned to me. "A drink?"

"No, thanks. Just came from lunch."

Conover waved me to a chair and sat down. "Well, we seem to be back to spirits, Mr. Hanrahan. Rhea's still shaken. I brought her here Friday morning and took the day off to be with her." He paused and smiled tentatively. "But she's recovered enough to be able to deal with Greg's editor, agent, brother, and lawyer. They're all here now." He paused again. "Thanks again for Thursday night, Mr. Hanrahan."

"No problem," I said. "Compton had a lawyer?"

"Yes," said Conover, lighting a cheroot. "Ted Gindel. Greg . . . didn't die intestate, I was relieved to learn. He drew up a will years ago, leaving his material possessions to his nearest living relative—that will be George Compton, his brother, nice man, that Sayres drove up with him from New York—and his literary estate to Rhea."

"He must have done that after he'd met her," I said.

"Yes. He amended his will six months after the Great Restaurant Clash. It even takes care of his unpublished work, which is several plays none of us knew anything about, and his just-finished novel. Pericles Press has a publication claim on it, and it will be published, but Rhea has control over it." Conover shrugged in contentment. "He made her his literary executor. I'm glad he did that."

"Will George Compton contest the will or make trouble?"

Conover shook his head. "No. He was a bit startled at Greg's success, and doesn't understand the first thing about publishing—I don't think he's a reading man—and doesn't want much to do with it. And he can't contest the will. It's pretty airtight." Conover smiled in appreciation. "Greg even thought of Miss Spendler. There was another amendment to the will that specified that she get her percentage from sales."

"Did he leave anything to Geoffrey Sayres, his friend?"

"Not that I'm aware of."

I lit a cigarette. "Why is Sayres here?"

Conover shrugged. "He drove the brother up in Greg's car. He'd come up once or twice with Greg and knew the way."

"I understand he and Rhea don't get along."

"True," remarked Conover. "He's all *Sturm und Drang* and no relief. His plays—two of which I've read—are the same way. I don't think the boy's known a happy day in his life. Can't conceive of happiness. If someone actually produced one of his dramas, he'd wrestle a neurosis out of it somehow. Worshipped Greg, of course."

"Compton wasn't like that?"

"Not in the least. He knew when the combat was over and could take success."

I smiled, remembering what Jerome Hixon said about Compton not being a combative novelist. I asked, "Why do you think Compton and Sayres were friends, then?"

"Greg saw a lot of potential in Geoffrey. It's there. How did Greg put it to me once? Oh, yes. He said that Geoffrey was still in his 'Bronze Age.'" Conover rose and poured himself a drink from a decanter. "Why are you still so curious about Greg, Mr. Hanrahan? Surely your job has been terminated."

I grinned. "It has been. But not my curiosity." I paused. "Do you think Compton should have won the Granville?"

Conover thought about it for a minute. "The odds were against his winning a poetry contest in the *Smalltown Courier*. But he won it. Like the Lord, the literati move in mysterious ways. It may have been an accident, or it may have been genuine recognition. I don't pretend to know which. I'm just glad."

My eyes narrowed a bit. "But was Compton?"

"I think he was," said Conover. "I spoke with him last Saturday morning. He was at a loss for words, but I think he was simply stunned." He sat down and leaned forward, closer to me. "What are you driving at, Mr. Hanrahan?"

"I can't say right now," I said. "Truthfully. All I have is a flock of suppositions looking for a place to roost."

"Would you mind sharing them with me?"

I sighed. "I'd mind it more if it turned out I was wrong. Then you wouldn't think I was very bright after all."

Conover merely smiled in defeat.

I smiled in turn, then glanced at the blueprints on the rug. "Have a name for it yet?"

"No. I've been toying with the idea of naming it after Rhea, but she said she'd sue me if I did," Conover said, chuckling.

Just then the study door opened and the subject came in. She was in a gray business suit and heels. I rose instinctively and stared at her. She stared back at me.

"Mr. Hanrahan," she said. "This is a surprise. I was thinking of you."

"How are you doing?"

"I'm fine, thank you." Rhea turned to her father. "We've finished our business, Father. I was wondering if you'd like to join us for a late lunch. You didn't have much of a breakfast this morning. Aunt Peggy's fixing some sandwiches."

"I'll have one," said Conover. "And how *did* your business go?"

"It went fine," said Rhea after a little pause.

"Anybody complain about having to trek up from the city?"

"No."

"Is something wrong?"

"Nothing's wrong, Father." Rhea turned to me. "Mr. Hanrahan, George Compton—Greg's brother—has agreed to let us bury Greg here, that is, in our grounds in Hansen, upstate. The funeral is Tuesday. You're welcome to come."

"Thank you."

"Will you join us for lunch?"

"Sure."

"We'll be in the den, Father," said Rhea.

When she had gone out, Conover said, "I thought you said you'd had lunch, Mr. Hanrahan."

I just grinned. "I didn't have sandwiches."

"You mean you'll be feeding your curiosity more than you will your stomach," said the shipbuilder.

The sandwiches, built in a circle on a silver platter, looked wonderful, but I had no appetite and just nibbled at one to look busy.

George Compton was, I supposed, a "nice" man, the adjective being a euphemism for undistinguished. He was about five years older than Greg but looked ten. He wore an old tweed suit that must have been his only suit. He seemed to be uncomfortably awed by his company and surroundings. I tried making conversation with him but our talk went as far as the weather. I couldn't determine whether it was shyness or simply mental inertia that made him seem so indifferent to the subject of his brother. He'd never read any of his brother's books and didn't seem to be in much of a hurry to do so. When I asked him what he thought of his brother's success, he said, "Oh, Greg was always dreamin'."

Earl Teague and Geoffrey Sayres both nodded hello to me but avoided conversation, Teague especially. Gussie Spendler introduced me to Ted Gindel, the lawyer, then took me aside. "Find the emperor yet, Mr. Hanrahan?"

"Not yet," I smiled. "How are you doing?"

She shrugged. "I was doing all right until Gindel read the will. Greg made me permanent agent for all his works. I didn't expect that."

"You did a lot for him."

"Would you mind giving me a lift home after this breaks up?" asked the agent. "Earl drove me up here, but you'd make better company."

"Sure."

"What are you doing here anyway?"

"I'm a friend of the family now."

Gussie Spendler finished her coffee then studied me for a moment. "I wonder for how long," she said. Then before I could ask her what she meant, she added, "Later."

I caught Teague pouring himself a drink at the sideboard. "Well, what was your reward, Editor?"

Teague studied me with a smug look. "What's that supposed to mean?"

"What did Compton leave you in his will?"

"Nothing," smiled Teague. "I already had the contract for his next book, and that's all I need. I'm only here to make sure it stays that way."

"Why would you worry about it?"

Teague shrugged. "You can never trust these seven-digit heiresses. I *know* there's a final manuscript of Compton's last book, and I don't want gold like that yanked from under me by some grieving would-be widow."

I smiled wickedly. "Compton made your reputation, Mr. Teague. Show a little gratitude."

Teague smiled back at me. "Hell, I'm grateful. And if it meant lining my pockets, I'd grieve from here to Hoboken. But there's no money in sentiment, my soft-boiled detective." Then he turned his back on me and walked away.

I fixed myself a drink and accepted a dish of chocolate mousse from Rhea's Aunt Peggy, then retreated to a corner to observe. The only active person in the room was Aunt Peggy herself, but it wasn't her fault that the lunch was a dud. Not in these circumstances. I noticed Sayres giving me a glance now and then, and after a while, when nobody else was around me, he wandered over and sat on a stool opposite me. "Are you going to Greg's funeral, too, Mr. Hanrahan?"

"I might. How are you doing?"

"Okay," said Sayres with a sigh. "I'll get over this, I guess."

"Where were you last night?" I asked. "I came over to talk to you, but you weren't home."

"Oh," said Sayres, surprised. "Well, you know, it's crazy. I had dinner with a producer who's interested in my last play. He . . . might put up some money for a production if he can find another partner. It's crazy because it had to happen *now*. It looks pretty serious and I should have butterflies in my stomach, but I can't feel anything."

"Did you have Compton's car keys all this while?"

Sayres frowned for a brief moment, then said. "No. Greg usually left them on a ring beneath one of the planters by his front door. They were there all along." He paused. "Why?"

"I didn't know you could drive. You drove George Compton up here, didn't you?"

"Yes, I did."

I finished the mousse and put the dish aside. "Think you can tell me now why you think it could have hurt Compton to accept the Granville?"

Sayres smiled sadly. "He's beyond being hurt now, isn't he? Never mind what I said before. I was wrong."

"I was thinking of his reputation, of him being lumped in together with all the other Granville clowns."

Sayres twisted his mouth in concession. "Well, that's more or less what I meant." He paused, glanced around, saw Rhea talking with her father and Gussie Spendler, then turned to me and with a lowered voice said, "That letter of refusal Greg wrote—I found it, Mr. Hanrahan."

I leaned forward. "Oh? Where?"

"In the glove compartment of Greg's car. I found it late this morning, with some road maps I wanted to look at to make sure of the way up here."

I sat back, then took a sip of my port. Now the reason I'd fibbed to Sayres about having gone over to talk to him last night was because all the while Bartlett and I were there, going over Compton's Mercedes, I didn't notice him at his window. His rooms had been dark, and I'd wondered where this somber, moody young man might have gone on a Friday night. I'd simply been trying to make conversation. Then he goes and volunteers a lie of his own, one much more serious than he imagined. There were maps in that glove compartment last night, but no letter. I asked, "Where is the letter now?"

"I gave it to Rhea," said Sayres. "She knows now. It's up

to her whether she tells the Granville Foundation. Greg made her his literary executor."

"What do you mean, it's up to her?"

Sayres shrugged, almost in amusement. "That *letter* is his last will and testament, in a manner of speaking. Greg didn't want the Granville. Has she enough character to respect his wish? Has she enough to respect him?"

"When did you give it to her?"

"Right after Gindel finished the reading. I called her aside and watched her open the envelope and read the letter." Sayres's eyes left mine and gazed into a distance. "It's up to her," he repeated.

I must have been silent for so long, thinking over the implications of what he had told me, that Sayres rose and nodded good-bye. I nursed my port and watched as everybody began a general leave-taking. Sayres and George Compton spoke with Conover and Rhea before they left, then Teague. Gussie Spendler glanced at me once as she spoke with Conover's sister. I got up and went to Rhea and her father.

"I'm sorry we didn't have time to talk, Mr. Hanrahan," said Rhea. "Perhaps tomorrow, over dinner? I feel I owe you something."

"I'm open," I said. "Call anytime. I'll be home most of the day."

"Fine." Rhea raised her hand and I grasped it, smiling into her lovely hazel eyes. My hand lingered in hers a second more than it should have, then I let go and shook hands with Conover.

"Good luck gathering those suppositions, Mr. Hanrahan," he said.

I told Gussie Spendler that I'd wait for her outside. When she came, she inspected my car with approval. "What model is this?" she asked as we climbed in.

"An MG Magnette," I said, turning over the engine. "Bought it a year ago, secondhand." I looked at her. "Don't you drive?"

"No. Never bothered to learn. Could you drop me off at my office, Mr. Hanrahan?"

"Sure," I said. When we reached Pheasant Road, I asked, "Well, what have you got for me, trouper?"

"What do you think of Rhea Hamilton?" asked the agent, lighting a cigarette.

"Greg did all right for himself. Anything else I'd have to say about her you wouldn't appreciate, you being a woman."

"She *is* attractive."

I chuckled. "That's like saying the mousse was edible." I paused. "What do *you* think of her?"

"Well, considering her obvious assets, and my being a woman, you wouldn't appreciate what *I* had to say about her."

"Jealous?"

"What else?" smiled Gussie in generous defeat. "She's a powerful woman, Mr. Hanrahan. Powerful. And she can be ruthless, too."

"How so?"

"Well, she didn't have to be at the reading back there. Greg handed it to her on a silver platter. But, I'm telling you, if he'd made me or Earl or that Sayres boy his literary executor, she'd have bought any one of us off—or tried to." Gussie paused. "Yes, Greg did all right for himself. He found a woman who had all the qualities of a Compton heroine."

My mouth twisted a little in passing bitterness. "Question is, Gussie: do women still look for heroes?"

The agent glanced at me. "Do you consider yourself one?"

I smiled. "I don't boast."

"Neither did Greg." Gussie reached over and patted my arm lightly. "I don't know if women these days look for heroes anymore, Mr. Hanrahan. I don't think many do, or ever have. From the looks of most married men, women don't even look for the illusion of a hero. That's in answer to *your* question. *My* question is: why do women do with heroes what they do when they've found them?"

"Which is?" If Gussie gave me an honest answer, I resolved, she could handle my memoirs.

"Make them common," she said. "Sap their courage, make the courage to be common the price of bliss and companionship and everything else a woman can ration out to a man who's not careful. Make them put their dreams and ideals in an attic or garage. Help them find the wrong answers."

I'd heard other men voice that complaint—I'd made it myself often enough—but never another woman. Well, she had my business. I wondered if she knew any good ghostwriters. I said, "A man who'd allow that to be done to him isn't a hero." I paused to light my own cigarette. "Are you saying that Rhea Hamilton tried that with Compton?"

"I don't know what to say—except that I think that she bribed Earl to submit Greg's book to the Granville people."

"Why do you think that?"

Gussie shook her head disgustedly. "Earl kept making little comments on our way up here. Wouldn't come out and say it, of course, just kept hinting. I didn't think twice about it—Earl would read something dirty into a girl eating an ice cream cone—until I met *her*."

"What kind of comments did he make?"

"Well, he started right off on his plans for his writers' retreat, how he'd name each cabin after a famous writer. I gave him some serious ribbing about Babbling Brooks, but he just laughed and said that maybe he ought to change the name to 'Compton Farms,' or something like that, because he owed a lot to Greg."

"What you're saying is that you suspect her of giving him enough money to buy the land, in exchange for his submitting Compton's book to the Foundation. Right?"

Gussie nodded.

I shook my head. "It doesn't wash, trouper. That's a pretty high price to pay on three hundred to one odds."

Then I shook my head again. "Besides, if that were true, why would Teague be stupid enough to suggest it?"

"Because it's beyond proof, and, Earl being Earl, nothing is clean in this world. He likes disabusing people of their ideas. He enjoys robbing people of their moments of triumph. He's grown creepier since the Granville announcement. I almost expect him to come into my office someday and do a victory jig, à la Hitler in Paris."

I laughed. "I don't much like him, either, Gussie."

14

fter I dropped Gussie Spendler off at her office in midtown I went home and took a nap. I needed a rest from today's revelations. It was about five-thirty when I opened my eyes. Walker had climbed on top of my chest and was still snoozing. "Food," I said, and his eyes opened instantly. I could have said "Einstein" or "eschatology" just as well. We play-fought for a while, then I picked him up and cradled him. "If I settled down, Walker, would you still love me?" I asked him, peering into wary eyes. He batted my cheek a couple of times with his paw, then meowed to be let down. I took it for an answer in the negative and let him go.

Of course, the first words out of my mouth had to have something to do with what was bothering me, not only in personal terms, but in terms of my investigation as well. "Settle down." I'd been asked to do that by a few women in the past. What it had always meant was to surrender, to retreat, to remove the centerpiece of my life out of the way of things and consign it to the attic or garage, as Gussie Spendler would say. Some men found it easy to "settle down," to abandon their dreams, ideals, or goals; they'd never taken those things seriously, they were mere pretences. Others let themselves be talked into "settling down" from fear—fear of being alone, fear of failure—hell, even fear of success, because success carried with it responsibility.

Sure, the times put a premium on independence. We lived in a welfare state that sucked as much out of it as it could get away with. That and other things seemed to suborn one's desires, courage, and determination. But should any of that make a difference? I didn't think so. Compton did it with the whole damned deck stacked against him. I had money, but that didn't make a difference, either. It was what was inside oneself that was suborned, bought off, frightened. It paid to belong. People grew up in that kind of society or culture and took the surrender and the anxieties for normal. Or most people did.

Compton didn't.

Compton's hero, Stridivant, had struggled with the same torture. Near the middle of *Walk Around the Sun*, Compton had written: "Why had human warmth, love, all the thousand little pleasures of living been monopolized by the faltering, the hesitant, by all those who were not able to look beyond their doorsteps? That boy down there, thought Stridivant: he'll devote the fire of his life to meeting her terms. And the girl he's embracing: she'll devote the fire of her life to convention and security. The things they were experiencing were genuine now—and would remain so until they became shackles. Tenderness, wondered Stridivant: why did it seem to be so inimical to passion? Why are all those things so alien to my life? Are they necessary enemies? He remembered Anne and all the things she had taken with her—all the things he had known for the first time—and closed his eyes. When he opened them, the boy and girl were still there. Stridivant moved away from the window to fix a cup of coffee he did not need."

The phone rang, startling me enough that I dropped the

book to the floor. It was six o'clock. I went to the phone at my desk. It was William Leif, office manager at Tyle Properties. "Mr. Leif, thanks for returning my call. Are you back in the city?"

"Yes, in fact, I'm still at the office, going through all my call slips. I understand you want to speak to me about Gregory Compton."

"Yes, if you don't mind."

"In what capacity, may I ask?"

"I'm a private investigator. I was looking into his disappearance when he was found last week."

"That's a shame," sighed Leif. "I mean, that he had to die so soon after he'd made it."

It might have been more than a shame, I thought to myself, but didn't tell Leif that. "I understand he worked in your office through a temporary employment agency?"

"Why, yes, he did."

"What was he like?"

"Well, I couldn't have asked for a better employee. He was somewhat overqualified for the kind of work I understand he did. But then he was older and more responsible than most temps we're sent. He was marvelous."

"When did he last work for you?"

"Oh, about a week or so before he won that Prize. But I saw him the day after the announcement. A Saturday morning. He called to ask me if he could ask me some questions about the real estate business."

"Real estate?"

"He said he was researching the background of a character for a new novel. I agreed to see him. We had brunch, and then he came up with me to the office for a while. He asked me some questions about property law and then he left around noontime."

Leif went on about how sharp and competent Compton had been. Five minutes later I said thanks and good-bye. Well, I thought, that was something. Compton had been busy to the last.

But why hadn't Compton mailed that letter of refusal? Had he simply forgotten to? Or had he a sudden change of mind? Well, Sayres was a liar, so I couldn't answer those questions now. Teague was a liar, too. And Rhea? I hoped with every atom of my body that Gussie Spendler had been misreading Earl Teague. The last person in the world I wanted to suspect was Rhea Hamilton. But I made myself think of it. If she'd bribed Teague, then could she have somehow bribed Victor Neary, the chairman of the Granville committee? With what? And for what? A paperweight and an amount of money which, to her, was a drop in the bucket?

Besides, Neary and his colleagues were supposed to be above that sort of thing.

I poured myself a glass of wine and sat down at my desk to outline all the possible scenarios I could think of, all the combinations, all the conclusions. Most of them didn't look very pretty. The simplest one, of course, was that Compton was the victim of a genuine hit-and-run. When I was finished with that, I made a list of things to do on Monday. For one thing, I was determined to learn how the Granville jurors voted. If the vote had been honest and not engineered, then my case was over. If it hadn't been, then someone was in trouble. Besides Geoffrey Sayres.

Geoffrey Sayres, dramatist. Moody Young Man. Liar. The only thing he'd told me so far and which I didn't question now was that he'd given Compton's unmailed letter of refusal to Rhea. Why had he lied to me? What was he up to? I couldn't for a minute believe that he'd murdered his best friend. For what? I burned my brain trying to imagine a reason, and only succeeded in making myself groggy.

And I had to suspect Rhea, Teague, and even Conover. They all might have had reasons to murder Compton. Then my head began to spin again and I threw my pencil down. I got up, changed, decided on a walk and maybe a movie, but then, in the elevator, pushed the garage level button.

Sayres deserved a surprise visit. He still hadn't answered my question.

It was a Saturday night, but apparently none of the residents in his neighborhood was in the habit of going anywhere. Even the driveways were blocked with parked cars. I wound up leaving my car five blocks away next to a fire hydrant. Sayres's lights weren't on, but Compton's were. A labored handwritten tab over a doorbell read *Second Floor*. I pushed the bell, not certain that it worked because I heard nothing. But a moment later I heard footsteps in the hallway, the front door opened, and there was Geoffrey Sayres.

He blinked at me once, then said, "Hi."

"Hello, Mr. Sayres."

"You missed her by about twenty minutes."

"Missed who?"

"Her. Rhea Almighty Hamilton. She and Gindel followed us down from Tarrytown to collect Greg's manuscripts and papers."

I asked, "Why do you think I'm here to see her?"

Sayres looked perplexed. "Wrong assumption, I guess," he shrugged.

I just smiled. "Mind if I come up anyway for a coffee?"

"No, not at all." On our way up the steps, Sayres said, "I'm here helping George Compton pack Greg's things. The landlord downstairs wants to move a new tenant in by the end of next week."

George Compton and I exchanged nods. He seemed to have undergone a change. There was a look of resignation in his face now, a sense of loss. He stood holding what I guessed was one of his brother's sweaters. The place was full of empty and packed cartons they'd probably hauled from a supermarket. All the shelves in Compton's study were bare now. I waited there while Sayres went to the kitchen. George stood near the couch and dropped the sweater on a pile of slacks and jackets. He sighed once and looked uncomfortable. He smiled at me without amusement. "This is like destroying a life," he said.

"How so?"

"It's like tearing someone apart and scattering the pieces all over. I don't like doing this—getting rid of his stuff. We never got along, but I still don't like it."

"You were at each other's throats when you were kids?"

Compton grinned briefly in recollection. "That's right. I was older and always picking on him. He never put up with it, though. I used to hate him. Pop was always strappin' us for fighting." He paused. "But we lost touch. I didn't even know he was still alive until I read the papers." He picked up a jacket and felt the material. "We were never close, but now this is the closest I'll ever get to him. Damn."

"Well," I said, glancing around the room, "it's all yours now."

"I'm giving most of the books to Mr. Sayres," said Compton. "I'm even thinking of letting him have Greg's royalties from his books. I might see this Gindel fellow before I leave."

"Why would you do that?"

Compton shrugged. "This young fellow seemed to be Greg's best friend. More of a friend than I was. It wouldn't be fair for me to start collecting money that way. I mean, I never gave a damn about Greg until now, so why should I benefit? I made life miserable for him, and it seems he lived pretty miserably after he left home. It might seem silly to cut myself out that way, but I wouldn't ever feel right if I didn't."

"Going to keep the Granville award?"

Compton shook his head. "No. Gindel said I had legal title to it, but that girlfriend of Greg's seems eager to have it, and she can. But she insisted I get that check Greg won, too." He shrugged. "Well, I could use it. The garage back home needs overhauling. She's paying for Greg's funeral, you know."

"What about his car outside?"

"Mr. Compton is selling it to me," said Sayres, coming into the room. "For a dollar." He sat down on a stool in the middle of the room and began sorting through stacks of books, putting a few into one carton, most into another. "Coffee'll be ready in a minute. I fixed some for you, too, George." As Sayres glanced at and distributed the titles, he asked, "Well, what can I do for you, Mr. Hanrahan?"

"Our conversation keeps being interrupted," I said, lighting a cigarette. "You never did tell me why you thought the Granville would hurt Compton."

"Well, didn't we agree that it would hurt Greg's literary reputation?"

"I suggested that as *my* reasoning. What's yours?"

"It's the same," said Sayres, annoyed. "I'll explain that. When you're in a minority such as Greg was, you have to have an extra-spotless reputation. It was Emerson who wrote that if you're a hero, you shouldn't try to reconcile yourself with the world. Well, the world tried to force a reconciliation on Greg. It might have worked if Greg gave in and accepted the Granville."

"Why do you think he didn't mail that letter of refusal?"

"He probably got together with Rhea to talk about it, then forgot about it."

"Do you think she knew beforehand about this intention to refuse the award?"

"Yes, I think she did. And she probably put him through hell, too. I think she wanted it more than Greg did."

"How did she react when she read it?"

"She didn't say anything, but she wasn't very happy about it."

"What do you think about it now?"

"It's too late," sighed Sayres. "It's up to her."

"*You* could have mailed that letter yourself, Sayres. If you felt so strongly about Compton's acceptance of the Granville, you could have easily dropped it in some mailbox and settled it."

"I *do* feel strongly about it!" said Sayres. "But I'm tired of doing other people's thinking for them. I'm tired of living on the fringes while everybody else is whooping it up. Let *them* decide for once. I've done more than my share, damn it."

I just stood there and absorbed the outburst. The kettle in the kitchen began screaming then and Sayres threw a book down, got up, and went out. Up until now George Compton didn't show any interest in our conversation, but when Sayres left, he asked, "What letter are you two talking about?"

"The letter that was in the glove compartment of your brother's car," I said. "The one with the road maps this morning."

"I took those maps out, Mr. Hanrahan, and there was no letter with them."

"Must've been some other time," I said. "It's not important."

Like hell it wasn't important. But I didn't want Compton thinking about it now and I didn't want Sayres to suspect that I thought differently on the subject. So I got him into a conversation about his garage business back in Michigan and he was in the middle of telling me about the time he helped the police nab a couple of car thieves who were using his place as a drop when Sayres came back with a tray of coffees. He put it on the desk and said, "Help yourselves."

We chitchatted over coffee for a while. Compton said, "What was your interest in Greg, Mr. Hanrahan?"

"I was hired to look for him," I said.

"Did *you* find him?"

"No. The police did. I've read his books, though, and I don't think he should've won the Granville, either."

"Oh," said Compton, frowning. "Who else didn't?"

"Mr. Sayres here, for one. And other people." I paused. "The thing's a mess, though. I don't think I'll ever straighten it out."

"There's nothing to straighten out, Mr. Hanrahan," said Sayres.

"No," I said, glancing at my watch. "I guess not. I've done my share. Well, I'll be leaving now. When are you heading back for Michigan, Mr. Compton?"

"This Wednesday. The day after the funeral. Will you be there, too?"

"Probably." I stood up. "Oh. Just one thing. You've claimed your brother's things from the county people out on the island, haven't you, Mr. Compton?"

"This morning. Mr. Sayres was kind enough to drive me out there."

"Was there a lighter?"

"No. Everything that was on that list the clerk made me sign for was there."

"Not even a pack of matches?"

"No."

Sayres said, "Rhea gave Greg a gold lighter, Mr. Hanrahan. One of those expensive electric models. Plain but elegant. His initials were on it."

"Well, that's interesting. Guess someone in Little Port kept it."

Sayres looked doubtful. "Maybe," he said. "Except that I saw it sitting on a table up in Tarrytown. In fact, on the one you were sitting next to, on the other side of the lamp. I didn't think of it. I mean, I just thought that Greg had left it there." The dramatist studied me for a moment and I studied him. "Why are you still asking people questions? It's over."

I shrugged. "Maybe it isn't, Mr. Sayres. And maybe it is. It won't be over until the last bill is paid."

"Mr. Sayres," said Compton. "What should we do about all this mail? There are some bills and things and even a check from this agency he worked for."

"Well, you could pay the bills with his last temp check. You'd probably have to go to the agency and have a new one issued, though."

"Why didn't Compton pick up his check at work?" I asked.

"With these agencies you have a choice of picking it up at the agency or having it mailed to you. Greg always had his mailed to him. He didn't like wasting an hour standing in line at a bank or at one of these check-cashing outfits."

"What agency did he work for?"

"What was its name?" mused Sayres. "Aristo Temps. They're in some building near Grand Central."

I recognized the name of the agency. The envelope was one of the ones I'd picked up from the table downstairs Wednesday night. My God, I thought to myself. Sayres had told the truth for once. "You ever work for them?"

"Once, a long time ago. You have to be able to type at least eighty words a minute or else they won't sign you up. The pay's worth it, though."

I started buttoning up my coat. "Good night, gentlemen," I said. "I'll let myself out."

On the porch outside I glanced at the planters on the wall next to the front door. There were three of them, each holding some evergreen shrubbery whose needles were half green and half brown. Well, I wouldn't thrive in this neighborhood, either. I picked one up and felt underneath, then did the same with the other two. Compton couldn't have put a penny beneath any one of them, let along a key. They were all flat-bottomed.

As I drove back to the city, I thought about how much of a pinball game this was turning out to be. Just like the Mackie case up at Sloane University had been. I had to bounce questions off of people without tipping them off that I was on the trail of something serious. As the case dragged on I began to feel more and more like the steel ball itself. I had that feeling now, too, chiefly because I suspected that Sayres had just "flippered" me again. I'd like to make him account for his whereabouts all day last Saturday, but I knew of nobody I could use to alibi or contradict his claims. He was a loner, a wild card. He was also a liar. And he was being cagey about something. But even if I didn't know him to be a liar, I hadn't liked him much in the beginning and I was liking him less and less with each encounter. He'd also volunteered information about the missing lighter. If Sayres wasn't lying about that, did Rhea know that she had it?

I'd reached a point where everything seemed so congested that it could never be unclogged. Mental lethargy was beginning to set in like a dead weight, and I couldn't let that happen. When I reached Manhattan I wound up going to a movie anyway, and saw *Henry V* with Olivier at a revival theater down in the Village. It was like a book so enchanting that you lost track of the page numbers and the time. It didn't let out until one-fifteen in the morning. It left me tired but also feeling like a million bucks.

15

Again I woke up ready to take on the world. Or at least re-enact Agincourt, with an option to appear at Rorke's Drift, Quatre Bras, and Tripoli. I was in a wonderfully heady mood and couldn't understand why. *Henry V* couldn't have done it alone. Nor could it have been the prospect of having dinner with Rhea Hamilton later in the evening. I thought about it over eggs and bacon and came to the conclusion that it was simply because I was beginning to make progress in the case. I was getting closer to the murderer. I was unraveling a paradox, untying a Gordian knot. I, Chess Hanrahan, all by myself. That a man had been murdered wasn't what made me feel good about myself. It was just the act of pure problem solving—problem solving that mattered.

Walker seemed to sense my mood and started batting my leg with his paw. Then he'd dash off to hide, inviting a chase. So I chased him and he'd ambush me and dash off again. Once I cornered him and he came out, eyes narrowed, advancing on me sideways, tail whipping back and forth. So I rolled over on the rug and played dead.

Soon he was licking my face. We were both a couple of fools.

By nine o'clock I was on my way out to Little Port. Captain Farrell wasn't in, but he'd left instructions with his sergeant to let me read the county police report on Compton. I didn't expect to discover anything startling in it, and didn't. The list of Compton's personal effects didn't include a lighter. I took notes, then handed the report back to the sergeant with a thanks and a good day.

I drove up to Freehold Road again, drawn by a residual determination to find some trace of the accident. A button, a penny, or even the heel of one of Compton's shoes would satisfy me. I just couldn't accept the idea of so clean an accident.

I parked the Magnette on the gravel and went over the scene again, my eyes scanning every square inch of grass, weed, and bare earth. But the only things I saw after an hour and a half were three cigarette filters—mine.

I sat on the guardrail and conceded defeat by lighting a fourth cigarette. I studied my own lighter and wondered about the one Sayres claimed he'd seen in Conover's home yesterday. Had Compton actually left it there or had Sayres put it there? If he had, where had he found it, and why would he leave it where he said he'd seen it?

Then I did see a button, a big, brown one such as might have come off of a raincoat. It was half buried in the dirt in a break in the grass, about two inches from my right foot. I reached down and pulled it out.

"This your car, mister?"

I turned around. It was a boy, maybe ten years old, in a corduroy coat and jeans. He had big round black eyes and a mop of black hair, and he was inspecting the Magnette. "It's mine," I said. I noticed a bicycle he'd laid on the gravel a few yards away.

"My uncle has one, too," said the kid. "He lives in Commack. How old is yours?"

"Twenty-one years."

"Got the chassis coated?"

"Of course," I grinned.

"That road salt's murder on cars, isn't it?"

"Sure is."

"You belong to an antique car club? You might know my uncle."

I shook my head. "I don't belong to a club, so I doubt if I know him."

"My uncle's an architect, that's how he can afford a Magnette. What do you do?"

"I'm a detective," I said. "That's how I can afford mine."

"A *private* detective?" asked the kid hopefully, his eyes growing bigger.

"Yep," I answered, secretly flattered by his reaction.

"Just like Marlowe and Spade and Holmes?"

"And all the others, too."

"On a murder case?"

"I think so."

"Awh, come on! Don't you even know if there's been a murder or not? Marlowe and Holmes'd know right off the bat!"

I shrugged. "It's not always that simple. A murder can be camouflaged to look like suicide or an accident."

"Yeah," said the kid, breathless. "You looking for clues?"

"No. Evidence."

The kid stared at me, his eyes praying. "Can I help you look?"

"Sure," I said. "If you can find anything other than cigarette butts in that grass down there, I'll mention you in my report."

"Wow!" The kid ran back and picked up his bike and was about to lug it over the guardrail when my eyes grew as big as his. I asked, pointing to it, "Where did you get that?"

"That" was a Mercedes mascot glued or bolted somehow to the mudguard of the front wheel of the kid's bike. He glanced down, then he looked even more excited. "I found it here, mister. Jimmy told me there'd been an accident right here, last week. When I was coming home from school I stopped to look around."

"When was this?"

The kid squinted his eyes in recollection. "Uh, last Thursday. About three-thirty. The guy they found here was *murdered?*"

"Maybe. Bring that bike closer."

I examined the mascot. Half the stem was there, and I was willing to bet that it would fit the other half on the Mercedes in Flushing. "How did you put this on?" I asked.

"I didn't. My brother did. He used some of that Super-Stick glue for metal."

"Where here did you find it?"

"Down there," said the kid, pointing to a spot just before a clump of saplings but not far away from where Compton's body had been found.

"Show me," I said, laying the bike on its side. As we walked down the slope, I asked, "What's your name?"

"Christian. Christian Kanewski. You can call me Chris."

"Who's Jimmy?"

"My big brother. He's in high school."

"Why didn't you take that mascot to the cops here, Chris?"

"I didn't know it had anything to do with that guy!" protested Chris desperately. "It was just junk." He paused. "What's your name, mister?"

"Hanrahan. Chess Hanrahan."

"*Chess?* I never heard of a name like that before."

I smiled. "It's the game I play with my suspects," I said, not wanting to resist it. And I wasn't about to tell him it was short for Chester.

"Wow," said the kid. "Can I have your autograph?"

"When I solve the mystery," I laughed.

"You think my mascot's really connected with a murder?"

"Maybe it was," I said.

We stopped in front of the saplings. Chris nudged a slice

of bark with his tennis shoe. "That's where I found it, Mr. Hanrahan. It was peeking out from under that."

I'd have missed it, too, I guessed. The spot was a full ten feet away from the spot where Compton had landed. "Where do you live, Chris?" I asked. "I'd like to take that mascot with me."

"There's some solvent in my dad's garage. We can take it off with that. I live only a block away."

"Lead the way," I smiled.

I followed in my car and waited half a hilly block away while the kid disappeared inside a big stone house that was a four-minute drive from Freehold Road. Chris came back out fifteen minutes later with the mascot and handed it to me through my window. "I'll return this if it has nothing to do with my case, Chris," I said. "But if it's evidence . . . well, you'll read about it in the papers. You might even get your name mentioned." I paused to light a cigarette. "By the way, what does your dad do?"

"Oh, he's just the assistant district attorney of Suffolk County, that's all."

That's all? I almost gagged on my smoke. "Look," I said. "Don't mention any of this to your dad, will you? He'll be involved in it sooner or later."

"Sure thing, Mr. Hanrahan."

I headed straight for Flushing with the intention of waiting for Sayres to leave his place before I approached the Mercedes. But I saw him coming out of a donut place with George Compton four blocks away on Middlefield. I zipped over to his block, saw the Mercedes still parked in Compton's driveway, stopped the Magnette, and jumped out with the mascot. I fitted the jagged stem of the mascot from the kid's bike onto the stem of the ornament's base on the hood. They meshed so well I could have left the mascot balanced there. A wave of excitement chilled my body. I'd found the murder machine. This was it. I ran back to my car and closed the door. Glancing back at the Mercedes once more, I was startled to see someone standing at the front window of the apartment below Compton's, an old man in a brown sweater. So somebody did live there. I wondered if he could tell me anything useful. From the impassive, almost stupid look on his face, I doubted it. But he might be worth a few questions later on. Through my rearview mirror I saw Sayres and Compton turn the corner. I drove off.

"There was a time when I couldn't stand the sound of the human voice in song. It was usually what was being sung that digusted me."

"Was there a time when it didn't? You must've had a favorite song."

"Sure. When I was a kid my favorite was 'The Shrimp Boats Are Coming.' I used to sit in our attic at home and listen to old 78 records on an even older crankup machine, and I played that one the most. I can't remember her name—the singer's, that is. I don't like shrimp, by the way, but that's beside the point."

The restaurant Rhea Hamilton and I were sitting in was not beside the point. Called Twilight, it was perched on the top floor of a downtown office building near Wall Street, while its prices perched on the top scale of what could possibly be charged in any premium restaurant, anywhere. She'd called me at five for dinner at eight, picked me up at seven in her Porsche, and we were in the cocktail lounge at seven-fifteen waiting for our table near a broad window with a view of the city north of Wall Street.

Rhea was in a soft brown, shoulderless gown which might not have left anything to imagination except that the flickering candles on our table made sharp, mysterious shadows and only spurred mine on. She also wore a diamond necklace and a diamond bracelet, both of which glittered with every little movement of hers and competed with the blazing lights of the city beyond. And I was back in my tuxedo—and in heaven, telling her my life story. It was easy for me to do that. When you see a vision, and if you're clean inside, your first desire is to bare your soul, willingly, gladly, happily. And I was clean, happy, and at home with her.

"What else did you like?" she asked.

A waiter came just then to clear away our china and I didn't answer until he'd gone. "The 'Soldiers' Chorus' from *Faust*. Heard it on the radio once and it became my personal theme song. It was in French, of course, and I still don't understand a word of it, and that's beside the point, too."

"What happened?"

I shrugged. "Over time I got worn down by the world. Living in it today is like living in a constant war zone. Nothing but destruction, nothing but tension, nothing but bracing yourself for the next artillery barrage or suicide charge. So I forgot, first what it meant to me, and then that it ever existed. I chose police work over law just out of an animal desire to fight back somehow at whatever was stalling me and making a Somme of civilization." I smiled in memory of my hard-won wisdom. "But it was the wrong choice. The wrong criminals. The hardcore cases aren't the flotsam out on the street. No. The hardcore are in different income and brain brackets. Like that professor I nailed up in Massachusetts and a few other choice souls. But I didn't figure that out until recently. I may be slow but I get there. Then my engine came back to life and I began remembering things. And I'm back."

"So I was right," said Rhea. "You *are* a man being reborn."

I simply smiled in agreement and appreciation. "What about you, Rhea? I've been doing most of the talking. What do you live for?"

If I'd asked that of virtually anybody else I knew, I'd have touched a sore spot and gotten dagger eyes. It was an innocent enough question; I supposed most people today didn't have innocent answers. But Rhea could be asked the question. I'd sensed it and much more that evening in my apartment.

She said, "I've lived mostly out of sheer curiosity. Most people who haven't yet identified or picked a purpose do that."

"Curiosity for what?"

"For the fact that in the whole world one can't believe that there's nothing or no one interesting in it. You're born into the world and once you accept the fact that it's there, your biggest and earliest act in life is your decision to do something with it. And being born rich is a greater handicap than most people think. On one hand you have everything others want and strive to have—or think they ought to have. On the other hand, you think you have everything that can be had and that there's nothing else. That's why I think most wealthy children grow up to be alcoholics, drug addicts, or philanthropists, or politicians. It's because they never develop a personal purpose."

I laughed. She was right, because she made me think of all the kids I grew up with and what had happened to some of them.

"It's not funny, Chess," she said. "It's tragic."

I took a sip of my brandy. "I know. It doesn't amuse me. I was laughing because it's a matter of shared wisdom. I don't have the experience every day."

"Did you have many friends when you were younger?"

"No. Did you?"

"No."

"Did your curiosity end when you found Gregory Compton?"

She smiled. "No. Oddly enough, finding him only whetted my curiosity. Not about the world, though. I wanted to see if he and the world were compatible. And if not, why not. Greg lived for his books. They were his purpose, his only reason for moving, acting, breathing, thinking—living."

"Exclusive of you?"

"Yes . . . I felt almost incidental to his purpose. It hurt sometimes but I didn't mind it so much. I loved him, I had him, and he was the most interesting thing ever to enter my life. But his purpose . . . it was so much stronger in him. It never seemed to leave him, not even while he was asleep. It wasn't long after we met that the odd idea occurred to me that if ever his purpose were taken away from him, he would vanish—literally dematerialize. Other men would turn to drink, or drugs—as my first husband did—if that happened to them. But not Greg. Greg would simply vanish. . . . " Rhea paused to take a sip of her drink. "I hope that doesn't sound silly to you, Chess. But that aspect of him was very real to me."

I shook my head. "No, it isn't silly. But weren't you jealous of that? Of his purpose, I mean."

Rhea smiled again. "Of course I was jealous. Only occasionally, though. I was happy that he loved me. He did love me. But when I grew jealous, I would stop and think of what it was I was jealous of, and then the jealousy would slink away."

I remembered how her father had put the same sentiment to me on the evening of his dinner up in Tarrytown. I asked, "Did you ever try to help him? With money, a job, introductions, anything like that?"

"I was tempted to," said Rhea after a moment. "You can't imagine how much of a temptation it was. And I wanted to so much, just to get him away from the stupidities he encountered every day, to give him time to work, to write, to think." She shook her head. "But I disciplined myself not to. I had to invent excuses to give him things, aside from his birthday and Christmas. But I knew that if I did everything for him that was within my power to do, I might destroy him, or he would turn on me. . . . No, I left him alone, as I think he should have been left alone. . . . " Her voice faded away then and an odd, dull pang sank inside me. I couldn't understand why but suddenly Rhea was a stranger sitting across the table from me. The bond had been broken.

"Left alone in what respect?"

"Left alone to win."

"Do you think he fed off of resistance?"

"No, he wasn't one of those at all. I asked him that once myself, when I wondered how he had been able to last so long. He said that the resistance was secondary—incidental—that his purpose was too important, too essential for resistance to matter to him. He said that his victories must be his own, that they must come from within himself. Otherwise they would be false."

Rhea looked away then, averting my eyes and my attentive expression. Something connected in my mind and I asked, "What happened between you two last Saturday?"

She frowned. "What makes you think something happened between us?"

"The fact that he was alone on a country road during a snowstorm that night."

Rhea studied me for a long while. The waiter came and I ordered coffee. When he was gone, she said, "I picked Greg up at his place and we drove out to the Island. We had dinner in a seafood restaurant in some town—"

"Taradash's, in Middleport?" I prompted.

"I don't remember," said Rhea.

"Okay. You had dinner. Then what?"

Rhea's features froze in sudden realization of the kinds of questions I was asking her. "That can't concern you," she said.

"Did you argue about the Granville? About whether he should accept it or not?"

"That can't concern you, either."

"It can if Compton was murdered," I said.

Rhea whispered, "That's impossible."

I shook my head, fighting my own temptation to tell her how it was probably done. Instead I asked, "That letter

Sayres gave you yesterday: are you going to show it to the Granville Foundation?"

"What letter are you talking about?"

"Compton's letter of refusal."

Rhea's eyes narrowed. "No such letter exists."

I said, "But you won't deny that Sayres gave it to you."

She said nothing.

"If you don't show that letter to the Foundation, you'll be perpetrating a fraud I don't think Compton would've wanted any part of."

Rhea's brow creased in wicked concentration. "Greg's beyond caring about frauds, Mr. Hanrahan," she said. "But *I'm* not. It's my business now and no one else's. If there is a fraud involved, *I'll* live with it. They're going to give Greg his due, damn them all. They're going to *pay* for making him *wait.*"

"It's *his* name and reputation, Rhea. Not yours. When the truth comes out, it's his name that will be compromised."

"There's *no* truth to come out, Mr. Hanrahan." Rhea glanced away and signaled the waiter for the check with a single flick of her wrist. Her action distracted me for a moment. I thought of how easily I could bruise that wrist between my thumb and middle finger, and of how much power that wrist commanded.

The waiter came and presented the check to her on a salver. She glanced at it, reached inside her purse, took out a pen, and signed it. The waiter frowned, took the check, read her signature, then smiled. "Thank you, Miss Hamilton," he said, then turned and left. Rhea took out two twenty-dollar bills and left them on the tablecloth, then rose. We said nothing more as we made our way to the foyer and elevator bank. The maître d' wished her good night as we passed him at the restaurant door. When we were in front of the elevators, I patted my coat, felt my cigarette case, then said, "Wait a moment, Rhea, I'm missing something."

I went back inside and approached the maître d'. "Say, do you know Miss Hamilton?"

"Of course we know her," he said congenially. "She comes here often."

"Oh," I said. "So she has an account here?"

The maître d' chuckled. "You could say that. You see, she's our landlord. Or should I say landlady?"

Just then our waiter rushed up from our table, which a couple of busboys were busy clearing. "Excuse me," he said, "you came back for this, I presume. Glad you remembered it but we would have let Miss Hamilton know that we had it." He handed me a slim gold lighter. It was a plain but elegant thing, the one I'd seen her use after dinner. In flowing script on one side of it were the engraved initials G.C. I thanked him and the maître d', stood for a moment to think, then pocketed the lighter and rejoined Rhea.

The only thing she asked me when we reached her Porsche was whether I wanted to be dropped off at my place or somewhere else. "After that," she said, "I don't want to see you again. If you come to Greg's funeral, please don't ask me any questions. Any questions at all. Thank you for your interest—but no thanks."

"I have a purpose, too, Rhea," I said. The late March evening wind blew between us on the curb. "One as private and grand as Compton's. I'll say this now: I feel something for you. More than the etiquette of the moment permits me to say. But for my own sake it must stay unsaid and incidental to my purpose."

She shook her arm free of the grip I hadn't realized I held her in. "Damn you," she said softly, then ran around the side of her car, got in, and roared off.

I stood there with the knowledge that it was not me she had cursed, but herself. I took the lighter out of my pocket. Maybe Sayres had told me the truth for once; maybe he *had* seen it on the table at Conover's place in Tarrytown. I wondered why Rhea had brought it with her tonight.

Perhaps she didn't know I attached some significance to it. Did she attach any importance to it herself? Just what was she doing with Compton's lighter? Had she borrowed it and forgotten to give it back? Or had he returned it to her? She was in such a rush to end our conversation that she'd left it behind on the table. That was clear enough. She would miss it soon and call the restaurant, and the restaurant would tell her that I had it. Would she ever ask for it back? I decided to keep the lighter for a while, to see who moved first.

I pressed the little button on its side and a strong, straight flame shot up. Then a breeze whipped up the street and snuffed it out.

16

Of course, in due time over another coffee I would have gotten around to asking her whether she had bribed Earl Teague into submitting Compton's book to the Granville committee. It's not the kind of question that you can ask and expect a truthful answer to unless you've got someone's confidence. For a while, I thought I'd had Rhea's. I was wrong. Every time I raised a sensitive issue, she bolted. Literally and figuratively.

Maybe I'd been wrong about her having recovered a bit from Compton's death. Perhaps it would take her longer. And maybe her unpredictability and mercurial moods had nothing to do with Compton.

So I stood on the curb and watched her Porsche disappear up the sinuous alley of Nassau Street. A cold wind blew around me and dispersed the lingering scent of her presence. I realized that at my present rate I might solve the mystery of Compton's death in perhaps two years. I realized that I had to stop being a gentle fellow and start flinging mud around regardless of people's feelings. The subtle, coy tactic had gotten me as far as I was going to get. It was time to shift into third gear.

I turned and searched for the plaque on the building we had just come out of. There it was, screwed in high above on the wall of the exterior foyer. It read: TYLE PROPERTIES, OWNER-MANAGER. Thirty stories of prime real estate.

I walked back home. Up Nassau Street to the Brooklyn Bridge. Straight up Broadway to Union Square. Up Park Avenue to Grand Central. Over to Vanderbilt and then to Madison. New York was the greatest place in the world to walk and think. I did lots of thinking. On Sunday nights its sidewalks and avenues were virtually deserted. I had nothing but red lights all the way up but didn't stop once because there simply wasn't any traffic. I wondered if Compton had walked the same route. Up from the soaring towers, through the grimy, made-over tawdriness of the city's midsection, past the bright display windows of midtown, to the discreet townhouses and piles of guarded privacy of the Upper East Side. Probably he had. He'd been a walker, just as I was. I wondered if this was the route he'd taken when he decided whose symphonies were to be the models for Stridivant's. Rachmaninoff's First? Beethoven's Fifth? Brahms's Third? Something in his own image and in that of the world as he wanted to live in it.

Yes, he'd probably walked this same route. Only he couldn't ignore the red lights. There was someone there at every intersection to make sure that he obeyed, traffic or no traffic. Until he walked alone along some desolate country road and some bastard ran him over.

I stopped in front of the Granville building on Madison and looked for another plaque. No, there was only the one listing the tenants. Below it was a bare, unsooted space where another had been removed.

At nine on the button the next morning I picked up my office phone, dialed a number, and when the receptionist asked me whom I was calling, I said, "Adele, please."

"Adele, sir?"

"In Accounting."

"Oh. One moment, please."

When Adele picked up her phone after two rings, she said, "Accounting department, Adele speaking."

"Hi," I said. "You don't know me. I visited your offices last week. You said you wouldn't miss Victor Neary, who'd been promoted. I'd like to know why."

"Who is this?" demanded Adele.

"Someone who doesn't have much use for him, either. My name's Chess Hanrahan. I'm a private detective."

"Oh," said Adele after a moment. "You're the one Atherton had in."

"The same."

"Well, what would you like to know?"

"Nothing that I'd want to discuss over the phone," I said. "I'll stand you lunch."

"Sure. I go at one," said Adele, sounding intrigued. "Where? There's a Big Burger right across the street from us."

"I was thinking more along the lines of Kurian's."

"Wow," said Adele quietly. "Sure, Kurian's is fine."

"Good. How will I know you?"

"I'll be in a brown trench coat. I'm a redhead."

"Good. I'll make the reservations for one-fifteen. If you get there first, just give the guy my name and take the table."

"See you there at one-fifteen."

"Wait a minute," I said before she could hang up. "Don't mention any of this to anyone in your office. All right?"

"It won't go beyond my cubicle."

After using the telephone directory, I took a cab from my office up to Grand Central and went into the Graybar Building. The Aristo Temp Agency was on the tenth floor at the end of a long wide corridor. In a gray decor reception area were about ten chairs occupied by people who were either filling out applications, flipping through month-old magazines, or looking impatient or very earnest. The woman at the desk looked besieged by them and by an enormous phone switchboard with twenty button extensions that never stopped ringing. Well, it didn't quite ring; it made a sound much like a drowning turkey. Half of her calls were from people asking about work and the other half were from people asking about their paychecks. It was only nine-thirty, but the woman looked as though she was about to pull her hair out. Finally she looked up at me with a sigh. "Can I help you?"

"Yes, I'd—"

Before I could finish, the turkey cried again. And again. And again. Three of the people filling out applications came up to the counter and put their clipboards down. Four newcomers had collected behind me. And again the woman glanced up at me in between calls. I said, "I'd like to talk to someone here about Gregory Compton. He worked for you people."

"Oh," said the woman. "*Him.* May I ask why?"

I took out my wallet and showed her my license. A New York private investigator's license isn't very impressive looking. That's why I had my old NYPD identification card in a window opposite it, and it looked very impressive. People could always take their pick when I flipped my wallet open. The woman was quite impressed. She said, "I . . . see. Would you excuse me for a minute, please?" She rose from her chair and disappeared through a door.

Five minutes later I was in Vivian Brewer's office. Vivian Brewer was an attractive but nervous brunette about my age, and president of the agency.

"Busy place you have here," I remarked.

"We never have enough people," said Vivian. "All those people you saw out front will have been sent out on assignments by the time you leave. Can you type?" she smiled.

"Not fast enough, I'm afraid. Maybe twenty words a minute under the threat of death."

"You have to do at least seventy words a minute with no errors and score ninety percent or better on our verbal and math tests. Otherwise you'd never be put on our payroll."

"Guess I'll have to stick to washing dishes," I grinned. "No doubt Gregory Compton qualified."

"He was one of our best people," said the president. "And he earned our top rates. Older than most of our people but none of our clients seemed to mind, and we certainly didn't."

"No complaints from your clients? I mean, he was a writer, and he might have had a habit of staring into space instead of burning up a keyboard."

Vivian Brewer shook her head. "No complaints at all, Mr. Hanrahan. Didn't have a negative attitude, was a better dresser than most of the executives he worked for, and was probably smarter, too. No college, but he could discuss any subject you could imagine—finance, foreign affairs, women's fashions, music, Canadian politics—anything."

I grunted in appreciation. "Do you get many like him?"

"Not *that* good. People from all walks of life temp for a while or for a living. I'd say that about sixty percent of our people are actors, actresses, writers, models, singers, directors, stage managers, what have you, all waiting for steady work in their professions or for the big break. Some of them can be temperamental or flighty or even snobbish. Most aren't, though, and many of them make a good living working temps."

"What kinds of jobs was Compton sent out on?"

"All kinds," shrugged Vivian. "He usually shocked the people we sent him to, because companies today are so used to semiliteracy and overall ignorance, not to mention the indifference their own and other contract employees bring to their jobs. Each of those problems has been growing, even among the people we put onto our payroll. But Greg . . . well, companies would keep him on even when his assignments were finished, just to have him around. Sometimes he'd spend weeks at one place doing make-work that would take him half an hour to do instead of a day and a half, and spend the rest of the time writing or reading." Vivian Brewer stopped long enough to light a cigarette, and so did I. She said, "What kinds of jobs? Mostly typing jobs with banks, publishers, insurance companies, broadcasters—statistical jobs that called for speed, volume, and accuracy. And many times he'd wind up doing other work, like designing a better way to handle information, or he'd correct other people's messes, messes an MBA or vice president didn't spot. He could do anything, outperform everyone, and took more to his jobs than any other temp I've known."

"Any of your clients ever offer him a permanent job?"

Vivian Brewer laughed. "They *all* did," she said. "Or they'd put in special requests for him. But he worked for us for a year and a half and showed no interest in permanent employment. He made more money working temps, and he said the variety of jobs we sent him to gave him material or ideas for his books. A permanent job would give him claustrophobia, he told me once. A 'job' wasn't what he was after. Only writing his books."

"Read any of them?"

"Not yet," said the president. "I wasn't even aware that he'd been published until I read about the Granville Prize, and I wouldn't have known about that if one of our counsellors hadn't brought it to my attention. He simply didn't advertise himself. I had planned to ask him why he was working temps when he was a published author and a pretty highly regarded one, too."

"He got a screwing-over from his publishers," I said. "By the way, did a Geoffrey Sayres ever work for you people?"

Vivian Brewer frowned in thought, then said, "Let me check," and picked up her phone and dialed an extension. A moment later she cradled the receiver and shook her head. "No, no one by that name is registered with us."

"So you knew Compton personally," I said. "What were your impressions of him?"

Vivian Brewer smiled and thought about it for a moment. "I could never make up my mind about him, *personally*. No one here could ever get him to chitchat. I couldn't imagine him having a personal life. He was too much of a monomaniac. He rarely talked about his writing; that's just the impression you got from just watching him. Everything outside of whatever made him tick was incidental. He was like a living monument to logic and purpose—cold and humorless and unapproachable—but you knew instinctively that anybody so cold and humorless and unapproachable had to be burning with some kind of passion."

I smiled. "'You' in general, or 'you' personally?"

"How do you mean?"

"Most people wouldn't bother to analyze a rejection to that extent."

Vivian Brewer blushed a shade. "I . . . didn't get very far." She paused. "He is . . . was an attractive man."

"And he was also engaged elsewhere. She got farther, but had the same complaint, I think."

Vivian Brewer fidgeted awkwardly with a paperweight near her, then asked, "Was there anything else you'd like to know, Mr. Hanrahan?"

I shrugged. "Where he worked for the last couple of months. That ought to do it."

The president rose. "I'll be right back." She went out and came back a minute later with a folder. Back at her desk, she said, "Would you like me to write out a list?"

"No. Just read off the company names."

Vivien Brewer sighed. "Okay. Bryant Savings, American Standard Office Products, First City Bank, Hawthorne Paper, Marine Trust, Sun Cable Network, Tyle Properties—"

"Tyle Properties," I interrupted. "When?"

"That was his next-to-last assignment," said Vivian Brewer. "A two-week job just before we sent him to Tempest Cosmetics, where he spent a week and never returned . . ."

"How long was he at Tyle?"

"A month and a half. The next week they wanted him back but we'd already committed him to Tempest."

"How big is Tyle?"

"It's a medium-sized firm. I don't know much about it, except that I think it's privately held and that it's been one of our steadier clients. It's up on Fifty-Seventh Street, near Carnegie Hall."

I wrote a few things in my notebook, then slapped it shut. "Well, I guess that'll be all for now."

"Why are you investigating Gregory Compton?"

"I don't think he should've died."

"Accidents are accidents, Mr. Hanrahan. They're not rules of life."

I shrugged. "Neither should be murder—if that's what it was."

"Why would anyone want to murder Greg—Compton? Except from envy?"

I was beginning to like Vivian Brewer. "Maybe not from envy. Maybe it was from jealousy, or hate, or some insane idea of justice. I don't know yet."

Tyle Properties, I thought to myself as I strode through the Graybar lobby. I wondered whether Compton had known whose company Tyle was. Of course. He had to have known. I checked my watch to find it was ten-thirty.

When I got back to my office I called my answering service for messages. There were six: five from prospective clients and one from Gussie Spendler. I called her first. "Hi, trouper. What's up?"

"Chess, can you meet me in ten minutes at the Lantern?"

"Sure. What about?"

"You'll see."

Back I went uptown. The morning breakfast rush was long over and I saw Gussie sitting in a booth in a virtually empty side of the restaurant with a man perhaps ten years my senior. When I slid in beside him, she introduced me.

"Mr. Hanrahan, this is Spencer Durand. Spencer, Chess Hanrahan."

Durand eyed me warily but offered his hand. We shook.

"Spencer is an editor with Euler and Shaw, a *very* conservative publishing house, Chess," said Gussie with a grin at Durand. "And I've been telling him all about you."

"About me and what else?"

A waitress came and I ordered coffee. When she was gone, Gussie said, "About Greg, and Rhea Hamilton . . . and Earl's allusions."

"Oh?"

"Spencer worked in Earl's department up until six months ago, Chess. I had an idea Saturday night after you dropped me off. I remembered one of the more civil persons at Pericles Press. I called him the first thing this morning."

"And?"

Durand said, "I think Rhea Hamilton bribed Earl to submit Compton's book to the Granville Foundation, Mr. Hanrahan. I couldn't prove it, of course, but I overheard some odd telephone calls—I had the office right next to Earl's—and then I saw him in a restaurant with her."

"How did you know he was speaking to Rhea Hamilton?"

Durand chuckled. "Earl's voice carries, Mr. Hanrahan. It would carry over a Park Avenue traffic jam."

He was right about that. "So what made you think she bribed Earl Teague?"

"I didn't think anything of it then . . . and would never have thought of it again but for Gussie here. When she told me half an hour ago that this woman was Gregory Compton's fiancée, Earl's decision to submit Compton's book made sense. So did his sudden money to buy this writers' colony of his."

"Where did you see them together?"

"Domino's, over on Second Avenue."

"Why didn't it make sense for Teague to be submitting Compton's book?"

Durand laughed. "Because he hated it. So did most everyone else at Pericles. In fact, mine was the only favorable editor's report on *Walk Around the Sun*. Earl got some kind of quiet kick out of sending it back to Gussie here."

I turned and studied Gussie for a moment. Then she said, "Spencer knows why Earl took it back, Chess. He knew then."

"The trade with Grackle's book?"

The agent nodded.

I asked Durand, "Why did you leave Pericles?"

"I was waiting for a spot to open at a more reputable publisher, Mr. Hanrahan. I left about a month after Compton's book was sent to the Granville Foundation. I've no regrets."

"I take it you had no fondness for Earl Teague."

"Couldn't stand the man," said the editor. "He's what gives publishing a bad name. His type, I mean. A close-minded, supposedly omniscient, dictatorial, cynical, cackling pragmatist."

I asked Gussie, "Earl's in Pennsylvania?"

"Probably," sighed the agent.

"Corrupting the rattlesnakes," remarked Durand.

17

When I returned to my office and called to reserve a table at Kurian's, it was too late. There would be no free tables until three o'clock. In a way, I was glad; I was getting sick of talking to people in restaurants. I didn't even have the beginnings of an appetite, even though I'd had a skimpy breakfast. But Adele might be very hungry, so I picked up the phone again and dialed another restaurant.

Adele was easy to intercept. Punctually at one-fifteen she bustled up the sidewalk from around the corner on Madison and paused in front of the marquee. I stepped out from under it and introduced myself, using my license to prove who I was. "I *knew* there had to be a catch," she said when I told her the bad news. She was a redhead all right, a short, trim, compact little woman who was a younger version of Gussie Spendler. Her full name was Adele Hubbard, and she was the assistant supervisor of the accounting department at the Granville Foundation. "Any cracks about Mother Hubbard and I'll kick you in the shins," she warned me. "After we leave whatever expensive restaurant you're taking me to, that is."

I laughed. "No, I won't make any cracks," I said, then escorted her to the cafe in the Pierre Hotel.

After we were settled and when I concluded that her big green saucer eyes wouldn't get any smaller, I drew my napkin from the ring and put it on my lap. "Order anything you like."

Once we had ordered, Adele said in a hushed voice, "You sure know how to disappoint a girl, Mr. Hanrahan."

"I do my best." I lit a cigarette, then Adele's. "Let me ask you this first," I said. "Are you loyal to the Foundation? Does it mean anything more to you than just a job?"

"No. It keeps me in money and sends me through school, that's all. Why do you want to know?"

"Because I'm investigating a fraud. Or a possible fraud."

"You don't know for sure yet?"

"It all depends on how much help you can give me."

"If you're a private detective, then you must be working for someone. Who?"

"In any other circumstances, I wouldn't tell you. Let's just say I'm working for Gregory Compton."

"Oh," said Adele, frowning. "That writer who was run over."

"Read any of his books?"

Adele shook her head. "No, and I don't plan to. I tried reading the books Neary and his gang burn incense for but they're all boring—or worse."

"Why won't you miss Victor Neary?"

Adele made a face. "Stuck-up old boob. He's one of these artsy old airheads who writes his memos like Chaucer. Thinks he's being cultural or witty. They're all like that, practically everybody outside my department. Not of this world, too rare for mere mortals. Won't say good morning to you on the elevator. It's either that or they're too friendly when they're really being nosy."

So over lunch, wine, and some strong Turkish coffee I had Adele give me a picture of the Granville Foundation. It was a radically different picture than the one Edgar

Atherton might have given me. I could see why Adele Hubbard might terrify Neary and even Atherton's secretary. She was a no-nonsense package of facts.

"What about your department supervisor?" I asked. "What's she like?"

"Heloise Byrd," said Adele. "She's a phoney, too, which figures, since she's a distant cousin of Atherton's. She went to some fancy women's college in New Hampshire. Worked for nothing but nonprofit organizations all her life, but she has trouble balancing her own checkbook. *I* run the department."

"Why do you stay?"

Adele shrugged. "I can take it. When I get my degree in June, I'm gone."

"A degree in what?"

"Finance. I'll be a real MBA."

"Atherton have any other relatives working at the Foundation?" I asked, pouring us both another cup of coffee.

"No, just Her Highness Heloise," said Adele. "But he has brothers all over the country. Horace Atherton is president of some charity trust in Boston, Delbert Atherton runs some kind of nature preservation group in Denver, and—what's his name?—Edmund Atherton is chairman of the English department at Regina University, down in Virginia. Old Edgar was a practicing lawyer once. In fact, his whole family is a distant relation of the Granville family. I think."

"Did you say *Regina* University?"

"Regina University," repeated Adele. "Atherton makes sure that some favorite of Edmund's down there gets a fellowship every year."

"How do you know?"

"*I* cut the checks, Mr. Hanrahan. Every one of them. And people gossip."

I ordered another pot of coffee from the waiter. Adele checked her watch. She said, "God, it's almost two-thirty! I should be getting back."

"Work overtime," I suggested.

"I planned to anyway," said Adele. "It's quarterly report time and I have to start getting ready to send money to all the fellowship winners."

"All by yourself?"

"No. I have four people under me. Heloise doesn't count, of course."

The waiter came with a fresh pot of coffee and new cups. When I finished pouring Adele a cup, I asked, "Is Atherton anything like your Heloise Byrd? Is he really the president or is he just pretending?"

Adele smiled. "This is the first time I've heard of someone wheedling information out of a woman with coffee. Isn't it usually done with liquor?"

I grinned. "That's the traditional method. I'll order some, if you like, but I can't guarantee that your debits and credits won't start playing musical chairs on your mind when you get back to your desk."

Adele nodded in agreement and took a sip of her coffee. "Wow, that is strong stuff!" She put her cup down. "Old Edgar? Well, he was there when I started at the Foundation three years ago. I suppose he's a good president. I guess anybody could be if his only job was to administer the giving away of money. There were rumors that he was in trouble with the Granville heirs, though. The Foundation has two annual budgets, you see: an endowment budget and an operating budget, both drawn on the principal, which is held separately and invested by another trust in the four corners of the earth. Atherton has control only over his operating budget, and he's abused it the last two years. He had to dip into the principal to make ends meet and keep the ship afloat. We heard that the Granvilles were seriously considering dumping him. But he pulled off a real coup."

"How so?"

"He somehow got the owners of our building to sell it to the Foundation for a dollar. That must have taken a lot of talking."

"Who did you pay the rent to?"

"To Tyle Properties," said Adele. "I *have* to be impressed with Old Edgar. We'd heard that Tyle was going to sell the building to a developer, that they'd been holding out for years. Our building and the one next door were the last parcels left to buy before the developer could move in with the wrecking crews."

I made my hand stop shaking and picked up my cup for a sip. "When did this happen?"

"A week ago last Friday. Atherton was all smiles the whole day, and nobody knew why until late in the day. Then word got around about the Tyle deal." Adele paused and screwed up her face in thought. "It was weird. Any other time we'd have put out a press release, or Atherton would have had an internal memo circulated. But if it hadn't been for the office grapevine, we'd never have known."

I told myself that I could have done this much earlier, that Adele could have saved me a lot of time and puzzlement. My first instinct was to kick myself. But I didn't, because you build on knowledge. Flashes of blinding insight weren't my habit. Sometimes I was *very* slow, but I always got there.

"You all right, Mr. Hanrahan?" asked Adele.

"Yes, I'm fine, thanks." I studied the assistant supervisor of the accounting department for a while, then asked, "Would you do some spying for me, Adele?"

"It depends."

"I'd like you to find out for me how the vote went for the Prize Gregory Compton won. I need to know how all the jurors voted."

Adele gave me a devilish grin. "I'll bet you're thinking that the voting was rigged," she said. "*Of course* it was rigged. These prizes are always rigged."

"Explain that, if you would."

"Well, they just stack the committees in favor of whatever author or poet or writer they want to win, that's all.

How else could any of these literary zombies make big? Certainly not because they're any good. I've met a lot of these prizewinners. They're either certified sleaze, complete phonies, or escapees from the funny farm. So are a lot of the jurors."

I smiled at Adele, but actually I was smiling at myself. She was what I was years ago. Scared of the scarecrow. Well, not scared. Just disgusted. I said, "Compton was good, Adele. He wrote for the people who make the world move. People like ourselves. That's why he shouldn't have won the Granville. Try him some time." I paused. "Think you can get me that information?"

"I'll try," said Adele. "The votes are all locked up in a different department. It'll be difficult. You want copies?"

I shook my head. "No. I know the names of the people who were on Compton's committee. I just need to know how they voted."

"Well, like I said, I was planning on staying tonight anyway. Neary's old secretary owes me a favor, and she and the new committee chairman are the only ones who have keys to that cabinet."

"You could get it for me tonight?"

Adele nodded. I took a cafe matchbook and wrote my home and office numbers on it after my name, then handed it to her. "Call me first thing. If I'm not at either of those numbers, leave a message to meet me somewhere."

"Will do."

I walked her back to the Granville building a few blocks away. "Can you find out how long Tyle owned your building?"

"I can tell you now. Granville's been a tenant for over fifty years and the rent's always been paid to Tyle. We were near the end of our lease—it ended in July—and there was talk that Tyle wasn't going to offer another. Tyle has buildings all over the city. It's a family-held company." Adele paused. "It's funny, now that I think of it. That very Friday, after word got around that the Foundation had been given the building, Mr. Trayner, our office manager, came up and took all the Tyle files away for storage. Everything—all the old leases, the rent receipts, maintenance correspondence, the works."

"Why do you think that's curious?"

Adele shrugged. "What was the hurry?"

I thought I knew what the hurry was. And Adele's big round eyes grew rounder and she made the connection. I shook my head. "Don't let the thought out of your head, Adele," I said. "Don't ask questions around the office. Don't even give Atherton a dirty look."

"It might mean my job if you're right, Mr. Hanrahan," said Adele as we stopped in front of the building.

"If I'm right about what happened, I'll pay you your salary until you find something else." I nodded in the direction of the entrance. "When was the Tyle Properties plaque taken down?"

"Last week. Wednesday morning, I think. At least that's when I noticed it was gone as I was coming to work that morning." Adele glanced up at me. "You've got that mad look on your face again, Mr. Hanrahan."

"Tragedies usually do that to me." I touched her elbow. "All right. I'll talk with you later, Adele. Okay?"

"Sure. Take it easy, Mr. Hanrahan?"

I just winked at her and walked away. I didn't know if what I was feeling showed. I went on for a while, too mentally numbed to think. After a while I realized that I had walked as far as First Avenue. I stopped in one of the tony bars that line that street and sat at the counter. "A Black Russian," I told the bartender. When I finished it, I ordered another.

"You look like you've just lost your best friend," remarked the bartender when he brought it to me.

I guess it did show, and he'd more or less summed up what I felt. But it made sense, all of it. Oh, Rhea, I thought to myself, how could you? What was the point? Wasn't he real enough to you? Did that goddamned Prize make him more real? For some strange reason, I recalled the title of one of Ruth Marchessini's books, *Accidental Judgments, Casual Slaughters.* Whose judgment? I asked myself. Whose slaughter? God, how she must have planned it! Months ago she must have looked into a way of giving Compton the ultimate gift, and discovered Atherton's financial problems. Promised him a way out if he'd guarantee that Compton won. And had that guarantee even before she approached Earl Teague with a simple cash bribe. How could she have misjudged Compton? After all that expense—the surrender of valuable real estate and the cash she handed over to Teague—Compton didn't want it. Hadn't even known what his closest admirer was up to.

But, no, Gregory Compton was going to get his due, damn them all.

So I sat in the bar for a while longer and thought about what I couldn't bear to contemplate. Helped a bit by the Black Russians. They were served in thick, squat little glasses. My grip on my now empty one grew tighter as I tried to contain my anger. No, channel it, I thought.

Who had murdered Compton? Sayres? Or Rhea? Sayres was a liar and an emotional mess. So was Rhea, I had to admit now. I made myself sit tight because I wanted a complete picture. I wanted to know how they all voted. It was only four o'clock and I couldn't expect to hear from Adele Hubbard until at least seven. Wait, I told myself. Wait.

The bartender was staring at me. I stared back. "Give me a coffee," I said. "Black."

The bartender brought me a black coffee. He wound up bringing me four more. I made myself sit on that stool for two more hours; I smoked a pack of cigarettes. I sat through the after–office hours Happy Hour and listened to all the gossip and laughter. I scowled at one nice-looking woman who tried to pick me up. "No," I told her, "I don't come here often."

At quarter to seven I left the place and took a cab to my

apartment. The answering service had a message for me taken not ten minutes before. I dialed the number and said, "Hi. It's Hanrahan," to Adele.

"Got a pencil ready?" she answered.

I had that and a big yellow pad sitting in front of me on the coffee table. "Shoot."

"You understand this is the final vote, Mr. Hanrahan," said Adele.

"What do you mean, *final* vote?"

"Well, there was a summary report in with these files, signed by Neary. There were ten books they all had to read and vote on, you know, and after three votes they narrowed it down to Gregory Compton and William Grackle."

That must have taken some fancy engineering by Neary, I thought to myself. But then the whole thing was supposed to be a secret vote with the jurors scattered across the country. Who was to challenge it? "So the fourth round was the final, right?"

"Right," said Adele. "Compton, five. Grackle, four."

"Read them off, Adele."

"Guest jurors first. Hector Chamblee—Grackle. Evelyn Zirbel—Grackle. Jerome Hixon—Compton. Ruth, ah, Marchessini—Compton. Oliver Gullum—Compton. Now for my office buddies. Neary—Compton. Shelby Roth—Grackle. Sean O'Scully—Grackle. Lisa Yeager—Compton."

"You're sure Gullum voted for Compton?"

"Got his and everybody else's ballot sitting here in front of me. Let's see here," said Adele over some papers she was rustling. "Ah, Hixon, Marchessini, Gullum, and Neary were the only ones to vote for Compton straight through all four eliminations. Lisa the Louse—she's a real backstabber, that one, cost a friend of mine her job a year ago—she voted for Grackle right up until the final vote. Then she switched to Compton. Say!" exclaimed Adele over the receiver. "That might explain why she got that raise! Got the memo for it the day before they notified the press."

"And Neary got the promotion he wanted," I added.

"Boy, you were right about this one!" said Adele.

"Look, Adele. Thanks. Don't let on that you know anything."

"Sure you don't want copies?"

"If you can do it without getting caught," I said.

"There's no one else here but me."

"Do it. What time are you leaving there?"

"In an hour."

"Where do you live?"

"Forest Hills, on Yellowstone Boulevard."

"I'll be waiting outside your building in my car. See you then."

Then I called Wallace Conover, who gave me the details of the funeral tomorrow. There would be a short service in the cemetery chapel—by invitation only—followed by the burial, and then a drive back to Tarrytown. I asked him who would be there.

"Well, Greg's brother, of course. Mr. Sayres, Miss Spendler, yourself, I hope, my sister, and I. Oh, yes, Atherton and his wife asked to come. And many of Greg's former work colleagues responded to last week's newspaper report and they'll be coming. It seems he had more friends than any one of us realized."

"See you tomorrow, Mr. Conover," I said, wanting instead to ask him whether he knew that Rhea had once owned the Granville building. But I made myself wait. I made a few more calls, but Oliver Gullum, distinguished critic, was unlisted. That was all right; I'd pay him a call in his office tomorrow. First thing in the morning.

I picked Adele up in front of her building at eight-fifteen. She gave me a fat manila envelope, then looked at my face. "You look like hell," she said.

"Thanks."

"I wouldn't want to be whoever you're thinking about."

"Oliver Gullum, honey," I said, pulling onto Fifty-seventh Street and heading east for the Queensboro

Bridge. "His was the key vote. He gave Compton the Granville."

"Who's Oliver Gullum, aside from being a book critic for the *Times*?"

"*The* book critic," I said. "But that won't be for much longer."

"You mean Neary bought his vote somehow?"

"No. Atherton did. Months and months ago. Through his brother Edmund at Regina University. Gave him a nice, juicy job."

"Why would Gullum do that?" asked Adele. "He doesn't need anything."

I smiled. "That's what I'm going to find out." My fingers flexed on the steering wheel. "How did you manage to pull it off, Adele?"

"I decided not to ask June—Neary's old secretary—for that favor. I just watched her like a hawk for the rest of the day, then took the key from the cabinet lock when she went to answer her phone. I think I'll keep it for a while."

"Start looking for a new job, Adele," I said. "The Granville Foundation isn't going to be a nice place to work for—starting tomorrow."

"Probably not," sighed Adele. "The Granville heirs visited Atherton and took him to lunch, too, while I was out today. They told him to give himself a raise. The Foundation won't have to pay rent now, you know. Good old Edgar."

After I dropped her off on Yellowstone Boulevard, I drove on to Flushing. Sayres's lights were on, but I didn't care. I wasn't here to see him or Compton's brother. I knocked on Compton's landlord's door until he opened it. He was a short, wizened man way past sixty years old, and he eyed my identification warily. Then he invited me in and told me that he was Hungarian, that he'd escaped from Hungary twenty years ago, and that he'd never liked the police. I settled back in some ratty armchair and listened to his life story. He was a lonely old man and I could wait. Two hours later my ears were fractured with his broken English and my throat raw from three cups of his thick, spiced coffee, but I managed to get out of him what he'd seen that Saturday afternoon at his window—my comings and goings, Sayres's, Rhea's, and Gregory Compton's.

And when I said good night and thanks to him, I had it all figured out.

Then I changed my mind and knocked on Compton's door anyway. Those Black Russians had slowed my thinking down. Compton answered the summons in his bathrobe. "I want to see the raincoat your brother was wearing," I said.

"You're in luck," said Compton. "I wanted to give it to Mr. Sayres—it's a fine coat, I think Miss Hamilton bought it for Greg—but he didn't want it. So I'm keeping it. Got it back from the cleaners today."

He took it off the hanger in a hall closet. And I took out the button I'd found out on Freehold Road. It was a nice coat, a trench coat, a tailored coat, of a quality and cut Gregory Compton would've had to work three weeks to afford, tax not included, whatever his top rate was at Aristo Temps. And the button I had matched the rest. It wasn't one of the functional buttons, but one that was missing from among all the extras on the front and at the bottom inside the lining. I handed Compton the missing button. "I don't blame Mr. Sayres for not wanting this coat."

"Why not?"

I shook my head. "I'll see you tomorrow, Mr. Compton. Good night."

I sat up at home very late, watching the city go to sleep beyond my living room window, twirling the stem of my souvenir goblet, thinking a lot and wiping away the occasional tear.

I wondered what music they'd play at Gregory Compton's funeral.

18

"Well, Mr. Sturgis, it's only a year's appointment, and while I'll have to spend half my time at Regina, I'll still be doing my column for this paper and for my syndicate, though only twice a month. It's essentially a research position, you know. The Olcutt Chair goes to someone new every year. I'll be following Sidney Froygenberg, editor of *The Cultural Quarterly*."

"Will you be writing anymore on William Grackle?"

"Yes. In fact, I'm doing a major piece right now for the *Times Sunday Magazine*, which will feature Grackle and many of his contemporaries of the New Naturalist School of Fiction. I'm using Grackle as my archetypal example."

"Then, of course, you won't be discussing Gregory Compton?" I smiled conspiratorially.

"No, of course not. That's one scrivener I won't waste another word on."

I'd had a preconception of Oliver Gullum. I'd imagined an over-the-hill pipsqueak, about five feet five, balding, prim and proper, weighing in at one-twenty. Someone most likely to "walk away" from anything that didn't measure up—or measure down—to his beady-eyed view of the world. But he was bigger than I was by about twenty pounds and three inches, and even seated behind his desk he could stare down at me from over the top of his Franklin bifocals. He was about fifty-five, tanned, and had a full head of black hair. And he was in good shape; he could have walked through a plate glass window and thought it was a thick fog.

But Oliver Gullum didn't believe in violence. He was a pacifist, even in the war of ideas. He was a little man in spite of his size. I'd called him up at the *Times*, and after I spoke with his secretary, was switched over to him. I had them both believing that I was Donald Sturgis, owner and publisher of *Vignettes*, a new literary monthly published in Chicago. Ruth Marhcessini had taught me a lesson on that score. I'd told him that I read his column religiously in the Chicago papers, wanted to know more about his Olcutt Professor of American Literature appointment, and that I was on my way to Paris on business. After some hemming and hawing, he bought it, and agreed to give me thirty minutes. I came prepared this time. I had a ring-binder legal notepad, and went out and bought the loudest silk tie I could find at Bloomingdale's, one that had orange, yellow, and purple cartouches. Gullum loved it. It was the first thing he noticed about me. I guess it said that I was literary and sensitive and uncommon.

I said, "Would you say that Grackle is our new James Farrell, Mr. Gullum?"

Gullum smiled. "In a manner of speaking, Mr. Sturgis. Different style, same message; different setting, same verve. You know something, I make the same comparison in my Sunday piece, though I don't dwell on it because I don't entirely agree with it."

I wanted to laugh. I didn't have much use for Farrell, either. "Nor do I," I said. "So, what *will* you be doing at Regina?"

"Consolidating my notes for a book on American literary criticism."

My eyes almost narrowed. "It's an honorable profession, literary criticism."

"Without a doubt, Mr. Sturgis, as you may well know. It's one of the few professions left in our commericalized culture that hasn't been corrupted. The responsibilities of criticism are enormous and without comparison. I sometimes find myself wishing I had chosen a more mundane career path."

"Have a publisher lined up yet?"

"Goodness, no, Mr. Sturgis. *I* don't have to worry about such things. There are seven houses waiting for my decision already, and by the time I finish my first draft in six months or so, that number will have doubled."

"You were pretty hard on Compton, weren't you, Mr. Gullum?"

"Compton? Well, there's an example of the responsibilities I was speaking to you about. One finds oneself in some very awkward positions when it comes to new writers. I feel myself duty-bound to discourage certain books and trends."

"I guess you're upset that Grackle didn't win the Granville Prize."

"*Very* upset, Mr. Sturgis. If I hadn't been one of the jurors myself, I'd have called for an investigation, or an explanation. But, since I *was* one of the jurors, I had to satisfy myself with a letter of support to Grackle instead. I assured him that his time will come, that he will be remembered when Compton is long forgotten."

Then I let Gullum have it. "That's very curious, Mr. Gullum. If that's the way you feel, then how do you explain this?" I reached inside my notepad and took out a folded photocopy of his Granville ballot and handed it to him.

Gullum looked at it and sat very still. Then his eyes rose and drilled me from over his bifocals. "How did you come by this, Mr. Sturgis?"

"The name's Hanrahan," I said, slipping the silk tie off. "Chess Hanrahan. I'm a private detective, and you're a liar and a fraud." Then I balled the silk up in my hand, stood up, and threw it into his face. The tie unwound to drape over one of his shoulders and arms.

Gullum's eyes were still closed. "Get out of my office immediately," he said.

"Speaking of responsibilities, I came here just to let you know that you're indirectly responsible for the murder of Gregory Compton, who shouldn't have won the Granville. It's nothing you could be hauled into court for—you were just a pawn—but you're finished, Gullum. You traded your alleged principles in for a mess of pottage at Regina. Why is that?"

"It's none of your business," said Gullum.

"Whatever," I chuckled. "It'll come out. Didn't it matter to you, how you voted?"

"I don't have to discuss anything with you," said Gullum. "I'm not obliged to explain anything to anyone, especially not to . . . to *your* level of mentality."

I laughed. "Tell you what I'm going to do, Gullum." I picked up my notepad and briefcase and went to the door. "I'm going to *walk away*. How do you like that? One second, though." I stopped, reached into my briefcase, and took out one of my regular ties. As I slipped it through my collar and knotted it, I said, "You're a peach, Gullum. A distinguished peach. A rotten peach. I mean, it wasn't bad enough that you were a cringing critic, ready to pour your brain dung on anything good that managed to break through the crust of your stinking literary world. At least you did that on principle. Or so everybody thought. But I've figured it out, Gullum. You don't have any principles. For the precise reason that you're scrofulous."

"Get out!!" yelled Gullum, whipping the cartouche tie off of himself but forgetting to throw it back at me.

"Sure," I smiled, giving the knot of my tie one last tug. "Don't forget to include this little incident in your book about your honored profession. Keep the tie, Gullum. It suits you." Then I opened the door and walked out. He could keep the photocopy of his ballot, too. There were plenty more where that had come from. And he couldn't go crying to Atherton. Atherton was miles away in upstate, attending Gregory Compton's funeral.

No, I thought as I strode through the halls of the *Times*, maybe what Gullum was doing right now was flipping through his dictionary in search of "scrofulous." *My* level of mentality? He was lucky I couldn't stay the whole thirty minutes. I had things to do, one of which was another chat with William Leif at Tyle.

When I was finished with him I pulled my car from the garage and headed up to Tarrytown and Conover's mansion to light another fuse. I stopped at a diner along the way for a late breakfast but I was still early. The funeral party hadn't returned yet. Conover's butler let me wait in the study. There was a copy of yesterday's *Times* on the table and I read it. On the bottom of the front page, ironically, was an article about some committee of novelists, playwrights, and poets who were upset that first, there weren't enough awards like the Granville Prize, but also that the whole idea of awards was faintly "elitist" to them and that they were against it. William Henry Grackle, lately a loser, was quoted as saying, "What happened recently is just another example of cultural discrimination, an example of the chaotic environment writers must endure. My colleagues and I are the true representatives of American culture, we've worked hard at it. But reactionaries refuse to acknowledge the new standards and fling blind recognition to the first passing ship-in-the-night. People wonder why so many writers have problems or get discouraged."

Don't worry, Grackle, I thought. Oliver Gullum will take good care of you.

An hour later, from one of Conover's windows, I watched the procession of cars come up the winding road and pull into the courtyard. Conover and Rhea noticed my Magnette, then came up the steps, followed by all the others.

There were about ten cars and perhaps forty people. I smiled a little when I saw Vivian Brewer among them.

Conover came into the study a moment later. I shook his hand and said, "Sorry I couldn't make it. I had business in the city."

The shipper nodded and slipped out of his coat. "Drink?" he asked.

"A cream sherry, thanks."

As he poured two glasses, he said, "And thank you for not asking How was it? I've never understood how one is expected to evaluate a funeral and then deliver a critique on it as though it were a Broadway play." Conover came over and handed me a glass. "Cheers, Mr. Hanrahan," he said.

"Cheers," I smiled. We both took a gulp of our drinks.

"I will say, though, that Rhea's choice of chapel music left me . . . not very happy, under the circumstances."

I sat down in a chair opposite Conover. "Barber's Adagio for Strings?"

Conover shook his head. "No. Something just as eerie. The Swan of Tuonela. Sibelius." He sighed, then shrugged. "It just wasn't right. But it seemed to fit her mood. She's grown more withdrawn, Mr. Hanrahan. I don't understand it. I thought she'd be stronger."

I understood it, but didn't want to tell him. Not yet. So I said, "I'd have picked the first section of the *Allegro con fuoco* of Rachmaninoff's First."

Conover grunted with interest. "Why?" he asked.

"It could have been a score by Stridivant. It could have summed up Compton's life. I mean, it's the kind of music I hear when I think of Stridivant."

Conover smiled. "I like that. You're right. That—or something like it—would have been more appropriate. I'll mention it to her. I'd have preferred it myself." He studied me for a while. I felt transparent. "How are the suppositions coming, Mr. Hanrahan? They must be why you're here."

I shook my head. "They're certainties now, Mr. Conover." I paused to finish my sherry. "Can you tell me anything about Rhea's real estate holdings?"

Conover sighed again. "I used to know everything about them. But as time went by and I became more and more caught up in my container business, I lost track of them, even while her mother was alive. It's been so long and it's strictly Rhea's business now. Most of those holdings go back sixty, seventy years. Some even much further. My wife's family—the Tyles of Tarrytown—invested heavily in midtown Manhattan property around the turn of the century." He gestured to the study at large and the rest of the mansion. "They finished this place the same week Custer's bugles blew their last at Little Big Horn." He paused, then frowned. "Why do you ask?"

"Did you know that Tyle Properties owned the Granville building?"

Conover didn't answer. He simply sat there and stared at me, long after I knew that he'd made the connection.

I said, "Rhea doesn't own that building anymore, Mr. Conover. The Foundation does. She deeded it to them the day after the final votes were tabulated for the Prize."

Still Conover said nothing. Then he slumped back in his chair, his sherry glass dangling between two fingers on an outstretched, limp arm. He closed his eyes. "God, what a fool I've been . . ." he whispered. He sat like that for a while, then his eyes opened. "Atherton," he said. "Atherton. . . . No wonder he was so agreeable, so damned agreeable. . . . That useless, boot-licking bastard. . . ." Then he inhaled sharply. "Rhea . . . Rhea, what have you done? Why? What for?"

I looked away. Conover didn't know the worst of it yet. He would, in time. When it was over.

The study door opened and Edgar Atherton looked in. "Mr. Conover, will you be joining us soon? Oh," he said, seeing me. "You have . . . company."

Conover shot up. "Atherton, come here! I want a few words with you!"

Atherton, a banal, unsuspecting look on his face, obliged.

Conover turned to me. "Mr. Hanrahan, you needn't witness this. Would you please excuse us?"

I nodded. "No more tragedies, though, Mr. Conover."

He nodded but his hands were still clenched into fists. Atherton didn't notice them; he was still mesmerized by my presence. I walked out and closed the door gently behind me.

I followed the surge of voices through the hallways to the main dining room. Conover's sister and some servants were busy setting up an impromptu buffet on the long table. I saw Gussie Spendler, Vivian Brewer, and George Compton, but neither Rhea nor Sayres. Spencer Durand was there, and so was somebody I recognized from Pericles Press. Earl Teague, of course, was not present; he was busy counting rattlesnakes in Pennsylvania. I approached Conover's sister and asked her where Rhea had gone.

"I don't know, honey," she said, "but I wish she'd come back and see to her guests."

I said thanks, nodded hello to Gussie and Vivian Brewer, and left the room.

I roamed through the hallways again and the voices subsided. I passed Conover's study and heard the shipper yelling at Atherton. Three rooms and a turn in the hallway later I heard Rhea speaking loudly, distinctly, and angrily from behind a door that was not completely closed.

". . . And I don't ever want to see or hear from you again, Sayres. Do you understand? After tonight, that's it. *That's it*! Here!" There was a sound like she'd hit him with something.

After a moment, Sayres said, "Sure. *You* just be sure to bring that check, that's all." Then he chuckled. "How much you want to bet that goof detective hits you up for some money, too, Rhea? He can't match his own socks but some day he'll figure you out."

"He's a *man*, Sayres, which is more than I can say for you."

"Just like Greg?"

This time I heard a slap so hard and solid that I almost felt the sting myself. "Mention Greg's name in my presence again and I'll kill you, Sayres. I mean it."

I heard movement for the door and ducked into an alcove. Geoffrey Sayres came out of the room, a big fat manila envelope tucked under his arm. He turned the corner and was gone. A long moment later I heard a sob, and then Rhea came out and followed him.

I didn't follow at all but stayed behind to listen to her muffled steps on the carpet and to sigh at my good fortune. Aside from good manners, one reason for my being here was to warn Sayres of the criminal liabilities of extortion by intimidation, otherwise known as blackmail, and to ask kindly or otherwise for Compton's letter of refusal. Another reason was to size up Rhea and decide on how to handle her now. I'd lighted one fuse here and that was enough. I was certain that she'd see Sayres tonight and that was as good a time as any to light the last one.

Without attracting anyone's attention I intercepted the butler and had him retrieve my coat, then slipped out of the mansion to my car. On Pheasant Road I parked again near some bushes and waited.

An hour later a Continental rolled out of the private road, driven by Edgar Atherton, accompanied by his white-haired wife. The look on his face was anything but gentlemanly now. Two more cars drove out, and finally the Mercedes, Sayres behind the wheel and George Compton beside him.

They drove to White Plains and stopped at a downtown restaurant. I parked not far away and waited. I wasn't hungry. Another hour passed. When they came out again I followed them all the way into Flushing. There was a space right in front of Compton's former apartment and that's where Sayres parked. I found a spot at the end of the block. Sayres and Compton got out and talked for a few minutes across the roof of the Mercedes, then Sayres gave Compton a see-you-later wave and crossed the street. That's when I locked my car door and started walking. It was five forty-five.

The front door was unlocked and I went in. I guess Sayres had just reached the top of the stairs when I rapped on his door. I could hear him skipping back down the steps. When he opened the door he had a smile ready, probably thinking that it was George Compton. The smile vanished when he saw that it was me. His expression became tired and unfriendly.

"Upstairs," I said before he could open his mouth.

Sayres shook his head. "I can't see you now, Mr. Hanrahan. I'm busy."

I pushed him inside and closed the door behind me. He tried to push me back but before he knew it I'd spun him around with a wallop on his right shoulder that made him trip on the first step and let me grab his right arm and bend it up behind his back. "Upstairs," I said again, exerting pressure on the arm, and this time he listened, dancing up the steps to lessen the pain. I walked him right into his kitchen where I let him go. The big envelope was on the table.

Then he jumped me, throwing a punch that whistled past my ear. He was close enough so I simply hammered his stomach once and he doubled over. I cut one of my knuckles on his belt buckle. I sat down in a chair and waited for him to recover.

When he did, he saw me sitting there calmly with a cigarette. He slid across the floor and leaned against the refrigerator door. "You . . . you don't have any right to do this. . . . Why are you . . . doing this?"

"Take your raincoat off and make yourself at home, Sayres," I said. "We have things to talk about. This, for example." I picked up the envelope and took out its contents. There were two bound manuscripts and a letter-size envelope. The manuscripts were plays, one entitled *Standard of Excellence* and the other *In the Cold Light of Day*. Both were by Gregory Compton. I asked, "Did he write others?"

Sayres nodded.

"What are you doing with these?"

"What do you think?" replied Sayres sarcastically.

"You planned to type new title pages that would read 'by Geoffrey Sayres.'"

Sayres's jaw literally dropped.

I smiled. "Of course, you'd have done that sooner, only you first had to determine whether or not anybody else knew about Compton's plays. And nobody else did, not even his agent. If you'd taken any of his plays before Rhea had a chance to claim Compton's papers and went ahead with a production—well, that would have been very embarrassing indeed." I paused. "I don't know if your own plays are any good, Sayres," I said, waving the two thin playscripts in the air, "but these are bound to be better."

Sayres looked away.

I took the smaller envelope and opened it. Inside was a cashier's check for fifty thousand dollars. I looked at Sayres. "And she's bringing you *another*?"

Sayres began to get up, his face twisted in rage. Before he could get very far I was above him and I backhanded him with all I could give it. He fell back between the refrigerator door and the wall. I must have clipped his nose because it was bleeding now. Then I sat down again. There was a roll of paper towels on the table and I tossed it to him. "Of course, you must have read all his plays—you being his best friend—and decided these two were the best. That's what I like, Sayres, a man of good taste, good judgment. But Compton was a poor judge of you, though. Either that, or you were a damned fine actor." I shrugged.

"I can't fault Compton for his error, though. I've fallen for some pretty fine acts myself."

Sayres's eyes grew watery. "I . . . I wasn't . . . acting," he said with a sound that was not quite a sob. He tore off a towel and dabbed with it at his nose.

"Now, Mr. Sayres," I said, "if you want to see how much blood that roll of towels can soak up, *don't* show me where his letter of refusal is."

"I told you!" said Sayres. "I gave it to Rhea! *She* has it!"

I shook my head. "You gave her a photocopy of it. You'd never have gotten to first base with her if she had the original." I stood up and walked over to the dramatist. "Well?"

"I don't—" I leaned forward a little and poised the back of my hand. "It's . . . it's in my study."

"Show me."

He showed me. It was in an envelope dropped behind one of his bookcases. "Sit down," I said when he handed me the envelope.

I opened the envelope and took out the original and ten photocopies. Compton's stamped envelope, addressed to Atherton at the Granville Foundation, was clipped to the original. And both the original and the envelope were Tyle Properties stationery.

Now it made sense. Now I understood why Compton had visited Leif that Saturday morning. He hadn't gone there to ask questions about real estate for some new novel. He'd gone there to lift some Tyle Properties stationery, so he could send his letter of refusal to the Granville Foundation on it. He wanted Atherton and Rhea to know that he knew the truth.

The letter read exactly as Sayres had quoted it to me last week. "You didn't lie to me when you said you found this in Compton's glove compartment, did you?" I asked him.

Sayres shook his head.

"But you lied to me when you said you'd found it last

Saturday, before you drove up to Tarrytown with his brother."

Sayres nodded once.

"So when *did* you find it?"

"That day . . . the Sunday he didn't come back. . . ."

"And you had a key to the Mercedes all along, right? Compton had another. They usually come in pairs, or he had a duplicate made. Just for you. Because you were his best friend." I studied Sayres for a moment. "You know something? This letter," I said, shaking it in front of his face, "was more important than anything he'd ever written. What I read here—in this single sentence—made possible everything else he'd ever written. All his books. All his plays. Hell—his *life*."

Sayres's face slowly wrinkled up in emotion. "*Then why didn't he mail it?*" he screamed. "*Why didn't the sonofa-bitch mail it?*"

I wasn't impressed anymore with Sayres's emotional outbursts, so I didn't give him a second glance. "Because he had more on his mind than just his career or future, Sayres. Something perhaps just as important to him as his work."

"*What?*" demanded Sayres with an outrage that was just short of a snarl.

"That's no longer any of your business. Just accept the fact that he forgot to mail it. I'd have forgotten, too, in the circumstances." I looked at Sayres and studied him again. "You pose an interesting hypothesis, Sayres," I said. "I mean, your character does."

"Well, that's none of *your* business!" Sayres rose from the couch. I pushed him back down.

"But you're wrong. It *is* my business. You had me stumped for a while, Sayres. You didn't make any sense until I pieced together everything you've said, from Wednesday night onward. I'll forgo the details and just give you the sum: as long as Compton was fighting impossi- ble odds, as long as he had the strength of character to do that—you would. When he made it, saw some success, then things changed. You thought he'd sold out when he won the Granville. You thought he was being wise and practical. Well, it was a tough life, trying to break into the literary establishment. One of the toughest lives that could ever be led. Compton seemed to have finally given in. Well, why shouldn't he? And, hell, if *he* was ready to give in, why shouldn't you?"

Sayres was good-looking but he looked very ugly to me now. It wasn't my estimate of him that made me think that. It was the set of his face. I'd struck home. But I wasn't finished. "You *knew* what was demanded of that kind of life, didn't you, Sayres? You *knew* what was the good. And you'd meet the demands and pursue the good—so long as someone else did, too. You *knew* what were the right things. And as long as there was resistance to all that, you were okay. Persecution or neglect can be glorious, right? You can always feel better than your persecutors or the ignorant, especially if they truly are contemptible. But the biggest difference between you and Compton was that he didn't feed off of the resistance. He was indifferent to it. But that resistance—that was the bread and butter of your soul, wasn't it, Sayres? You had no goals, no reason to fight. All you were really doing was looking for an excuse *not* to fight for anything."

Sayres jumped up, his hands shooting straight for my throat, and I swung my fist at him more from anger than from any instinct for self-defense. Down he went again. No, I wasn't kidding around with this joker. I wanted to do a little strangling on *him*. I wanted justice, but there were better ways of getting it. I put one knee on his chest and held the knot of his tie hard on his throat. "Tell me, Sayres! Tell me why you'd want to foul the memory of your best friend!"

"I hated him when I was left alone!" he cried. "I hated him when I knew he was with *her*!"

"My God, Sayres! The man was alone most of his adult

life and *you* couldn't bear the thought of his being *happy* for once? Jesus Christ, did you think that recognition by Rhea or by those Granville people meant the end of his reason to live? Or did it mean the end of *your* reason? To be happy is to be corrupt?"

"No!" screamed Sayres, and then he began crying—crying in relief.

I got up from on top of him, my head spinning. You don't nail someone's soul like that and not feel something. I hadn't thought much about Sayres until I hustled him upstairs a while ago. Not consciously. Then it had just come out, logically, ineluctably. I felt invincible, and clean. Chalk up another paradox for Hanrahan.

"You don't . . . understand," sobbed Sayres. "You don't know what it's like . . . being alone. . . ."

I laughed. "You mean you only took on meaning when *he* was around?"

Sayres said nothing.

"You mean that you had to have someone around who was as beaten and terrified and messed up as you are? Or someone you *thought* was like that? But Compton wasn't, my boy. You misjudged him and he misjudged you." I shook my head. "He was no hero to you, Sayres. He was a narcotic. He could stand being alone. Probably preferred it, going by what passes for friendship these days. But you couldn't stand it. And when he was gone, when he was with Rhea, and when you learned it was forever, you began to climb the walls, like any other dope head."

Sayres cried softly, "He was . . . like a brother. . . ."

"No way was he any brother of yours." I turned away because I couldn't stand the sight of him anymore. I picked up Compton's letter and sat down at Sayres's typewriter. I rooted around his desk until I found some envelopes and a box of stamps. Then I typed up a new envelope addressed to the Granville Foundation.

"What are you doing?" asked Sayres from the couch.

"Doing what you should've done—other people's thinking for them. Only you were wrong about it being other people's."

"*She* wants it . . . she wants it worse than Greg ever did. . . ."

"He never wanted it, Sayres. Shut up."

When I was finished, I sealed and stamped the new envelope and stuffed it and all the photocopies inside my jacket. I left Sayres on the couch and went into the kitchen to fix myself a coffee. There was some liquor in the cabinet but I didn't touch it, even though I wanted to. While the water was on the burner, I tore up the cashier's check, dropped the bits into the ashtray, and put a match to the pile. Then I took off my coat, poured myself a coffee, and waited.

19

When my watch read seven o'clock, I went back to Sayres. He was still on the couch and still in his raincoat. All he had done was sit up and was staring furiously into space. "What time are you expecting her?" I asked him.

"Soon," he mumbled.

"What *time*?" I insisted.

"She said seven, or seven-thirty!" said the dramatist, his red-rimmed eyes flaring angrily at me.

For a moment I felt like enlightening Sayres about my true reason for being here. But then my interest in telling him anything reached bottom. Let him do his own thinking. I wondered how long he would last in his present state.

I was almost back in the kitchen when I heard the unmistakable roar of Rhea's Porsche as it changed from third to first gears outside the house. Instantly I jerked into my coat, grabbed the envelope with Compton's plays, and was headed downstairs when Sayres's buzzer rang. She was in as much of a hurry as I was.

I slammed Sayres's door behind me and opened the front

door, and there she was, dressed in slacks and that same black fur coat again. I didn't give her a chance to say anything, either. "Let's go, Rhea. Your car. I drive."

She simply looked at me with an incredulous expression. She must have known it was finished. Probably she'd had a terrible fight with her father. And she must have known why I was here, seeing the envelope she'd given Sayres in my hand.

For a moment she was rigid. And for a split second I pitied her. I don't think she noticed. And for a split second, too, her purposeful eyes widened and she looked at me as she must have once looked at Gregory Compton.

Then the look was gone and I was the intruder again. "Why should we go anywhere?" she asked.

I said, "I want you to give me one good reason why I shouldn't mail Compton's letter." I reached inside my jacket, took out the envelope so she could see it, then put it back. "Sayres is out of it," I added. "He won't be cashing your check. And I have all his copies."

After studying me for a moment, she said, "All right. Where to?" She turned and walked briskly back down the brick steps to her double-parked Porsche.

"Middleport."

She paused in midstep, then went on. I followed. She'd left her keys in the ignition again. As we drove away, I glanced up at Sayres's window. He was there, watching.

Neither of us said anything until I pulled onto the Parkway. Then Rhea asked, "If I can give you a good reason, will it stop you from mailing that letter?"

"No."

"Then why should I try to give you one?"

"Because I'm going to give you a chance to stop *me* from mailing it, Rhea. On the same spot you stopped Compton." I put the Porsche in the middle lane. "To help you make a decision, you should know that I didn't tell your father my suspicions or my conclusions. Sayres doesn't know, either. This is just between you and me."

"I think I knew that when my father told me who you were that night." She looked over at me with the hint of a smile. "I think I knew it then."

"Spare me the compliments."

"You . . . haven't any proof, Chess."

"Tell it to the district attorney."

I slowed down and cruised in the middle lane. I wasn't in any hurry now. I wanted to give her time to think of a good reason.

After a few miles, she said, "Can't you guess?"

I shook my head.

"How can't you *know*," said Rhea angrily, "if you've come this far?"

I shrugged. "I don't know what was going on inside your head when you did it, Rhea. All I've been working with are suppositions. Pretty solid suppositions, it turns out. You tell me."

"You're . . . wrong . . ."

"No, I'm not. I'll be generous and tell you how it probably happened. You did love Compton—once. You probably would've killed anybody who harmed him. But the minute you started getting him something he didn't want, something you knew he didn't want—that damned Prize—that's when the corruption set in, that's when you got canker of the soul.

"And that was a year ago when you had the idea to get him the Granville Prize. When you probably saw Atherton and promised him a way out of his financial troubles by guaranteeing him the building if he'd guarantee Compton the Prize. Then you bribed Earl Teague to submit his book. It was as simple as that. The rest is mere mechanics."

"Why are you so certain?"

"Because Compton should never have won the Granville Prize—and you're the only reason he could have won it."

Rhea said nothing. I said nothing. Minutes passed and so did thousands of lights. As I turned onto the Jericho

Turnpike, I said, "We'll drive around the Island all night if necessary, Rhea. We'll drive until I get a reason."

"You . . . didn't misjudge me, Chess," said Rhea quietly.

"Yes, I did," I said. "What I . . . was beginning to fall in love with was only what was left of you after the soul rot set in. That's all. My mistake." I gripped the steering wheel harder. "And you misjudged me, Rhea. You lied to me at your father's dinner party. You underestimated my intelligence—either that or you didn't think much of my rectitude. Maybe both. You should have believed me when I said I had a special interest in paradoxes. And you kept up the lie, not only with me, but with your father, with everyone you knew. And if I hadn't pursued the matter, if I hadn't taken the paradox seriously—you probably dismissed our talk as idle, intellectual chatter—everybody'd still be in the dark." I shook my head. "You didn't take me seriously, Rhea. Or maybe you didn't take a certain part of me seriously enough. Oh, you might have admired it, all right, but you probably thought it was as incidental to me as an extra pair of suede boots in your wardrobe."

"You . . . seem to speak from experience," said Rhea.

"It's happened before. But not this way." I glanced at her. "You didn't take Compton seriously, either. You couldn't have. Otherwise you'd never have tried to get him that damned Prize."

"That's not true . . . that I didn't take him seriously."

"Oh, you once might have. But when you set the ball in motion a year ago, you couldn't afford to feel about him what you might've once felt. You had lots of time to back out of your deal with Atherton. You chose not to. You didn't want to know, didn't want to believe it. You chose blindness."

Rhea seemed to withdraw into herself. "How . . . did you learn that I owned the building?"

I shrugged again. "I could say that I wouldn't have noticed anything if you hadn't signed your check in that restaurant downtown and waltzed out. The maître d' told me you were the restaurant's landlady. But I would've learned that you owned the Granville building yesterday anyway. I learned that Compton worked for a while at Tyle Properties, and I learned that Tyle until very, very recently owned the Granville building. Compton didn't know you owned Tyle until he worked there, and he didn't see any importance in your being the Foundation's landlord. And he'd worked in so many businesses that he didn't think to tell you that he was at Tyle. It just wasn't important enough to him. Or maybe he thought that you might be sensitive to it. He *didn't* tell you, did he?"

"No . . . I didn't know . . ."

"Did you see him at all the week before the Granville announcement?"

"No," said Rhea. "He was . . . busy. He was finishing his new book."

"Whatever his reason, he didn't tell you and you didn't know. Anyway, one of the reasons I didn't make the funeral this morning was because I had a little chat with William Leif, Tyle's office manager. Compton reported to him when he worked there. One of Compton's tasks was to type up new leases for tenants of some of your properties around town, and one of those leases was the Foundation's. That particular lease wasn't delivered, because Leif assumed a property sale was pending. Compton knew that, too, and had no reason to think any more of it—until he learned that he'd won the Granville Prize. He called Leif either Friday evening or Saturday morning, learned that Leif was putting in half a day on Saturday, then drove into the city to visit him. He told him that he was researching a new novel but what he actually wanted was to confirm the building sale. He and Leif talked about the Prize and Leif eventually told him that the Granville Foundation was no longer a tenant of the building, but its owner. He even showed Compton the memo you sent him, signed by you, advising him of the transfer. At some point during their talk, Compton laid hands on some Tyle letterhead, which he later used to type his refusal on. He'd put it all together by then," I paused. "I would've traced it back to you sooner or later, Rhea."

Rhea said nothing. She rooted through her purse for a cigarette. But before she could light it, I brought up Compton's lighter and pressed its button. She nodded thanks, and I lit one for myself. I said, "Here, keep this, it's the gift Compton gave back to you." I dropped it on her lap.

She picked it up and looked at it. "Where did you find this?" she demanded, a tinge of anger in her voice.

"You left it in the restaurant," I said. "There was a missing lighter in Compton's personal effects. I traced that back to you, too."

"He . . . he didn't give it back," said Rhea almost inaudibly. "I borrowed it . . . and forgot to give it back. . . ."

I shook my head. "Don't lie, Rhea. He gave it back— probably threw it at you." I glanced at her and she looked away. I went on. "So Compton came back to Flushing, drafted his letter, showed it to Sayres, then went back home to type it again. Then he called on you in Manhattan. You suggested dinner out here to celebrate the Granville Prize. Some time during or after that dinner he told you what he knew and asked you for the truth. Did *he* have to pry it out of you, too?"

"No . . ." whispered Rhea.

"But you must have argued with him."

"Yes . . . we argued."

I turned onto the Middleport exit. "I suppose the reason you gave him wasn't good enough," I said.

Rhea said nothing.

"How's your father?"

After a long silence, she said, "He won't speak to me. For the first time in my life, I saw . . . hate in his eyes. For me."

"Can you blame him? And he only knows that you rigged

the Granville for Compton." I stopped for one of Middle-port's two traffic lights. "By the way, no one else knows about that, either. But when I get home tonight, I'm going to fix Oliver Gullum."

"He . . . was on the jury."

"That's right. His was the deciding vote. Atherton bought it with some plum university job for the literary guardian. Atherton also bought some votes with a few in-house promotions. Compton should have lost by a landslide. In fact, his book shouldn't have even made it to the semifinals. Anyway, what I'm going to do is mail copies of Gullum's review of *Walk Around the Sun* along with copies of his ballot to some newspapers, including the *Times*, and to all the other guest jurors. Of course, when people start asking questions, it'll all come back to you again. That's another reason why I couldn't make the funeral. I was busy preparing my big mailing. And that's another reason why you'll want to stop me." I pulled the Porsche over to the curb and nodded to the marquee of Taradash's Seafood Corner. "Remember this place, Rhea?"

Rhea glanced out her window, then looked away. "I didn't know you could be this way."

"Which way is it this time?"

"Cruel."

I shook my head. "No. Just. This is where Compton had his last meal. Or did he have much of an appetite? I don't imagine he had." I put the Porsche in gear and moved on. As we talked, Rhea grew more and more distant, even though she sat but a foot away from me. She seemed to shrink in her own existence, diminishing herself somehow until she reminded me of a little girl trapped by a cobra. Her beauty remained, but now it was just a shell hiding a terrified, guilty soul.

"What gave you the idea to rig the Prize for Compton?"

"This time . . . last year . . . when I read about the Granville, about who won it. It was then."

I grunted in recollection. "I remember that, too. Let me

see. Yes. *Man With Knife*, by Jack Tasso. He's serving a sentence for armed robbery and second-degree murder in Georgia. Now he's writing screenplays and contributing to literary journals. He'll be paroled soon, I hear. I read the book. Grade A garbage with a hard-boiled Marxian twist. What about it?"

"Isn't that enough?"

"No."

"That was when I decided that Greg would win the Granville."

"And?"

"That was when I discovered that I owned the building the Foundation had occupied. I didn't know until then. It was just a street address, it had been in my mother's family for years. I also learned that the Foundation had been late with its rent frequently. And I learned why. Atherton was not a good manager. He'd spent a lot of money renovating the Foundation's offices. He'd given himself and his top executives unusual raises. And he'd spent money on public relations when no expense was necessary. That's when I knew that I could guarantee Greg the Granville Prize."

"Did he ever say that he wanted it?"

"No."

I went past Middleport's last light and made a left on Freehold Road. "When did Sayres approach you about the letter?" I asked.

"Last Saturday . . ."

"You know, for a while I suspected Sayres. But I have a witness who saw Compton get into his Mercedes the previous Saturday afternoon and drive off—and saw you bring that car back early Sunday morning. Around one o'clock. And you were alone." I started slowly up the hill, then pressed the accelerator and climbed Freehold at sixty miles an hour, made the hairpin turn—where Farrell said the carload of kids had gone off the edge—with all four wheels hugging the pavement, then raced straight up the road. I drew up to the spot where Compton had been hit and stopped with a lurch that tested the strength of Rhea's right arm braced on the dashboard. "There," I said, cutting the ignition. "We're here."

The road was still. The only sounds were the cooling metal of the engine and the wash of the surf. I switched on the dome light. There were tears on Rhea's cheeks. I reached over with my right hand, held her chin and jaws in a tight grip, and yanked her head around to face me. "*Why . . . didn't . . . you . . . leave . . . it . . . alone?*" I demanded with an anger I couldn't hold back. Then I let her go and looked away.

She sobbed once, then said, "I . . . wanted him to be . . . happy . . . Chess . . ."

I closed my eyes. "He had you, Rhea, and he had his work. That was enough." I looked over at her. "Whatever order he placed you and his work in, you should have been grateful." A lone car passed us, and then it was still again. There was only the darkness and the mute reflectors on the long guardrail. "I didn't even know him, and I'm grateful."

Rhea slammed the top of the dashboard with her two fists. "I gave him a victory—a *victory*—and he . . . he treated it as though . . . as though it was something with gangrene!"

"You knew what he felt about it before that," I said. "Why should his reaction to it have surprised you? You knew what he thought about the Prize, about how his winning it was like being nominated to be installed in a wax museum of horrors." Then I sat back with a new thought. "Or did you think that was just his opinion?" I looked at Rhea. "Was it here that you gave him your reason?"

"Yes . . ."

"And what was it?"

Rhea only sobbed.

I said, "Whatever it was, he was already sick of you, wasn't he? Sick of the sight of you and sick with what you'd done to his life. Sick of the knowledge that for a whole year you knew about it and said nothing. Sick from the knowledge that you betrayed him, betrayed what you professed to love and admire in him. He couldn't bear being with you. He'd stopped the car—or told you to stop—and he got out. He'd already told you he was going to write the Foundation and refuse the Prize. He left you sitting in the Mercedes, the gift from you he no longer wanted either."

"No . . ." whispered Rhea. "No . . ."

"It's strange," I said. "He was as determined to refuse the Prize as you were for him to accept it. And he'd written that letter. It was in the glove compartment of the Mercedes. Sayres found it the next afternoon, when my witness saw him come over to snoop through the car. You killed Compton to stop him from writing a letter he'd already written. But he wanted to get away from you so badly that he probably forgot to take it with him. Under the circumstances, I'd have forgotten it too." After a pause, I said, more to myself than to Rhea, "That was just about the only thing Sayres didn't lie about—that letter, and the lighter."

Rhea sat up and said bravely, "You're talking nonsense, Chess."

"Or tragedy," I said. "Well, Sayres had his lies, and you had your own. You wanted to drop on Compton and everyone else the lie that he'd won the Granville. That lie became a necessity, didn't it, Rhea? And to preserve the lie and keep it alive—you had to kill. Your behavior the night you were to have first learned that Compton was dead, the night I followed you all around the city and finally into that damned bar, it makes sense now. You weren't a woman in grief. You were someone with a lie to live and to live with— to preserve for as long as you lived. A lie—in Compton's name. A lie you began to draw me into the moment we met at your father's party, a damned, rotten lie . . ."

"It wasn't a lie . . . what I saw in you, Chess," said Rhea, her voice tight. "What I was beginning to feel for you, that wasn't a lie . . . not then, not the night you came after me . . . not when we sat and talked about ourselves . . ."

"Compton was dead when we met, Rhea, and you *knew* it. Yet you went on, speaking of him as though he were still alive somewhere, standing there comparing him with me, saying that we'd like each other. . . . Damn you, Rhea . . ."

"What I said about you, Chess, that wasn't false, not that and not what I said about Greg . . . I wouldn't have spent two minutes alone with you if you were less than what you are, what I saw then . . . I couldn't help but talk to you the way I did that night, because . . . because I thought I'd never see the likes of it again. . . ."

"Damn you, Rhea! Don't you understand? That should've been *Compton* in that room with you, not me. But he was dead, and you knew it. It's something you can't reconcile, Rhea, and you had no right to poison me, or to lie to him, or any of it! No right, and no *reason* to. No good reason, that is."

Rhea risked a short glance at me. "I've hurt you deeply, haven't I, Chess?" she asked.

I turned and looked at her. "As much as you hurt Compton."

Another car passed down the road, and we were quiet for a while. A gust of wind buffeted the car and made us both shiver. Rhea said, "Have you a quotation for the occasion, Chess? I . . . I've probably earned one by now, haven't I?"

"If you want," I said. "'When vice prevails, and impious men bear sway, the post of honor is a private station.' Addison. I'd have substituted 'dishonest,' 'lying,' 'mediocre' for 'impious,' but you get the picture."

"You . . . have a remarkable memory."

"I ought to. That's the quotation Compton used at the beginning of Part One of *Walk Around the Sun*." When Rhea said nothing, I asked, "What about your reason, Rhea?"

"I . . . I was ashamed of him," she began in a whimper. "I was . . . *ashamed* of him." Then her voice rose. "There!" she cried. "I've said it! I was ashamed of him! Ashamed of his being a failure! Of his always being beaten, and cheated, and ignored . . . and beaten! I wanted a hero, a live, conquering hero who smashed the world. I wanted to make it accept him, to acknowledge him . . . and it would have . . . it will . . ."

"And dead or alive, he was going to accept that Prize, wasn't he? Damn you, wasn't he real enough to you without it?"

"No!" cried Rhea savagely. "No. He was nothing without that . . . that acknowledgment. Nothing but a failure!"

"Was there ever a moment you hated him because he was indifferent to the Prize?"

"Every time I read about some literary award . . . I hated him because . . . because he wouldn't even laugh at it, he wouldn't be hurt by it. . . . He'd read about it with the same interest he'd read about some . . . Hollywood divorce!"

"But dead or alive, willing or kicking and screaming, he was going to be Gregory Compton, recipient of the Granville Prize. Right?"

"That's right! Alive . . . or dead!"

I shook my head. "Wrong." I put my hand on the door. Rhea grabbed my wrist. Her face had changed from angular fury to soft earnestness. "In . . . in the name of his memory, Chess, you mustn't send that letter. If you value what he stands for, please, don't . . ."

"But I do," I said. "Stop me if you can." I picked up the envelope with Compton's plays and opened my door. I shook off Rhea's grip, stepped out, and slammed the door shut, then began walking down the road back to Middleport. When I'd gone about thirty feet, the Porsche's lights flickered on, and then the engine turned over. I heard the tires crunch the gravel, and the lights swept me once as it passed me and roared back down Freehold.

At the time, I was simply driven by anger, disgust, and my sense of justice. It wasn't an issue of giving Rhea a chance to redeem herself; it was a wild desire to give Compton a second chance to defend himself.

The Porsche reached the bend, stopped for a moment, then turned sharply and raced back up the road—for me.

I stood frozen by the reality of it, and braced myself to dive to my left over the guardrail and the slope where it couldn't follow me. Compton hadn't had time to think of that. He hadn't expected it. I had.

When the Porsche was thirty feet away from me, I turned to jump. But then it braked suddenly and slid to within ten feet of where I stood. I squinted over the blinding headlights, trying to see Rhea's face. I took a few steps forward. Then the Porsche roared again and backed away from me into a tight U-turn. I caught a glimpse of her face then, the anguished, knowledge-wracked face of a woman who'd lost everything. As I shouted her name, she gunned her motor and the Porsche rocketed away down the road again. As it gained speed it angled to the left across the median strip, accelerated, rammed into the guardrail at the bend, and flew over the edge out of sight.

As I ran down the road, there was an explosion and an orange glare lit up the neighboring cliffside. By the time I reached the edge, it had died and there was nothing to be seen in the darkness below but the ghostly whitecaps of the breakers as they washed over the shadowy rocks.

I don't know how long I stood there. Perhaps it was a minute. Perhaps it was an hour. But I found myself saying tiredly to the void, "I'll take that as a compliment, Rhea. Good-bye."

Epilogue

I didn't mail the letter.

By the time I trudged back into Middleport and found a mailbox at the railroad station, I had a better idea. A much better idea.

I delivered it myself.

The next morning. I simply barged past the receptionist and secretary into Edgar Atherton's office and handed it to him. I said, "Open it," and waited until he did and read Compton's letter of refusal. He glanced up at his anxious secretary, and then scowled at me. "So what, Mr. Hanrahan?"

I turned to the secretary and said, "You're a witness to his having received that letter." And to Atherton I said, "There are notarized copies of that in the mail, going to all the same people I sent copies of Gullum's review and ballot to. You'd better announce the refusal before they do."

"What if I don't?" sneered Atherton, tossing the letter down.

I shrugged, turned, and walked out. I didn't come here to educate him.

Wallace Conover became Compton's literary heir. He

ignored the ensuing Granville scandal the best he could, and steeled himself against the smear campaign against Compton that went on even after publication of the letter. He was chilly toward me, and I understood that. Jerome Hixon took up Compton's cause, as did some other critics, and eventually the letter made a difference.

Oliver Gullum was roasted, too. Many other critics and literary lights came to his defense, some even painting him as a "victim of capitalism"—though careful to omit mention of his Hamptons estate, his private house on Saint Kitts in the Virgin Islands, and his twice-yearly junkets to Europe, among other things. But all the tears and testimonials failed to make a difference. Oliver Gullum's column never appeared in the *Times* again. I learned, too, from Ruth Marchessini, that the board of governors of Regina University had prevailed upon Edmund Atherton to withdraw Gullum's appointment as Olcutt Professor of American Literature.

Edgar Atherton remained president of the Granville Foundation for exactly a week after I visited him. The next I heard of him was when it was reported that he'd been appointed an executive of the National Arts Endowment in Washington. Which is where he belonged.

Earl Teague was fired from Pericles Press. He was fired because Wallace Conover suddenly bought the publisher and made sure Teague was out the door the same day. And the next day Conover turned around and sold Pericles to a conglomerate. Pericles was dissolved three months later. Teague found a job as a book reviewer for some left-wing weekly that was largely subsidized by wealthy fools and by the National Arts Endowment.

Before Pericles closed down it auctioned off its books. Spencer Durand, of Euler and Shaw, was the high bidder for all of Compton's books, including the contract for his forthcoming *Defender of the Realm*. Durand also made arrangements to publish all of Compton's plays.

Adele Hubbard did not lose her job at the Granville

Foundation. In fact, she was offered the supervisor's position after the Granville heirs decided to clean the Foundation out. She took it. And I took her to Kurian's to celebrate, making sure I had the best table in the house.

I never saw Geoffrey Sayres again. I think. On one of my nocturnal wanderings I passed a fellow who stood on a curb down in the Village. He may have wanted to cross the street, but he just stood there, his body weaving back and forth, his head nodding. Shot to the gills with dope. His face had a week's growth, and his hair hadn't been cut in months. His clothes hadn't seen soap and water for that long, too, and smelled it. I couldn't be sure it was Sayres. I turned away from trying to determine whether or not it was. It didn't matter.

The souvenir brandy goblet with the lipstick on the rim sat on my desk at home until it was just another souvenir of another resolved paradox. I would study it in the evenings and think of Rhea. There was a bitterness to purge from my system, one that clung to my idea of elegance, of beauty, of nobility, of stature, of desire. For a while after it was over, every time I thought of those things—every time I saw them, or experienced them—I'd feel a cloying revulsion rooted in distrust, contempt, and pain. The bitterness. But every time I felt those things, I'd remember what I said to Rhea about canker of the soul. When I could smile at myself again, and think to myself in all seriousness— "Hanrahan, your eloquence improves by the day, what are you worried about?"—I knew it was time to put the goblet away.

I got a letter from Christian Kanewski—the kid who'd found the Mercedes mascot—telling me that his father wouldn't let him have the mascot ("He said it was still state's evidence and wasn't a nice thing for me to have"), but could he please have my autograph. So I sent him a studio photo of myself inscribed, *To Chris K., the knight on bicycle who helped me to checkmate. Fondest, Chess H*.

I read Shakespeare's *Twelfth Night*—just in case Ruth

Marchessini popped into town and tested me on Sir Toby—and some of his sonnets, too. In one of them, I ran across the line: "Nor thou with public kindness honor me, unless thou take that honor from thy name." I stopped there because I recognized the line from somewhere else, and then realized that Compton had used it in *Walk Around the Sun*, in a dinner party scene where Stridivant replied to some critic's profuse compliments on his music. The critic had the previous evening lavished the same compliments on another composer's atonal film scores. The critic, of course, became Stridivant's newest and most rabid enemy. Compton had substituted the *thou*'s and *thy* with *you* and *your*, and I wrote Marchessini a short note about it. She replied with a long letter of appreciation for both Compton and my powers of observation, saying that she'd noted the line when she first read *Walk* and that it was too bad I didn't actually write for a magazine. "You have the makings of a promising novice," she finished, and referred me to her collected works—which came with the letter.

I recovered from Rhea's death—or rather from my disillusionment—faster than did her father. I hadn't seen him since we sat across a bare table from each other in the conference room of the Suffolk County District Attorney's office to discuss the circumstances behind her "accident." When I left him then I knew he'd fought a desire to punish me for everything with a fist in my face. One day I called on him at his lower Manhattan office. He agreed to see me, but only out of cold courtesy. His office was still cluttered with blueprints of his new container ship. The biggest one was still where I'd seen it the first time, on the rug held down by the same books and the statue of Nike.

"Good morning, Mr. Conover," I said, sitting down. "Thought I'd drop by and see how you were."

Very formally, with enough frost in his voice to chill a champagne bottle, he replied, "I'm fine, thank you. Yourself?"

I studied his drawn, hostile face for a while, then said, "I'm over it."

It was only then, I think, that it occurred to him what his daughter might have meant to me. He simply looked at me for a long moment, then swiveled in his chair to stare out of his window. "I . . . didn't know."

I fumbled for words and found them. "What happened to Compton, could've happened to me," I said. "It didn't. Give her that much, at least."

Conover swiveled back to face me. "Are you suggesting forgiveness, Mr. Hanrahan?"

"No. Because Compton can't sit here and suggest that he misjudged her, as you had. As I had."

Conover frowned at me. "Are you comparing yourself with Greg?"

I shook my head. "No, not that, either. What I'm saying is that when I made her face a choice—that night, on that same road—I think I made her take Compton seriously for the first time. And she did."

Conover swiveled in his chair again and sat with his back to me, alone with his thoughts. After a moment, I asked, "Found a name for that ship yet?"

"No, Mr. Hanrahan. I haven't given it much thought lately."

I stood up and took one of his fine-line pens from the desk. "Look," I said, "I have an idea for that."

Conover didn't respond. I walked over to the print on the rug and stooped down, then uncapped the pen and printed *Stridivant* in neat capital letters on the bow. I paused for a second to admire my handiwork, and glanced up to see Conover watching me with curiosity. I rose and put his pen back. "See you around," I said, and then I left his office.

Walk Around the Sun was still on the best-seller lists when I heard from Conover two weeks later. There was a knock on my office door one morning, just as I was getting ready to leave for a late breakfast with Gussie Spendler. It was a messenger with an envelope from Polaris Shipping. I signed for it, then slit the envelope open. Inside was a handwritten note clipped to a certificate, in my name, for five hundred preferred shares of Polaris Shipping. The note read, "Hope to see you at the launching of the Polaris *Stridivant* in two or so years. Meanwhile, with my compliments, and take care. Conover."

Over breakfast a few blocks away, Gussie said, "I dropped William Grackle, Chess. Dorothy Resnick down the street snapped him right up, of course. But I thought it was time I got the taste of Earl out of my mouth. Grackle was furious for all of two minutes."

"Good for you, trouper," I smiled.

"So you're seeing Vivian Brewer," remarked the agent with sudden slyness.

"How did you know?" I asked.

"I called her to send me a temp for next week. My secretary is going on vacation." Gussie sipped her orange juice. "I mentioned that we were having breakfast and she mentioned that you two were having dinner tonight."

I stirred my coffee. "She's giving me typing lessons."

"And you're introducing her to literature," sniffed Gussie.

The waitress came with our orders then and the agent and I talked about our businesses. Then she asked, "Why did she do it, Chess? Rhea Hamilton, I mean. You never told me."

I shrugged. "She wanted a trophy, Gussie. A greater trophy than anybody else would've dared to see and want—but still a trophy. And he refused to sit still on anybody's mantel, empty, dusty, and dead."

I suppose my voice had been a little harsh. The needlessness of the tragedy still made me mad when I thought of it. Gussie changed the subject. "Ever find that emperor? Compton's emperor?"

"He was a runt," I said. "He bit my toe and ran away."

"I'm sorry, Chess," said the agent after a long moment.

She said it with a woman's perception, letting me know that she'd guessed what Rhea had meant to me.

I looked up at her. "I'm not."

She wanted to ask me what I meant by that. But she didn't ask, and I didn't tell her.